DON'T FORGET TO BREATHE

CATHRINA CONSTANTINE

ALSO BY CATHRINA CONSTANTINE

The Upside Down of Nora Gaines
Incense and Peppermints
Marly In Pieces

WICKEDLY SERIES
Wickedly It Begins
Wickedly They Come
Wickedly They Dream

TALLAS SERIES
Tallas
Snow On Cinders

Copyright © 2021 Cathrina Constantine

All rights reserved. This book or any portion thereof may not be reproduced or used in any manner whatsoever without the express written permission of the publisher except for the use of brief quotations in a book review.

Printed in the United States of America
Second Printing, 2021

ISBN 978-1-63795-403-4

Editor
Melissa Levine of Red Pen Editing, LLC
Cover Designer
Melissa Stevens of The Illustrated Author Design Services
Interior Design and Typesetting
Melissa Stevens of The Illustrated Author Design Services

ACKNOWLEDGEMENTS

In all things, I thank God first.

I am extremely grateful for those who have supported me. Not only my family and friends, but the hundreds of wonderful readers and reviewers. Over the years I have received such wonderful compliments from complete strangers. People who go out of their way to email me with glowing praises. Those kind things brightens and encourages my writing journey.

Thank you to Melissa Levine of Red Pen Editing, LLC. Her professional editing services are outstanding, polishing and tightening this novel until it shined. She is easy to work with and I highly recommend Melissa.

On a side note, typos have an affinity of haunting all of my manuscripts. And after rereading this story a gazillion times, I can only imagine what ghostly spirits tampered with my writing.

One day I'd like to meet my Fabulous Cover Artist, Melissa Stevens of the Illustrated Author Design Services. Melissa. I'm sending you a virtual hug for all that you have created for me over the years. Not only has she designed this phenomenal cover for Don't Forget To Breathe, formatted and designed the interior, she also designed many of my amazing book covers.

Niki

My Princess
I Love You More

CHAPTER 1

Moonlight played tricks with my eyes as we circumvented the graveyard like an obstacle course. Pluming fog licked my legs and misty ghosts danced on marbleized stones. My breath shuddered as Henry nudged my shoulder, leading the way.

"Hurry," he whispered, passing me.

Goosebumps pebbled my skin as I picked up the pace. I cranked my head to the left. Dark moving shapes appeared in the distance and moaning floated past my ears. *Is it the wind or my imagination?* I stumbled over an urn and Henry lugged me up, urging me on.

"What are we running from?" I said on a gush of breath and quietly so not to wake the dead.

"Them, over there." Henry jerked his chin and the lenses of his glasses captured raining moonbeams. "I think it's cops."

His hand reached back, palm up. I latched hold. "Why would the police be patrolling the cemetery?"

We whipped around a mammoth tombstone, a squared foundation for a glorious angel. He halted and threw me unceremoniously toward the solid concrete. My heartbeat migrated up my esophagus to pound at the base of my throat. Henry covered my mouth with his hand. "Shh... Don't breathe so loud."

My clanging heart had little intention of slowing. Henry squashed his body into mine. Too close. Cold leached into my back as his speeding heartbeat harmonized with my own. I cringed at the discomfort of being pressed between his chest and the stone.

Seconds later, Henry's hand stroked my torso and then he nuzzled his head into the side of my neck, kissing my throat. "What. Are. You. Doing?" I said, voice stilted.

When he raised his head from my shoulder, I glared at his shadowed silhouette. Before I had a chance to protest, he pancaked his hands on my cheeks, and his mouth mashed my lips. Confounded and then irritated, I pushed on his chest, but he clutched tighter, deepening his kiss, his tongue prying apart my lips. His hand gravitated along my shoulder to wedge between my back and the tombstone while his other hand scrounged about to cop a feel. I was stuck between a rock and a hormonal boy.

Rather than submit to his unwanted groping, my fingers grabbed what little belly flesh of Henry's I could muster and twisted hard.

"Owww—" He backed off. "What the hell, Leo?"

"You wanna screw me? Is that the real reason for hiding behind this tombstone? Why did we have to run?"

"I didn't have to make you run for that. I practically had you on the ground a minute ago." He shoved a hand through his short hair and then tweaked his glasses up his nose. Then, glancing to the right and then the left, he said, "I did see something. It looked like a couple of guys walking through the graveyard along the ridge. It looked like cops and I wasn't taking any chances."

Whether he was lying or being truthful, I couldn't read his eyes in the dimness nor through his lenses. "We're not alone." I felt chilled. "How many people hang out in a graveyard?"

He shrugged and, not even trying to be subtle, he adjusted the zipper of his jeans. In a singsong tone, he said, "I thought we could drink beers, smoke a little weed, and you could take care of whatever popped up."

I fumed at his innuendo. Doing the naughty in a graveyard with Mom recently planted in aisle 113 pissed me off. "Our nighttime picnic is over." I went to move, but his hands came down on my shoulders.

"You're not leaving. We were having such a good time. Right here. Right now." He lowered his head to taste my lips. "Let's stay awhile." Stale beer breath washed over my face. "Hidden behind this statue, we could rock this place. Make it come alive."

I straightened my arms to hold him off. "I don't think so."

"C'mon, Leo. You're teasing me, right?" Henry swatted away my armed barrier. "Baby, we deserve this after our crappy week." His fingertips scored a groove along my spine. The deed generated a slight backbend, which pressed my chest into him. He thought it was an enticement. "This is an awesome high." He ground his pelvis into me, exhilarated. "The juices are flowing."

"Henry. No! You asshat." I discovered his dark libido that night, and how he could be a real dickhead. I wasn't attracted to him in that way. Every so often, I wish I were. *Life would be easier.* "Let's just go."

"Leo, I want you." He chafed his whiskered cheek on mine as his hand roamed under my shirt. "I've waited patiently. Don't you think?"

His touch made my skin crawl. "Stop it." Disengaging from his embrace, I ducked under his arm and loped to find the spot where we'd been drinking to gather my discarded hoodie. I wasn't drunk or high enough to put up with his baloney. Since he was probably lying about seeing cops, I stomped on the manicured lawn, not caring if I made any noise.

Not hearing Henry slogging behind me, I slowed and turned toward the angel tombstone. "Stop clowning around. Let's go."

Not a word.

"Okay. I'm sorry I called you a sick ass." I spied my hoodie draped over a headstone like a pall and headed that way. I kicked one of our empty beer cans by accident; the tinny rattle echoed throughout the cemetery. After shrugging into the hoodie, I stooped and collected the cans into the crook of my arm. "Now you're freaking me out. I'm leaving without you."

Strangled gurgling roiled over the dewy lawn. "Henry?" Aluminum cans tumbled from my arms. "Are you okay?"

"Go away!" His speech muffled as if he was choking.

I stood there, motionless. *Is he for real?* I heard huffing breath and what sounded like his fists or his body bashing against the concrete. Was he having a seizure, an epileptic fit and didn't want me to see? Somewhat wary, I paced back to find him.

"Henry? What's wrong?"

"Get the fuck out of here. Now!" There was a sound like ripping fabric. *Is he tearing his shirt?* "Run! Or I'm going to kill you."

Hairs on the nape of my neck prickled. I tore off as if hellhounds were nipping at my heels. Not slowing even when reaching the railroad tracks, I crashed and rolled on the wooden ties, scraping my hands and knees. A pungent scent of dead leaves and loamy dirt wafted in the air. I sprang up, grumbled at my clumsiness, and peered toward Hallow Saint's Cemetery.

Gulping down my fear, I hugged my arms around my waist, consoling myself. Coward came to mind. *How could I leave him like that? I have to go back.* A resigned breath splintered the seam of my lips. The shimmering moon lit my passage as my sneakers crunched on the wooden railroad ties. I stalled on the rails and stared down the swell of land, past the trees into the cemetery, searching for Henry. My ears were only picking up sounds of whispering leaves. I half expected him to make an appearance, laughing his ass off about his cruel joke.

Something caught the edge of my vision, but it scampered away. Squinting didn't help. Too dark. A flashlight might've been useful, if I had one. *Note to self, carry a flashlight.*

I trekked farther along the tracks. Using the high ground to observe the area, I could scarcely make out the tombstones that pocked the ground amidst the fog, looking eerie and lonesome. Then I spotted remote figures. It could be kids looking for a place to party in private. I crouched and balanced on my toes and wondered if one might be Henry.

They traveled behind a large monument, causing me to lose sight of them. To the left, a prowling cat distracted me until a sudden bloodcurdling scream scraped into my bones.

Not faltering, I dug a hand into my pocket for my cell and dialed 911. A man's voice answered. "What is the location of your emergency?"

"Hallow Saint's Cemetery," I whispered.

"Say again?"

"Hallow Saint's Cemetery."

"Can I have your name and address?"

Through panic-stricken eyes, I noticed a glowing headstone; someone must've dropped a flashlight. It remained in place like a beacon. "Follow the light." I disconnected the call and, wheeling around, I tripped. Scrabbling upright, I belted down the tracks.

It wasn't Henry. It wasn't Henry. Not again. Please, God, not again. This can't be happening. Henry is fine.

I ran like a crazed psycho. Sawing pain in my lungs constricted any decent airflow, and the stitch in my side felt like a knife. I rested beneath a streetlight. To quell the dizzies, I leaned forward and grabbed my knees. Using the sleeve of my hoodie, I mopped my sweaty face and neck, then plucked aside hair that was taped to my face.

Somewhat in control, I rolled my shoulders and scouted the familiar road. Tarpon Hill. With my pulse still skittery, I jogged home. Once I reached Westgate, I stopped outside of Henry's Dutch colonial house. His car was there, but that wasn't unusual. We had hiked to the cemetery with his pockets stuffed with brew and marijuana. I perceived the shining window on the upper right-hand corner. His bedroom. Not that I'd ever been in his room, but he'd pointed it out more than once and told me how he slept nude, like I needed to know. Henry beat me home.

Did I imagine the scream? A surge of water blurred my vision. Over the last year, I'd turned into such a crybaby.

Figuring it was past Dad's stupid curfew, I went for my phone to check the time. I wanted to call Henry to chew him out for being such a loser, but my cell wasn't in my back pocket. I impatiently patted the opposite pocket, then my front pockets and hoodie as well. Empty. No cell.

Swirling around, I stared down the winding street. Where did I lose my phone? I advanced a step with brainless thoughts of retracing my path to the scene of a possible crime. Did my phone flip out of my hand after I'd fallen? I didn't remember putting it into a pocket. *I can't go back. Not now.*

Peeved, I kicked a rock and sent it flying. Grasping my face, I squelched a maddening cry. I trudged up the road, passing two houses, and crossed the street to eighty-six Westgate. Dad had left the sidelight on, and cracking the screen door, it screeched like an alarm. I winced.

Shucking my sneakers, I padded into the kitchen where a small nightlight furnished a dull shine. I aimed for stealth and tiptoed along the hallway to the bathroom. I brushed beer breath and smoke from my face and mouth.

Quiet and feeling home free I went into my bedroom. I toggled on the lights and jumped out of my skin. A shriek plugged my throat. Seated on my bedroom chair with his fingers templed was Dad.

"I can't handle this, Leocadia." Exasperation whittled his features as he pinched the bridge of his nose. "I can't be worrying about you night after night, wondering if you're alright and coming home in one piece."

"I'm sorry, Dad, really, I am. We were fooling around and lost track of time. I'm sorry."

"You kids always know the time." He eased off the cushioned chair using the armrest for leverage. "Your cell phones are practically glued to your hands."

Not anymore. He'd rip me a good one if I said I lost my phone. "I said I'm sorry. It won't happen again."

"It will. You know it will." He lumbered forward and kissed the top of my head. "I can't lose you too." He sighed and left my room.

His painful reminder was more than I could bear, triggering tears to trample over my face. I just might have been a witness to a crime, and the anniversary of Mom's murder crept closer every day.

CHAPTER 2

The black corners of my room softened into a silvery gray. I turned my head to check the alarm clock, 4:45. I begged the heavens, "Please, let me sleep," and smothered my head underneath my downy pillow.

A nanosecond after slamming my eyelids closed, I was immediately transported to a year ago...

Hesitating on the wooden front porch, I peered at a watery substance. I made an effort not to touch the crud with my pristine leather boots, and for a change, the front door was unlocked.

"Mom, what's that stuff on the porch?"

Unfastening the messenger bag from my shoulder, I plunked it on the recliner. More red liquid stained the floor and the area carpet. "Mom, what is this? Are you painting the kitchen again? Dad is going to kill you. Red? Really?"

All was quiet as I walked into the kitchen. A cutting board sat on the counter amid a mound of carrot shavings. Bubbling and hissing drew my attention. Steam furled from a pot on the stove. I sped over and switched off the gas. The basement door was ajar; I yelled, "Mom?" My ear bent for her usual lyrical humming. Silence. Then I looked through the back window, but she wasn't in the perennial garden.

Is it...blood?

Maybe she had cut herself and ran out the front door? An uneasy zing cramped my bones. The counter and the dinner preparations all appeared normal as if she'd taken a break.

I retraced my steps to the living room. How did I miss the trail of blood, or whatever it was, bumping up the staircase? "Mom, are you up there?" My heart hammered in my chest as I toed each stair with foreboding. Every scary movie replayed in my mind.

First, I peeked into my bedroom. Exactly how I left it, a holy mess. Whenever I left my room like this, which was always, Mom would compulsively clean it. It never made sense to do it myself if she was willing to do it for me.

My walk down the hallway to my parents' bedroom became sluggish. She'd been complaining of not feeling well and had stayed home from work today. Was she sick and needed to rest and forgot about the boiling water? The door was shut. I knuckled the frame softly. "Mom?"

My hand twisted the knob and inched it open. I gagged on the smell.

An awkward, half-naked body draped the mattress—porcelain skin sliced apart, and silky blonde hair fanned the floor. Dripping red blood—gobs of blood. Eyes filled with terror watched me. Dead eyes. My jaw moved. Mommm—but no sound. I shuffled a foot forward and doubled over, spewing lunch. That was when I noticed a bloody dagger laid next to her fingers. Forged in a peculiar camber design like something I'd see in a museum.

Arms swallowed me from behind, "I'm not going to kill you. Not yet." Then everything faded to black.

I woke with a start and gasped. My heart ached. Struggling upright I crisscrossed my arms over my chest and gripped my shoulders. Tears sprinkled my face—sorry for my loss, sorry for myself. No longer in a dreamy state, my chaotic pulse throbbed. The dagger was a new addition to my dreams.

"Mom, what does this mean?" My voice broke and fell to pieces around me. "The police have given up. They can't find who did this to you. I need more," I cried, pressing my fingers to my eyes. "Why can't I remember anything else?"

Mellow light shirked the blinds and I glimpsed the time. 5:02. I dragged in a deep breath and my thundering heart regulated to a negligible thrum. I slumped my chin to my chest, sitting there like a worthless head case. The dreams were getting worse and repetitious. The police still hadn't found her killer, and I still couldn't remember jack-shit.

Tap. Tap. Frowning, I scanned my room for the source of the noise. This house we'd moved into had lots of creaky noises.

Tap tap tap.

There it was again. The sound was coming from the window. I peeled back the quilt and slipped out of bed. As my feet flattened on the hardwood, the morning chill embedded into my toes. I hunched and wrapped my arms around my cooled body and snuck toward the window.

Henry?

Levering the blinds, I gripped the windowsill. It wouldn't budge. I put my weight against the glass to loosen the frame and jimmied it up. He looked disjointed through the windows screen and since I'd been working through mixed emotions, I frowned at him. "What happened to you last night?"

"Let me in."

"Why should I?"

"We don't want to wake your dad, do we?"

He wasn't wearing his glasses. His eyes were cloudy like muddy water and there was a gash on his lip. He was completely disheveled and in need of a friend. Grudgingly,

I raised the screen and receded. Beneath my window was an ingenious tree stump, a steppingstone. Over the past year I have utilized it often. As soon as Henry grasped the frame, raw abrasions were noticeable on his knuckles. In an inelegant hop, he hauled himself in and lowered the window, barring the cold.

My bare feet felt like ice cubes as I skated on the floor to make sure my bedroom door was locked. Turning, Henry had already settled into the chair, leaving a path of dirt particles. The soles of his sneakers were caked with mud. I put a finger to my lips, warding off any loud talking, and scuttled to sit on my bed.

"I'm sorry," he uttered.

"You should be. You really freaked me out."

"I don't take rejection well. I lost it." He looked down and raked the thighs of his jeans with his fingers. "I've been a reject my entire life, and then when you—"

"First," I broke in, "I thought we were running from the police. Then you started pawing me. What was I supposed to think?"

His head snapped up, and he said, "I thought you liked me." He gave a careless shoulder lift. "And, I kind of have a temper problem."

"You're damn right you do." My fingers rolled into fists. "Don't ever do that again."

"Sorry." He massaged his brow, closing his eyes. I stared at the bruises on the back of his hands as his coppery hair caught the light of a new day.

"What was that sound last night? Like you were tearing your shirt or something?"

His eyebrows dipped downward, a dismal countenance. "I was controlling my anger by taking it out on myself."

"Is that why your knuckles are all beat up?" Not raising his hand to look at them—he knew what I meant. "And I thought I was the nutbar." My head moved from side to side. "You said you were going to kill me."

"I did? I don't remember saying that." He looked straight at me while beating his fingers rhythmically on the arm of the chair. "You must've imagined it."

"I didn't imagine it. You snarled it." I elevated my ice-cubed feet off the floor, sitting cross-legged with my arms balancing on my knees. "What did you do, punch yourself in the face too?"

He touched his knuckle to the gash on his lip, and it came away tinged with blood. "I walked into my dad's fist."

"Your dad hit you?"

"I lipped off. No big deal."

"It *is* a big deal."

"Leo, drop it. I deserved it."

I bit my tongue, understanding where his anger originated. After a moment of silence, I asked, "Did you really see people or the cops in the cemetery?"

He blinked before replying, "Yes, I thought I did."

"What did you do after I left?"

"You made me feel like such a loser." He extracted a curt breath as his fingers picked at the material on the chair. "Just in case it was the cops, I picked up our cans." He peered at me, wanting my approval. But I had none. "Then I went home. I couldn't sleep so I came over here." His gaze looped around my room. "To say I was sorry."

"Did you hear or see anyone else in the cemetery?"

"N-nope." He seemed to be studying the toe of his sneaker as he fidgeted in the chair. "Like I said, I left. Why?"

He sounded truthful and I wanted to believe him. Yet when he raised his eyes to meet mine, there was an indecipherable glint.

"Did you hear a scream?" Inquisitively, I slanted my head. Either he was tired or fed up because he pressed his fists to his brow.

"Leo," he whispered. "Spit it out."

Sometimes I couldn't tell what was real and what was a dream. I didn't want to be that lunatic, a person who saw and heard things that weren't really there. I had gone through enough psychotherapy to last a lifetime. Dreams were messing with my brain and I was in the process of hiding them. I had no intentions of going back to the psychiatrist. Did I imagine the bloodcurdling scream, the beam of light on the headstone? Did I dial 911? Even Henry looked odd, or was it an expression of fear.

"Must have dreamt it," I said. "Never mind." Bowing my head, a tangle of hair shuttered the sides of my face.

Henry released a breath as if he'd been holding it in. "I'm going home to get ready for school. I'll pick you up at seven-thirty?" As he stood to leave, he wiped down his face with tense fingers. "Oh, by the way. A little gift just for you." Stuffing a hand into his jeans, he slipped out a teeny-tiny plastic bag. He lobbed it and it landed between my legs.

I knew what it was and picked it up as if it might bite. "I...I told you, I quit."

"I thought you needed a jolt. You've been looking kind of mangy."

"Thanks...but...no..." I handed it back to him, but he shrugged my hand away.

"Keep it. Someday it'll come in handy."

He raised the sticky window generating a loud abrading noise. I recoiled, hoping it didn't wake Dad. After he climbed out, I watched him slink around the corner of the house and then lowered the window.

I still held the tiny bag in my fingertips. Treating the cocaine like poison, I flicked it into the drawer of my bedside table.

The house across the street, diagonal from mine, belonged to a man who once lived alone. I thought he had been a bachelor or divorced. Whether he was being nice or weird, he constantly watched me. For an older guy, he wasn't bad looking. Then this past August, Henry and an old lady had moved into the house. Being a nosy neighbor, I spied with interest as they unloaded the truck with their belongings. Henry was of average height, cropped coppery hair, neither fat nor skinny. We hadn't actually met until the first day of school when I walked to the corner to wait for the bus, and he was already there.

I had noted his hipsterish glasses: rectangular, golden-brown frames that matched his hair and a handprint limning his neck, which I declined to mention on our initial meeting.

As weeks passed, I learned the guy across the street was Henry's father. He provided evasive snippets as to why it took him and his mother over a year to move into the Hallow. I wasn't one to pry into his personal life and he hadn't pried into mine. That aspect had drawn me to him—he never inquired about my mom. His quirky dry sense of humor wasn't endearing to everyone and Henry was having a hard time fitting in. I befriended him because he didn't treat me like a headcase or look at me with soulful eyes. Two weeks ago, his dad purchased a used SUV for Henry, and I benefited from his good fortune.

Fitting into a pair of denim jeans and a snug plaid shirt over a tank top, I already felt wiped. When was the last time I had a restful night's sleep? I opened the drawer to my bedside table and split the lid of an embroidered box. My secret stash for extreme emergencies. The last time I *used* was August 2nd, when it would've been Mom's fortieth birthday. I added Henry's bag of coke to the contents. Tantalized by a modest pick-me-up, I toyed with a teeny white pill, then I contemplated the monotonous day ahead. I overcame my internal struggle as I slipped it into my pocket and made my way into the kitchen, late as usual.

Dad was in the process of opening the side door to depart for work, but he turned and said, "Have a glass of juice and a piece of toast before you leave. You're getting too skinny."

I stretched my neck easing stiff muscles. "Remember, I have cheerleading practice after school. I'll be late."

"I can't believe you stuck with it. You never cared for cheerleading. I still remember you and Mom squabbling about it."

"Yeah, well." I grabbed the toaster from the bottom shelf of the cupboard. "She thought it'd help get my nose out of my books. So I'm taking her advice...for now." In reality, after mom died, it had been Nona who insisted the regimented practice would keep me focused.

"Are you taking the bus home, or should I pick you up?"

Thinking, I untied the loaf of bread. "I wouldn't have to depend on anybody if you'd put mom's car on the road for me. Hint. Hint."

"I'll think about it," he said, surprising me. "What about tonight?"

"I don't know for sure. Maybe Henry will stay after and I can hitch a ride with him."

A crease formed between his brows.

"What?" I turned from his frowning expression and stuck a slice of bread into the toaster.

"That kid looks and *smells* like trouble, don't you think?"

"Dad, he's...he's a nice guy. Just shy."

His mouth rumpled, adding a resolute head nod. He walked out of the house and then stopped. Poised with one foot on the threshold, he said, "Were you anywhere near Tarpon Hill last night?"

"Why?" This wasn't good; he knew something. He'd warned me to stay clear of the Hill after dark. That section of the village was seedy and, admitting I was wetting myself on Tarpon would be suicidal.

"The morning news is broadcasting a story of a body found in the ditch between Tarpon and Erie Road."

I tried holding it together. The scream really happened? "Yuck! How awful." My throat tightened and I managed to squeak, "Do they know who it is?"

"Not saying until they reach next of kin." His lips thinned into a taut line. "See, Leo, that's why I don't want you wandering the streets at night. That's why I worry."

"You can't live like that, worrying about me all the time." I was relieved and sickened at the same time: relieved, I hadn't imagined it and sickened because a murder had taken place in the cemetery right after I ran away. "I'm good. Don't worry." After saying the reassuring words, I jabbed my fingers into my back pockets to stop the tremors.

CHAPTER 3

As soon as Dad clicked the door, my cool resolve vanished. I sheltered my face in my hands, huffing and puffing from one end of the kitchen to the other. My shoulders jolted at the pop of the toaster. I gaped at the slice of toast, and my stomach twisted.

The scream had been real. A body was found on Tarpon on the banks of the cemetery. Did someone drag the corpse to Tarpon—why? What would have happened if I'd stayed with Henry?

The honk of a car fragmented my thoughts. "Darn it, he's early." I darted to my bedroom for my messenger bag and burst out the side door, toast forgotten. Buckling in, I gazed at Henry's tired, droopy expression as he navigated the car down the driveway. Coppery-brown nubs marched along his chin; evidently, he hadn't found time to shave.

"Did you hear the news," I said, "about the dead body on Tarpon last night?"

His fingers hardened, circling the steering wheel in a firm grip. "I don't listen to the news. It's all bad."

"I agree, but my dad does." I combed through my rebellious hair and gazed through the windshield. A rising sun peeked over the horizon with streaking golden fingers. It was going to be a beautiful day—less one human.

I turned back to Henry. "Doesn't that freak you out?"

"Huh, what are you saying?"

"We were there, by Tarpon Hill."

"So? We don't know when the dude was murdered."

"I never said it was a dude." He was so blasé. Disturbing. "It could've been a female."

"Whatever."

"Wow, you're taking this information extremely light."

"Leo." His cadence was brusque. "What do you want me to say?" He forced his glasses up the bridge of his nose. "Yeah, it's a crime, happens every day. Get over it." His bruised knuckles advanced from bloody red to white as he held the wheel. "It's not like it's someone we know."

My innards churned. For all eternity, my memories would include Mom's gruesome murder scene. I absently smoothed my thumb over the little lump in my pocket, the pill. When the psychiatrist had failed me, I'd taken matters into my own hands—drowning my sorrows in any way possible. I couldn't, and didn't, speak the rest of the drive.

Henry parked, and I barged out of the SUV and jaunted into school without waiting for him. It took two hours to compose my internal war of contention.

"You're going to practice after school, right?" Nona asked in a low voice during English class.

I nodded and veered toward my friend.

"Mrs. Sweeny's teaching us a new routine." She showed me her gag face. "She wants it ready for the football game on Saturday."

"I hope it's not lame like the last one." Nona grinned.

"Miss Nelson," said Mr. Slepe, the teacher. "Do you have something to share with the class?"

Heads veered in my direction. "Uh...no."

"Then all eyes up here." He exhibited his eccentric two-finger point to his eyeballs and then flipped the double point at me. "I'm the teacher, not you."

Following class, we speed-walked to our favorite haunt, the third-floor restroom. Prior to lighting up, we pushed open the window to rid telltale signs of smoke. Nona fished in her purse and withdrew a pack of smokes. "Want one?" She offered the pack to me.

I slid out a cigarette, and then she torched the tobacco with her lighter.

"I can tell something's bothering you." Nona blew a torrent of smoke from her mouth.

In brief, I clarified my recent dream: The murder scene. The bloody prints. The dagger and being grabbed from behind.

"Leooo," she whispered, even though the restroom was empty, "you're starting to remember. You have to tell the police."

"The police didn't find the dagger. I...I'm not ready to... to..."

She prevented my stammering with a locked hug. "I'm here for you."

"It's probably nothing, but I went out with Henry last night—"

"Well, that explains it all." Her eyeballs bugged out of their sockets. "Why do you keep hanging with that boy?"

I joggled my head. "He's new and needs a friend. He's... okay." Her eyes crunched along with her face. "Why don't you like him?"

"He's...I don't know." Nona flicked her ash into the sink. "I can't put my finger on it. He's...different."

"Henry's introverted." Clouds wreathed our heads and we began fanning smoke toward the window. "So he's not Becket Kane or Joseph Andreessen."

"That'd be nice, though." Nona giggled, displaying a salacious brow wag. "I saw hottie looking you over at our last practice. If Henry hadn't been there, Becket might've made a move on you."

"You're dreaming." I tossed my cigarette into one of the toilet bowls. "Becket doesn't know I exist. Besides, he's a senior and we're inferior juniors."

"I hope you're speaking for yourself, hun. My Reggie is a senior and I'm nobody's inferior." White defined her big dark-brown eyes. "And yesterday Reggie asked me if you were going out with Henry."

"Why would Reggie ask you that?"

"C'mon, Leo. Are you dense?" She smiled, a tiger with a secret. "He was asking for someone."

"Oh, no." My shoulders slouched. "What creepazoid wants to know?"

"I told Reg that you friended that oddball because you felt sorry for him."

"Henry is...is...Henry. That's all." God forbid I acknowledged he tried making out with me last night. She'd hemorrhage. "So who's asking about me?" Eagerly, I clasped her arm. "No way, it's not Becket."

"I betcha it is." She included her butt with mine into the toilet bowl. "I couldn't shag it out of Reg. If I weren't taken, I'd be all over Becket like a bee on honey."

"Yeah, you and the whole swarm of queen bees."

"He hasn't gone steady with anybody since tenth grade," she harped. "Becket's one of those love 'em and leave 'em type of guys. Probably 'cause Joyce broke his heart. Do you remember Joyce Winter? We were freshman at the time."

"She was drop-dead gorgeous. I'm glad she moved to another state."

Nona folded a strand of ebony hair over her ear. "And you're gorgeous, too, hun."

I tsked, blowing air between my teeth.

"You're selling yourself short, girl!" Her hand came forward and pincered my chin between her thumb and forefinger, examining my face like a beauty consultant. "I was shocked when you cut your long hair. It was almost to your waist."

I remembered the day well. Ten months ago when I had considered breathing was overrated. I was a waste product hunkered in the corner of my bedroom on a psychedelic trip. My hair was like a shroud covering my body. I felt the need to free myself from its weight. Snatching a pair of scissors, I hacked away.

"It's kind of—unique." She sounded uncertain. "Red hair with orangy-blond highlights."

"Foiled dye job," I grumped.

"Makes you look badass with those long, gnarly razored layers."

"Real badass," I mocked, turning sour, "and pure candyass on the inside."

She persisted. "And your green eyes."

Emitting an exaggerated head loll, I nipped her embellished observation and said, "Did you hear about the body they found on Tarpon?"

"Nooo." She flinched. "That's not far from my house."

"I guess no one listens to the morning news around here." The bell pealed for the start of class.

"Oh, poop! I'm late again." Nona dashed from the restroom.

However, I didn't care about being late and inspected my face in the mirror while fingering the pill that hugged my pocket. "Mom," I said to my reflection, "how else can I put up with cheerleading today?"

Outfitted in school colors of red, white, and blue, the skimpy uniform molded to my body like shrink-wrap. The cheerleading squad gamboled onto the football field, flashing pom-poms as if their lives depended on their enthusiasm. Sloth-like, waiting for the pill to kick in, I feigned zeal and plastered a bogus smile on my face and shook that pom-pom for all it was worth.

Mrs. Sweeny, fists shelved on her hips, sturdy legs parted, resembling the jolly green giant in teal green sweats, supervised our every move. A shrill whistle twanged around the field, our signal. We lined up in our assigned formations, hands clasped behind our backs.

An abrupt clamor came from the fieldhouse, and a herd of buffalo stampeded over the field. Grunting and clanking of shoulder pads, a pack of twenty-something players galloped over the terrain. Helmets clutched in their hands, a team of muscular, broad-shouldered boys reeking of testosterone.

The boys had a mystical, magnetic pull as every head on the cheerleading squad turned to watch. Such remarkable synchronization that Mrs. Sweeny laughed. "Girls. Girls," her voice held a strict edge. "I wish all your routines were this choreographed, precise and neat."

It was, and always had been, my prerogative to zero in on Becket Kane. I trusted my ability to remain unnoticed. Except for this time when lancing vivid eyes met mine head-on and I was caught and tackled.

CHAPTER 4

"C'mon, stay with me," Nona pleaded, fifteen minutes after peeling off our uniforms. "I'm going to watch Reggie practice."

"I'm beat." The pill was a dud. "I just want to go home and sleeeep." We walked toward the bleachers to find Henry, my ride home. Several classmates and half of the cheerleading squad were there fawning over the boys. "Henry isn't here today," she said while canvassing the stands. "Reggie will give you a ride home. Then you won't have to take the late bus."

More than likely, Henry was home fast asleep, right where I'd like to be. I hated taking the smelly late bus. *I need my own car!* Sighing, I accepted her offer. We headed up the stairs to take a seat and heard, "Yo, Nona." We twisted and saw Reggie waving at us. "Love ya, baby."

Nona's face lit up like a Christmas tree. "Back at cha', Reg." She blew him a kiss.

"Pleeease," I droned. "You two are making me nauseous."

"You're just jealous."

I was.

When I had entered Star Hallow High as a freshman, Becket Kane was a sophomore. The grade gap didn't deter me and I became a discreet Becket observer. Morsels of spicy gossip regarding his escapades highlighted my days. Back then, he only had eyes for Joyce. It was fruitless for me to pine after the boy, but I couldn't help myself. There was something about him that gave me all kinds of feels.

What exacerbated my dilemma was that Nona had been privy to my obsession. We'd been hanging out less and less with Reggie in the picture and she'd been conniving to set me up with one of his friends.

Nona pinched my knee. "Did you see that pass Becket made to Reggie? Oh my gosh, that was phenomenal."

I smirked at her love of the game and, Reggie, a nice-looking boy, not quite reaching six feet tall and could run faster than a coyote. His black hair was snipped close to his head and he had an unforgettable smile. But, what held my interest were the boys' snug-fitting uniforms, in particular, Becket's. My eyes latched onto him like a boring tick.

Nona ruined my concentration. "You still got it bad for him, don't you?"

Masking my infatuation, I said, "Who's that?"

"Leo, you're not that cunning; give it up. I know you like the back of my hand."

Yes, Nona did know me, too well. We'd been friends since fifth grade. If it weren't for her, I'd have been in a sanitarium after Mom passed.

Dad had evolved into a slobbering, incoherent wreck, and I barricaded myself away from the world on a destructive mission to join Mom. Thanks to Dad's endless supply of alcohol, a good drink was always available. The psychiatrist was keen on doling out prescription drugs: one pill to speed me up, one pill to make me sleep, and more pills for depression. We'd toiled through endless months of juggling meds.

Then one day at school, the local druggies, Skip and Dave, had noticed I was a hurting puppy. So they hooked me up with something to wash away all my troubles.

Skipper had said, "What you need is a little Zen." The acid took me on some wild rollercoaster rides. I preferred cocaine to ecstasy, but beggars couldn't be choosy. School played second fiddle to my becoming a recluse. Hibernating in my bedroom for days didn't bode well with dad, as if he were in any shape to criticize. When my savings ran dry, Dave put the kibosh on any freebies.

I didn't know if I'd be alive today if it hadn't been for Nona's profound cajoling. Her ceaseless, uplifting prayers to the point of clinging to my heaving body as I puked, cried, screamed, and pulled my hair out. I was struggling to stay somewhat clean. I never constituted weed as a hard-hitting drug, but Nona wasn't pleased when I indulged. Perhaps that was her logic for disliking Henry, his tangy odor of hemp.

After practice, most of the guys took to the showers, and Nona and I lingered next to Reggie's car, waiting. My body wilted like my scraggly ponytail. It wasn't long before Reggie swaggered from school and, to my daunting bewilderment, Becket Kane sidled beside him.

I swerved to face Nona and complained, "Did you set me up?"

"Chill, Leo. I did *not* set you up." She overlapped her bottom lip on her top lip, thinking. "I have no idea why Becket is deliciously sauntering over here with my Reggie."

"I look like puke." I scooped the strands of hair that had escaped my ponytail, re-twisting them into my hair tie.

Nona etched a fake smile on her face and whispered out of the side of her mouth, "He knows you saw him. Turn around and be cool. Be nice."

"Oh, God."

"That's right, hun, you pray."

I revolved toward the boys heading our way and tensed. With a great effort of acting badass and not candyass, I leaned onto Reggie's car, crossed my ankles, and hooked my thumbs into the belt loops of my jeans.

Nona was accurate with her analysis: Becket didn't just walk—he prowled with graceful intent. Clad in delectable tight jeans that hugged him in all the right places and a black T-shirt stretched across his chest. His lengthy pale hair looked as if he'd just roughed a towel over his head. Wavy, damp golden strands caught a breeze exposing his flawless chiseled features. A strong jaw, full mouth, and as they neared, Becket flashed his periwinkle blue eyes in my direction, taking my breath away.

Becket gazed at me with a critical eye. I felt naked and vulnerable under his weighty check-out. Unlinking my thumbs from my belt loops, I crossed my arms over my skimpy chest. In stocking feet, I topped the charts at five feet six, although my ankle boots added two inches, but I still had to crane my neck to look up at him. Finally, after enduring his thorough scrutiny, those starry eyes delved into mine. The corner of his mouth quirked up. I apparently passed inspection and I countered with a smirk of my own.

"Hello, Leocadia." His arm rose, lean fingers pointed my way.

He said my full name. So. Fricking. Awesome. I reached forward and smoothed my palm into his. Warm, though callused, his touch jettisoned a current along my arm. Then like a true dorkatron, I corrected him, even though I liked the way he said my name. "It's Leo."

Grinning, he said, "Leo." His smile threw me over the edge. Heat stole into my face, and when he released my hand, I felt chilled.

My nitwit brain malfunctioned when Becket came within a foot of me, and I hadn't noticed Reggie and Nona sucking face. Not until a slurpy noise turned me in their direction. *Gross.*

Becket teased, "Get a room."

After a single lip-smacking peck, Nona said, "Of course it's alright, Reg. I don't mind, do you, Leo?"

"Huh?"

"Becket's car is at the mechanics on Rigley Street. Reggie's going to give him a ride over there before taking you home. Is that okay?"

"Sure, yes, fine." I sounded pathetic.

We climbed into the back seat of Reggie's compact car. Becket had to part his legs around the front seat to fit and his left knee rode high over the middle hump. With long-legged Becket sitting beside me, there was minor personal space. When his leg swerved and touched mine, I wrestled with wanting to touch him. Over the years, I'd conjured all sorts of daydreams about the boy, and now, I made myself as little as possible. I could talk to Henry, no problem, but Becket, no way.

Reggie and Nona chatted up a storm while Becket and I remained mum. I averted my eyes toward the side window, playing it cool, while Becket's scent encompassed me like a bewitching lariat. He smelled like clean soap and I whiffed in appreciation.

I caught Nona's turn of the head as she threw me a wry brow. Her eyeballs were casting me juvenile twitches. My interpretation—speak to the boy.

It was a little bit too late as Smith's Garage came into view. Reggie made a wide turn causing my shoulder to brush against Becket's arm.

"Leo." Becket's voice was assertive, eliciting my neck to kink in his direction. "Reggie said you live on Westgate; that's in my direction. I'll drive you home."

Even if I had a rebuttal, he elbowed the door and stepped out before I had a chance to answer. I'd heard rumors that he was a domineering quarterback and the team obeyed his every command. Yet, he hadn't sounded conceited or arrogant. I'd call it being a friend to Reggie—Becket offering to take me home so Reggie didn't have to go out of his way again for me. A favor for a favor?

My eyes cut to Nona. I had to have looked scared out of my mind because she encouraged me by saying, "Go, girl. Call me later." Her eyebrows jumped to her forehead, issuing me a go-get-'em smile.

Outside the mechanic's garage, I waved to a departing Reggie and Nona and steeled myself against performing a happy dance. The pitter-patter of my heart kept beat to an imaginary conga-line.

With keys juggling in his hand, Becket ambled from the garage to his car. In gentlemanly fashion, he held the passenger door open and looked for me. Still standing by the garage entrance, I hadn't followed him and felt like a ditz. Nevertheless, I scraped some dignity to walk toward him, his eyes watching my every move.

Once stationed behind the steering wheel, he turned to me with impassive eyes. "I'm an excellent driver. But you might want to put on your seatbelt."

"You live at eighty-six Westgate, right?" I nodded and wondered if Reggie told him my address.

"You're quiet, for a girl." His message was obvious—girls talk too much. I fiddled with the hem of my sleeve as my tongue glued itself to the roof of my mouth.

"Well, if you're not going to speak, mind if I put on some tunes?"

I initiated a simple shrug. He then furnished me with a smile, enhancing his features to the tenth degree. I had read a book recently where the protagonist swooned in her lover's arms, and I'd snickered. *I think I just swooned.*

I hadn't anticipated his choice of music as he leveled the radio's volume. I had him pegged as a headbanger, wild boy, but a baroque style of strings floated through the speakers.

My body relaxed, drawing in a peaceful breath.

"There, that's better." He watched me. "You're a pretty uptight girl."

"You don't know me."

"Ahh, she speaks," he said, awarding me another mind-blowing smile. "The next street is Westgate, right?" Disheartened with the short drive, I nodded.

Becket asked, "Did I say something wrong?"

Baffled, I looked at him. "No, why?"

"You were just opening up, getting all talkative. I could hardly get a word in edgewise." I offered him a tight-lipped grin.

We coasted along Westgate and I indicated where I lived. "That's my house on the right. The one with the green trim." Turning into the driveway, he let the car idle. "Thanks for the ride." I cracked open the door.

"Leo." I swiveled on the car seat, gazing at him over my shoulder. "Someday, would you like to get something to eat?"

My breath hit a snag. I nodded and said, "Sure." It sounded more like *shore*.

"Great, nice chatting with you." I liked his suggestive grin.

I waltzed into the house and found Dad in the living room watching the World News.

"Hey, Leo. Who was that?"

"Who was what?"

He repeated, "Who brought you home. It wasn't that Henry kid."

"Were you spying on me through the curtains?" I wasn't uptight; it struck me as silly.

"That's my job, kiddo."

"Becket Kane drove me home after practice."

"A boy from school, I assume."

I sighed. "Yes."

His mouth gathered to the side. I plopped onto the couch and pillowed an arm beneath my head.

"The local news is teeming with allegations about that dead body found on Tarpon Hill. They said it was badly mutilated."

Dad fractured my cheerful mood. "Did they say who it was yet?"

"Yeah, a guy that graduated from Star Hallow last year. Skipper Townsend. Do you remember him?"

My chest caved; of course, I knew Skipper. He was Star Hallow's renowned drug dealer. "I...I kind of remember seeing him around school."

"And they found a second body in Hallow Saint's Cemetery. He went by the name of David Galbraith. Did you know him too?"

In disbelief, I mumbled, "Ah-huh."

"Police are investigating. The news is presuming it's a drug-related crime. They interviewed Detective Dyl," Dad said, voice scratchy. "You...you remember him?"

I lay there like a corpse.

"He said they had an anonymous tip," Dad went on. "A garbled 911 call leading them to the cemetery. The detective is asking for anyone with information to...to, please, come forward."

After a tense pause, he cried, "Leo, I'm reliving it all over again."

CHAPTER 5

"It's not the same," I retorted and rolled off the couch. "Mom was an innocent victim."

Through his whimpering, Dad said, "So are those boys, so young."

"You can't take every murder to heart. It's not healthy."

"Leo, how many murders have occurred in Star Hallow in the last year?"

I was beginning to feel ill. His question had caught me off guard. "I...I don't know."

"Only one—Lily, your mother. Now two more." He hiccupped and drool dribbled from his mouth. "This is a sleepy little town. Murders don't happen in the Hallows."

"Dad, you're being overly sensitive." I couldn't stand looking at his crushed face as my stomach pitched. I hurried to the bathroom and barfed the paltry scraps I'd eaten that day.

While trying to ignore his wallowing sobs, I hobbled to my room like an old lady. Just as I flipped the lock, the telephone rang. Dad wasn't in any shape to answer so I raced into the kitchen to the landline.

"Where have you been?" Nona blared through the receiver. "I've been calling your cell for over an hour."

"I'm sorry, but I forgot to tell you, I lost my cell."

"Where'd you lose it?"

Hesitant to explain the incident in the cemetery, I sensed the need to keep it secret, at least for now. "I don't know."

"Will your dad fork out money to get you a new one?"

"I hope so."

She burst with impatience. "You know why I called, right?"

Nona knew nothing about my misery and I tried to absorb her gusto. My whole psyche flip-flopped as I relayed, "He asked if I wanted to get something to eat." I had to hold the phone away from my ear as she screeched like a banshee.

"I told you so." She pealed a redundant squeal. "Becket's been eyeing you for a while now."

"What did Reggie tell you?"

"He's close-mouthed. Won't nark on a friend," she said flippantly. "All I know is that Becket actually did need a ride to get his car. It was fate, Leo, plain and simple."

"Hah, that's what you call it? I call it a coincidence."

"I don't believe in coincidences." She was getting dramatic. "It was fate."

"Okay, fate then." I paused, thinking. "Becket asked me out, but he hadn't mentioned when and he didn't ask for my phone number."

"You mean he didn't make an actual date?"

"No."

"Don't worry, girl. If he's interested, nothing will stop that boy."

"Maybe he said that to be nice."

"Then why," Nona said, "did he want to drive you home if he wasn't interested?"

"Probably to repay Reggie for giving him a lift to his car."

"Leo, you're reading too much into this. Stop dissecting every little thing."

I didn't want to get my hopes up. Yet, I gambled a tiny squeal.

An hour later, while I lay on my bed, finishing my math homework, a tap sounded on the window. Not again. I raised the blinds to see Henry leaning with both hands on the house.

I drew up the window. "Hey, Henry. This is getting to be a habit."

"I've been trying to get a hold of you. Are you ignoring my calls?" I detected a trace of spite in his tone.

"No." I had an idea. "You want to go for a walk?"

His mouth curved. "Sure."

"I'll meet you out front." His head jerked up as an affirmative, and then he pushed away from the house.

I left my bedroom and walked into darkness. Dad had turned off the lights and went to bed early. If he woke up and found me gone, he'd have my head. So, I scrawled a note and placed it in the middle of the kitchen table. Snagging my hoodie and slipping a flashlight in the pocket, I went to meet Henry.

A blanketing cloud coverage obstructed the moon and stars, sheathing the avenue in murkiness. "It feels like rain," I said and browsed the menacing sky.

"It gets dark early, but this time of year rocks," Henry said while following my lead. "Halloween is the best. What do people do in the Hallows?"

"What do you mean, do?" I crossed the street and stalled on the sidewalk in front of Henry's house where

I had discovered my phone was missing. I kept my eyes lowered toward the ground, ready to retrace my footsteps from last night.

"New York's a virtual nightmare around Halloween. Every year there's kick-assing parties and the clubs are insane. We'd hit one of those haunted mansions or something." He unzipped his jacket and winged the sides as if he were too hot. "It's even better when you're flying high. I'm going to miss that."

"Star Hallow has haunted everything. People like to say their houses or farms are haunted and charge admission to scare the pants off you."

"Sweeeet. We're going, right?"

"Umm...I never liked Halloween," I lied and kept my gaze lowered.

"You're shitting me, right? We're definitely doing something. I'll bag us some good stuff so we can get really freaked out. I'll show you how we party in the city."

I had no intention of disclosing to the new boy that I'd essentially lived a nightmare the whole year. It had been right before Halloween when I found her.

That caged memory developed out of nowhere. I was picturing her body, again and again. I tried my best to wrangle it back into its cage and lock it.

Not that I participated last year, but Nona and the girls frequently had a master plan for celebrating Halloween. Besides, I didn't want to commit to Henry. Especially since Becket finally knew I existed. As an alternative, I explained, "There's this one decrepit place on Lucien Court. It's haunted and—"

"Are you looking for something?"

Lifting my head, I perceived his wondering expression. "Yeah, I lost my cell phone last night."

"Why didn't you tell me? We could've looked for it earlier when it was light out."

"I didn't get home from practice until almost seven."

"I never had to wait that long for you."

"I missed the late bus so Nona and Reggie gave me a ride," I answered with another petty fib. "I had to stay and watch the boy's practice."

His lips drew into an apologetic bumpy line. "I was so tired, I raced home and zonked out or I would've given you a ride. Sorry."

"It's not your job to chauffeur me around. I appreciate it, though, I can't wait until I have my own car." Returning my sights to the ground, I caught a glimpse of his cell lighting up as he was dialing a number. "Who you calling?"

"You." The rim of his lip perked up. "We'll hear it ring if it's close by."

Both of us stilled our feet. "Hmm, nothing."

Henry dialed again and brought his cell to his ear. "No voicemail or ringtone either."

"Figures," I said, disappointed. "It's dead."

The intermittent streetlamps aided in my search, showering the neighborhood until we reached Tarpon Hill. Unfortunately, vandals and kids liked to rock the lamps as a game and, over the years, Star Hallow seemed to give up on replacing them. The one surviving streetlamp I'd been standing under the night before had been snuffed out.

Henry matched my snail's pace, also hunting for my cell phone. As we walked, he brushed the blades of grass with his sneakers on either side of the concrete sidewalks. When I stopped to read the street sign, he looked up.

He asked, "Why do you always take the long route on Tarpon when Lucien Court's faster?"

"You've cut through the Court?"

"When we first moved here, I didn't have anything to do." The cold must've gotten to him because he zipped his gray jacket. "I came down this road a couple of times and crossed over the tracks into the cemetery and had a radical idea of hanging out there. Nobody to bother us." He snorted. "Get it? No body?" With what I imagined was a funny look on my face, he said, "Is it because of that haunted house?" He raised his arms and wiggled his fingers, making fun of me. "Ooooo... are you afraid?"

"That's part of the reason."

Henry hooked my arm and yanked me to the crossroads of Lucien and Tarpon. "I want to see this haunted house. C'mon."

Overshadowed with a wave of dread, I dug my heels into the ground. "No, Henry. I'm not going down that street." I yanked my arm from his hold. "I'm looking for my phone and it's not on Lucien Court."

"Come on, Leo. We'll come back and look for your phone. First, I want to see this house." He faced me with a wayward leer. "Do people live there?"

"It has a grisly reputation." I looked toward the street that gave out murky vibes. "Been vacant for years. I think the realtors have given up trying to unload it." I rubbed my hands over my long sleeve hoodie for warmth. "Last I heard, the Hallow was thinking of demolishing it."

"Crap, what a waste. Let's go before I miss all the fun." He dashed ahead.

"No, Henry." My voice dissipated in the faint wind. I watched him trot down the dismal street. He wheeled around, beckoning me to follow. With an overstressed shake of my head, I mouthed, *"No. Way."*

He wasn't taking no for an answer, and spinning frontward, he persisted along Lucien Court. I lost sight of him as he vanished behind a giant oak tree. Unsure, I begged my legs to move. Everyone in the Hallows had been well aware of the history of the Lucien Baskerville Estate erected in 1895. Its property buckled into the railroad, and Hallow Saint's Cemetery was practically in its backyard.

A cul-de-sac was named after the founder, Lucien Court, and it sustained only three houses: the Lucien Estate and two ancient shingled colonial homes. The Estate had been abandoned after several new homebuyers claimed inexplicable occurrences. Three years ago, the beige colonial situated on the east side of the Estate had burnt to the ground, more than likely squatters or kids. On the western side of the street, the unkempt green colonial was where I grew up—until Mom was murdered there.

CHAPTER 6

Making an effort to control the shakes, I removed the flashlight from my pocket and pressed the button; it didn't work. I smacked the cylinder tube onto the palm of my hand. Thankfully, it flickered on.

My light floated over weedy grass and along the curbless road. Imbued with reluctance, I grazed my feet over the familiar broken sidewalk, recollecting every crevice and irregular concrete pad. "Henry."

Rolling rumbling sounded in the distance and the threatening sky was caving in. I needed to look for my cell phone before it rained. It wasn't my desire to get stuck in a rainstorm, in particular, on the Court. "Henry, where are you?" I walked in a hurry, meaning to grab him and get the hell out of there.

It seemed instinctive for my body to stop and turn. A shroud of darkness engulfed my old homestead. Petrified and trapped in a mysterious spell, my legs had an inexorable gravitational pull to where I grew up. I toddled toward the porch like a zombie in motion and directed light on splattered crimson stains. It wasn't possible, was it? A horrific reminder, blood had leached into the craggy wood.

As if touching my sneakers on the stains was sinful, I sidestepped onto the porch. The suspended porch swing drew my vision. A flash of memories: Mom tucking a blanket around me. Mom reading while rocking back and forth. The squared picture window was now swathed in dusty dirt. I pocketed the flashlight and skated to the window. Using the sleeve of my hoodie, I erased a grimy patch.

I cupped my face like a pair of horse blinkers and mushed my nose to the cleaned patch. Too dark to see anything, I extracted the flashlight and affixed it to the glass. It didn't make a dent in the dark.

For sure, I saw something move. I huffed, fogging the pane and swiped at the condensation and looked again. A tongue-thrusting, open-mouthed face sneered at me from inside the house. I let loose a gut-wrangling scream. Backing away I hit the porch railing and fell to my knees.

"It's only me," the face yelled through the glass. "It's me—Henry." Less than a minute, he was leaning over me.

"Chill, Leo," he said through a chuckle. "Just a Halloween gag. What's with the fainty gig?"

"Oh my God, oh my God, oh my God." Severely hyperventilating, I struggled to get the words out. "You gave me a fucking heart attack." The world tipped upside down. Henry supported my elbows and carted me to the porch swing. "I think," I paused, gasping, "I think I'm going to kill you."

My body was tingling with pins and needles infesting my face. "How'd...how'd you...get in...the house?"

"I didn't break in if that's what you're thinking," he relayed. "The side door was open."

As far as I knew, the house was supposed to be locked up tight. It'd been on the seller's market for the past six months. Your average Joe normally didn't like to purchase a home where an unsolved murder had transpired, go figure.

"What's gotten into you?" He swept back my hair, allowing cool air to touch my face, which remained tingly. "I've never seen you like this before."

"How long have we known each other?" Not waiting for his answer, I said, "Two months, Henry. You don't really know me."

"I know that I like you. I know that I want to be with you." His brow puckered, turning sober and he reached for my hand.

Oh, no. I had created a monster just by being nice, friending the new kid, and now it was backfiring. When had I acquired such compelling charm? If Henry persisted in hounding me, Becket would think we were an item. "I do like you." I tried being earnest while putting the kibosh on the phony fixation he'd conceived. "Like a friend."

He grinned. "Friendship that's growing." He slanted into my body as his thumb stroked the top of my hand.

I pulled my hand away and scrubbed off his touch. To eliminate my current predicament, I leaped to my feet, sending him crashing to the ground. "You wanted to see the Lucien Estate." I indicated the way with a hop over the two front steps and ran through weedy grass. "Let's go, or are you a scaredy-cat?" I yelled over my shoulder.

He whooped while pole vaulting over the porch railing, running after me. The Lucien Baskerville Estate spread over twenty acres of land. The three-story Victorian structure resembled the classic haunted house. Weathered planks boarded a few of the first-story windows, where kids had thrown stones and rocks. I still remembered the day when I'd been cruising on my new two-wheeler bicycle and watching Star Hallow crewmen hammering boards over the broken windows. The structure consisted of four gables, a hexagonal turret, and at its summit, centering the facade, an exceptional circular stained-glass window. Pillars and posts upheld a wraparound porch and the second and third-story balconies. Sun-baked grime had obscured most of rectangular windows.

"Holy moly, this place rocks." His breathy phrase misted around his head. "I see a fun-ass Halloween bash. So what's the story on this crib?"

Henry and I lingered on the sidewalk staring at the mansion; tall stalks of brown grassy weeds infested the property. I inspected the windows for signs of recent break-ins and located a broken window on the second level.

"There's lots of stories. Probably most of them are fabricated nonsense." We stood shoulder to shoulder and I turned to look at him. His eyes squinted behind his lenses, peering upward.

"He strode over a bricked pathway toward the wraparound porch. "So, Leo, give me a history lesson."

Overgrown shrubbery encased the mansion, and mutinous vines twined the central pillars, bleeding over the roofline. Fronds dangled from gutters that weaved an intricate netting over the porch, and a rusty chain bolted the double-door entry.

"I'll give you the condensed version. It starts with Lucien Baskerville and his new bride, Monique." Weeds scraped at my jeans as I tracked Henry's footsteps. "Lucien started a cargo business and set up shop on Lake Erie. His investment paid off and he had shipyards all around the Great Lakes."

Henry fought with disentangling vines that ate the side of the house and the door as I went on, "He met Monique at Port Sault Ste. Marie. Lucien thought she was nobility, a daughter of a wealthy land baron. She told him that she'd accept his proposal of marriage if he built her a beautiful home, supporting her in the lifestyle she'd been accustomed to."

I spread my arms. "And here it is. After they married, Monique squandered Lucien's fortune. He pleaded to his wealthy father-in-law for a loan. Monique's father laughed in his face. That was when Lucien discovered Monique had been sending funds and gifts to her family in Sault Ste. Marie, leaving him penniless. With her task complete, Monique had another wealthy suitor waiting in the wings." I paused, waiting for Henry to look at me. "Her lover."

"You have the tale memorized. Awesome." Henry's fingers circled the rusty chain and wrenched the links devoid of results. Flexing his arm and squeezing his biceps, he said, in a Swedish dialect, "I need to pump some iron. Let's find another way in." The porch creaked underfoot as we trekked further. He swerved back to me. "Okay, go on. Her lover?"

I tweaked my eyebrow and strived for a cruel grin. "Before she left, Lucien had been drinking heavily and claimed to see ghostly people wandering around in the mansion. These ghosts told him about Monique's adultery. Nowadays, a psychiatrist would've called him a schizophrenic, but he only saw these people at the mansion, nowhere else."

"Are you making this shit up?"

"It's a major part of Star Hallow's history." A chill wrapped around me, and, again, I tugged on the long sleeves of my hoodie. "Pretty much every kid who grew up in the Hallow has memorized the story. If you don't believe me, you can learn about the mansion's history in the library."

"How do you know Lucien was schizophrenic?"

"It's documented but I'm adding flair just for you. Stop interrupting, okay?" I cleared my throat. "While Lucien was gone on his many business trips attempting to recoup his floundering company, Monique was having relations with her new conquest. One day Lucien surprised the staff and came home early. A servant confided to him of the mistress' illicit affairs.

"Lucien went berserk. He stomped into the study where his honored sword from the civil war hung on the wall and removing it from the mount, he marched up the staircase." I seized Henry's arm for emphasis. "It's said to this day, people who've been in the mansion can still hear the *clunk, clunk, clunk* of the sword hitting each step as he walked."

A shiver went through Henry's body as I released him. "When Lucien surprised Monique, a man jumped from the bed only to be sliced in two." Pretending I held a sword, my arm whooshed through the air. I stopped for a breather, actually frightening myself. Henry pried a wooden plank from one of the window frames, then fed his body through the opening.

"Hand me the flashlight," he said, sticking his arm out of the gap.

After handing over the light, I peeked in. A delicate shine milled over ghostly shawled furniture in white sheets.

"Come on in."

CHAPTER 7

As I crawled over the windowsill, a shard of glass ripped my jeans at the knee, gouging my skin. "Ouch." A dribble of blood ran down my shin and I swabbed the fluid with my fingers.

"You okay?" Henry asked.

"Fine, just a scratch." I glanced over the dusky room and trilled my voice, "Crreeepy."

"Haven't you ever been in this amazing place?" He held the flashlight beneath his chin where the light and shadow disfigured his face. Knowing how sinister he'd appear he cackled like a wicked witch.

"Stop it, Henry. This place doesn't need any encouragement."

"So truth. You've never been in here?"

"Truth." I lied. "Never."

"Our first adventure into creepsville. Cool." Moving the beam of light around the area, he sighed in disappointment. "Looks like a typical home with lots of crap."

"What did you expect?"

"I don't know. Something out of a horror flick."

"Looks pretty horrible to me." Stationed in the corner was an elegant grand piano. I swept my fingertips through the dust and raised the piano's lid and tapped the out-of-tune keys. The tinkling echoed throughout the room. Henry removed a sheet from a piece of furniture. Sooty particles became airborne, catching the light.

"This couch looks ancient." He ran his palm over the fabric, raising tons of dust motes.

"No one's lived here since the 1980s. My mom once told me that whenever people moved in, something bad always happened within five years."

"You're kidding?" Henry's shady features held a spark of joy. "You mean this mansion has been vacant that long?"

"It's prime property. Those other two houses on the street were originally built as servant's quarters in early 1896. Over the years, gullible out-of-towners wanted to transform the mansion into all sorts of excellent ideas. Buyers have been weirded out by the—"

"What idiots would actually believe that legend?" He spun around, taking the light with him and the dark shadows swallowed me. "This place is a goldmine. If I had the money, I'd buy it."

Whether it had been rehashing Lucien's tale or traversing back to the scene of Mom's murder, I felt a boding presence and didn't like it. "Henry, we should leave. There's something off with this place. Can't you feel it?"

"I love it." Out of the blue, he tore from of the room, taking my flashlight with him. Heavy thumping sounded as he headed up the winding staircase.

"Don't leave me." My skin itched as if worms squiggled beneath my skin as I ran after him. "Henry!"

"This way, Leo." He streamed light onto the stairs.

I held onto the banister, feeling mounds of dust and insect carcasses under my palm. When I reached the second-floor landing, I brushed my hands over my jeans and scowled at him. "You dirtbag, you left me in the dark."

"I got excited. C'mere, let's look around the old joint. Maybe we'll see a headless body or something."

"Hilarious." My hand darted out, stealing the flashlight from him. "It's my flashlight," I said rather surly.

"Damn, Leo. Don't get so hot and bothered—unless…" Swiveling toward me, Henry puckered his lips and zeroed in on me.

"Don't even think about it," I said, holding a hand up before he could get too close. "I'm not hot and bothered for you, Henry James. Nice try."

"Well, you can't blame a guy for trying. We'll just pretend that didn't happen. Let's start at the top of this shit heap." He started a two-step lope up the second flight of stairs where the gloom swallowed him.

"Henry, I want to leave," I whined after him. "Remember, we're supposed to be looking for my phone."

A peculiar shushing came through the walls, and I didn't like the sound of that.

Alone and defenseless, I felt like a human bull's eye. From somewhere deep within, I dredged up some courage and sped up the stairs, stalling once to sneeze. My feet struck the third floor with hope of finding Henry.

"Come out, come out, wherever you are." Frozen on the edge of the landing, I listened for his footsteps. I heard lightweight scuttling and aimed the light toward the baseboard.

Scurrying mice, nasty. Flashing the beam into a narrow hallway, it formed into a T at the end where a shadow was stirring. "Is that you?" It had been years and years since I explored the mansion but never in the dark.

I walked warily, depositing one wobbly leg in front of the other. A clothesline of flimsy cobwebs adhered to my face, and I swatted at them like a hare-brained loon. "Henry, I'm getting pissed," I said, suppressing a cry. "I want to leave."

"Up heeere..." hailed a faraway cadence.

I turned and witnessed white vapor breezing up the fourth flight of stairs. The sight causing icy fingernails to claw down my backbone. A ghost?

Then, in the opposite direction came another voice, "Leo. Leo. This way."

Relief strengthened my spine at hearing Henry. I swerved away from the fourth flight of stairs and the bizarre vapor, which I figured was a figment of my hypersensitive imagination. I headed into the hallway and stopped at the T, where it branched in either direction.

"Where are you?" Of course, he wasn't answering me. Inhaling for more courage, I choose to veer to the right.

Four six-paneled doors lined the walls. I twisted the first ornate knob and spilled light into a mishmash of clutter. I then traveled down the hall to the adjoining door and was enveloped by an unsavory smell. Rubbing the musty stink from my nose, I thought about avoiding this room. *What's that smell?*

There was a sound like water dripping and then splashing into a tinny pot. Perhaps the roof leaked? Curiosity got the best of me and I shouldered open the door. Pitch black, not a trace of light. The revolting stench heated the room. Was there a rotten animal in here? I plugged my nose to block the stench.

I guided my feet with the flashlight, but my sneakers stepped into a gooey substance. Suctioned to the floor, I pried them up; the goo looked reddish black. The cause of the stench? My paranoia reached its pinnacle. Let Henry find his own way out. *I'm leaving.* I turned toward the hall and the flashlight's beam sliced through the room. I was ready to flee when I caught sight of something. I cast the light upward, toward the high ceiling.

A bristly rope had been knotted around a chandelier. My light followed the line of rope and landed on a corpse. Not animal—human.

"Henry?!"

CHAPTER 8

My bumbling legs didn't register with my scattered brain as I choked on a scream. My sneakers swam in the goo and I fell on all fours. The rubber soles struggled to grip the floor, and when they did, I zoomed forward like a missile. Superman had nothing on me as I flew faster than the speed of light and surfed over three flights of stairs.

Throaty laughter followed me, ricocheting from wall to wall. "Leo. Leo. LEO!" Like hell—I wasn't stopping. On autopilot, my feet scrabbled on the main floor at warp speed. Remembering the front door was bolted and chained, I hightailed it for the living room where we came in.

Someone snatched me from behind. Gurgled shrieks clotted my throat as I operated the flashlight like a battering ram.

"Leo, stop!" He barred my attack with his arm and swiped the flashlight from my hand. "Get it together, girl."

"I hate you! I hate you! I hate you!" Fuming hotter than hellfire, I hissed through my teeth. "Is this your idea of a practical joke? You sick bastard."

"Calm down, Leo, please." Henry barnacled my flaying arms to my sides. "I wanted you to see the ingenious of it all."

"By scaring me into an early grave? You shithead. Let me go." I jostled from his grip. "Did you plan this whole charade? What was that up there?"

"We can make money," he said. "And you can buy that car you keep talking about."

"What do you mean? How?" I said, seething.

"I've been hanging out here. Coming up with fantastic ideas. I brought you here to show you what we could do with the place."

"Let's get out of here. I can't breathe." I wiggled through the broken window and Henry followed. Once outside I parted my lips, filling my lungs with air. Even the pressurized atmosphere was better than the decrepit airflow in the Lucien mansion. A bolt of lightning snared my eyes. The storm would be upon Star Hallow soon.

"Hurry," I said. "I want to check the railroad tracks for my phone before we get soaked." I began a rapid hike through the maze of vegetation behind the estate, not waiting for his answer and not caring if he followed me. Brambles, gorse bushes, and vines were attempting to trip me up. In the background, Henry was pulling and grumbling at the imprisoning shrubs.

"What about my idea?" he asked, his voice coming from close behind me.

"You're forgetting one thing. We don't own the property."

"We'll do it on the sly. Exclusive invitations to select people."

"The police will hear about it."

"You're such a downer, Leo." He hacked his arm at a sapling branch. "This is an outstanding opportunity. A haunted mansion and a party combined. Can't you imagine the possibilities? No limits! We can drink, smoke, do whatever."

Trekking to the railroad tracks, I turned toward him. "What was that scummy stuff on the floor, and who or what was hanging from the noose?"

"It was a mannequin wearing my old clothes. I axed the face and body and added red food dye to watery paste to make it look like blood." His tone was animated as he described his ploy. "That was real blood on the floor. I got it from the butcher. I told him my mom was making czarnina. That's Polish duck blood soup."

"Yuck. You mean my sneakers are covered in real blood?" I scraped my soles on the train ties hoping to rid them of the bloody residue.

"There were dozens of rooms," I said. "How did you know I would walk into that one?"

"Ah-hah—I locked most of the doors beforehand and left open only those three rooms."

"You locked the doors?"

An impish smirk slipped onto his face as he held up a key. "Skeleton key. Cool, huh?" He twirled a unique brass key between his fingers. "I found it wedged in one of the keyholes, but it doesn't work in all the locks."

"Hmm... But how'd you know I'd even end up on the third floor?"

"You heard me calling you, right? That's how. I purposely led you up there."

I mindfully mulled over that moment when I'd stalled on the third-floor landing. "When I reached the third floor, you said— 'Up here'—leading me to the fourth-floor attic. Then you called my name in the opposite direction. Which was weird." I pulled my earlobe in thought. "How did you get that vapor to flow up the stairs?" Shining the light beam at his neck, a cocktail of reactions decorated his face.

"You heard me say— Up here?"

"Yes," I said, bothered by his outrageous games. "Just tell me the truth. How did you do it?"

"I didn't."

"You didn't what?"

"I didn't say that. I don't know anything about this vapor thingy you're talking about." He shrugged, throwing his arms in the air, a gesture of dismissal.

"Are you for real?" A scowl pulled on my face. I didn't believe him.

"Just more reason why we have to have a cosmic party at the mansion. That sounds like a neat trick. I'll have to figure it out. Or the ghosts can do it for us." His eyes gleamed, probably pondering a spooktacular Halloween fest. "By the way, you never finished telling me the tale of Lucien and Monique."

In a zigzagging motion over the railroad tracks, I combed the area for my phone. "Just help me find my cell."

"You mean you're not going to tell me the whole story?"

"I'm going to leave you hanging."

He chuckled. "I get it."

I was disappointed after retracing my path to Tarpon Hill. No cell phone. "Shoot. Now I'll have to tell my dad."

"Hey, maybe he'll buy you a smartphone with a data package."

"I wouldn't bet on it, but that would be nice." A thunderous clap rocked my chest. "I wish it would rain already. My head is throbbing from the pressure." Although, I figured my headache was more than likely due to Henry's tricks.

"I love thunder and lightning storms. I once stood outside with a steel rod hoping to get hit."

"You're one cracked dude; you know that?" He snickered and pulled a joint out of his jacket pocket and lit up. "Are you serious? Right here, in public?"

"No streetlights on Tarpon. If anybody drives by, they'll think it's a cigarette." He handed it off. "Here, take a hit. It'll relax you. Take away that headache. Then you can finish the tale of Lucien."

If Nona found out I was smoking a joint, she'd beat me, but she won't, at least not by me. Fingering the joint, I inhaled a profound drag. After a measured exhale, I handed it back to him and retold the tragic end of Lucien and Monique.

"Lucien's mind was affected by the booze and morphine. After he murdered her lover, he tied Monique's arms and legs to their bed. She was his prisoner and tortured her for days."

"What do you mean by tortured?" His voice was raspy after inhaling and locking the smoke in his lungs. "How?"

"You really like this torture part, huh?"

"I want to know how he tortured her." Henry again handed off the ashy joint.

I hesitated relaying the nitty-gritty because it made me self-conscious. So I took another hit and then uttered, "He raped her."

"You can't rape your wife."

"Yes, you can!" I said, eyeing him with cynicism.

"Okay, I get it. Are you making this up just for me?"

"I read it," I said, vocalizing with a lungful of weed. "I don't know if it's all true or if the author made it up. But it's a good tale. Do you want to hear more?" A discharge of smoke slithered past my teeth.

He removed his glasses and shook his head. "Hell, yeah." He scrubbed the lenses with the border of his jacket and put them back on.

I smiled, taking pleasure in taunting him, especially after he shocked me to death. "Lucien wasn't done persecuting Monique. He carried her body to the fourth-floor attic while lugging his nifty sword." Henry's probing gaze was enthralled and hooked.

"Once in the attic, he dropped her to the floor and shattered the window overlooking the front yard. He ordered her to jump. Hysterically crying and screaming, she refused. Then, wielding the sword, he cut off her arm."

Henry coughed out, "Why didn't the servants help the poor woman?"

"Really?" I continued with a smug grin. "Again, he ordered her to jump. She tried running away but he chopped one of her legs." Reenacting the scene, I cleaved the air with my arm. "Yelling obscenities, he promised to cut her into pieces if she didn't jump. Somehow, she managed to drag what was left of her bleeding body to the window." Overplaying my role, I sagged and scuffed my left leg over the sidewalk, groping with my hands. Playing a drama queen, I hauntingly whispered, "On the night of the blood moon, you can still hear her dreadful screams as her body fluttered to the ground below." I smacked my hands together for effect and was pleased when Henry's shoulders twitched.

I adored retelling the tale to a newbie. "Lucien then reacted like the devil incarnate by raging through the mansion, slicing and dicing the servants. Only God knows what maggot drilled into his brain. Days later, it was written the mansion reeked of decaying death when Lucien put a gun into his mouth and pulled the trigger." Pantomiming, I lifted my hand to my mouth and pulled the trigger. I concluded my theatrical performance.

"What a totally repulsive story. I love it. How did anyone really know what happened?" We shared the joint until it sizzled into a microscopic butt. He let it sink to the sidewalk and ground it with the toe of his boot.

"That's the interesting part." I swatted at a bug buzzing around my face. "One of the servants had Lucien's illegitimate baby. Unknown to Lucien, the servant eventually made her living quarters in the attic. They were secretively hidden in the small, enclosed room when all hell broke loose. Supposedly, she bore witness to the entire thing."

Henry's mouth curled.

"Oh, there's more. Much more."

CHAPTER 9

"But those stories are for another day."

Henry's jaw sagged. "You mean you're going to leave me hanging like this?"

"Exactly." I loved the cute, vexing expression on his face before I twisted my mouth into a gotcha smile. He rolled his eyes. I could tell he was impressed with my story prowess.

"Hey, I have to get home," I said. "My dad was mad last night when I came in so late."

He took out his cell and checked the time. "It's only eleven o'clock."

"Time flies when you're being scared to death." We turned the corner onto Westgate. "You picking me up in the morning?"

"Yep, seven-thirty."

I waved goodbye and went down the street to my house. Entering the foyer, I toed off the heels of my yucky sneakers. I walked into the kitchen and stopped. *Crap*! Dad's upper body was sprawled over the kitchen table. Not good.

He popped up. His back hitting the chair, it rocked slightly. "Where the hell have you been? Two nights in a row." Bloodshot eyeballs fastened on me. "I let you run wild after your mother died. You think I'm blind? All the drugs you were using, getting plastered to forget. I figured you needed privacy and time to heal, but now I'm reining you in, kid."

"What's gotten into you?" I tugged off my hoodie and hung it on a peg behind the door. "I left you a note." His fingers had crumpled the piece of paper. "It's not that late, Dad. Barely eleven."

"I don't care," he slurred, either from drowsiness or being drunk. "I need to know where you are. Who you're with. You got that?"

"I'm almost seventeen."

"Don't pull the age card on me." He rose and wobbled, definitely drunk. "If you live in my house, you follow my rules. Got it?"

Since Mom died, he'd changed, and booze only made it worse. "Got it." It was better to agree than to disagree when he was like this. "I'm going to bed." As I went by, his fingers circled my arm.

"Who were you with?"

"Just Henry." His whiskey breath stung my nose.

"I don't like him snooping around here."

"He's my friend."

"I don't like him."

"You don't even know him," I said, perturbed. His drunken eyes watered. "Dad, why don't you go to bed? We can talk about this tomorrow."

"There's no debate. You mark my words."

"Okay. Fine."

"What do you mean by that punkass remark?"

"I'm not being a punkass. I said, okay. I understand."

He freed my arm and then staggered into his bedroom. His behavior had been getting unpredictable; one day he was caring and the next wired. I couldn't handle his changeable personalities. If Mom were here—but she wasn't.

Striving not to think about it, I went into my bedroom.

I flipped open the cover of an assigned novel and read a couple of chapters. Forty-five minutes later, I ballooned back the covers. Ready to snuggle into bed, a tap sounded on the window. *I can't believe it! Henry's pestering me, again.* I switched off the lights, hoping he'd get the hint. He didn't.

Ensuing through minutes of consecutive tapping, I grumbled and kicked off the covers. Garbed in my skuzzy tank top and boxer shorts and cussing under my breath, I zipped up the blinds and froze.

In all his glory, inclined on my house was Becket Kane.

Glad for my darkened room, I wondered if he could see my grungy clothes. He flipped his hand upward, a signal for me to open. I leaned into the glass and made another mental note—lubricate the window frame.

The wind had kicked up and his hair pranced about his head.

"May I make an observant suggestion?" he said. "Make sure the blinds are completely closed before changing your clothes." His mouth stretched attractively into his cheeks. "I tried not to watch, but I'd be lying if I said I didn't peek."

I was mortified. —*Where's the cape of invisibility when I need one?*

He swiped long strands of hair that had stuck to his eyelashes. "Reggie gave me your cell number, but I haven't been able to get through."

A blaze of lightning brightened the angry dark-gray clouds and thunder quaked the house, then an abrupt surge of pelting rain evolved into a mantle of falling water.

I weighted my shoulder into the frame and shoved the screen as wide as I could get it. "Get in before you get drenched." In a graceful swoop, Becket was in my bedroom and he helped me shut the window from the sleeting raindrops.

A waterslide of ropy hair dripped down his face. "Thanks, but I'm getting your floor wet." His hands thrust the hair off his forehead, plastering the strands to his head.

I raced to the chair and snatched my comfy robe and chucked it at him. He caught it and looked at me, arching one of his eyebrows. "What do you want me to do with this?" he said, amusement glittering in his eyes. "I'm not wearing your robe."

"Use it to wipe up the floor." I switched on the light and tugged at my top and boxers, wishing they'd magically change into something more appropriate.

I tried not to gawk as he mopped his face with my robe, then he crouched to the floor to mop the water. Rising to his full height, I felt dwarfed and my room suddenly became minuscule. He bunched my robe into a ball.

"I didn't expect to see you so soon." I went for the carefree pitch, but it was pitiful. Taking my robe from his hands, I threw it on the floor next to the doorway.

"Ah, she speaks."

Becket was unruffled as if jumping into a girl's bedroom window after midnight were common. He gave my room a onceover before his gaze landed on me. "Clean."

After Mom died, I'd inherited her clean freakdom and took that as a compliment. "Want to sit until the rain subsides?"

"In your bed?" he purred sarcastically. "Leo, what kind of guy do you take me for?"

"Um...chair. Sit." Punctuated words ejected from my mouth and heat torpedoed into every nook and cranny of my body.

"I was going to wait until tomorrow and catch you at school, but this was more fun. I just meant to knock on your window, not actually be invited in." He shoved out of his jacket and his sneakers and then heard my intake of breath because he paused. Elevating his arms expressing innocence, he stated, "They're wet and dirty. Don't have a fit. I didn't want to get mud all over your floor." In stockinged feet, he padded to the chair and sat. "Relax, Leo."

Ashamed by my timid-ass stupidity, I moved to the bed and balanced my backend on the edge. I crossed my ankles, and the act drew his attention to my feet. His pokerfaced gaze traveled the length of my legs, activating a full-body shiver.

"Nice."

"Nice what?"

"Legs, you have nice legs."

"Thanks." Flattery will get him everywhere. It was an insecure move, but I lifted my legs to my chest and wrapped my arms around my shins. I saw it in his pursing lips that spread into a rakish smile. He sensed my vulnerability.

We worked through an awkward silence, listening to the storm battering the roof of the ranch house. "The rain will let up in a minute."

He had a quick comeback. "In a hurry to get rid of me?" Baby-blue eyes, cool and alluring, fringed with black lashes, stared at me. No wonder every girl in school drooled when his name was mentioned.

"It's late," I said, for no reason other than to break the awkwardness.

He blasted me with a righteous smile. "Have to get your beauty rest, eh?"

His contagious smile willed my mouth to curl before reaching my eyes. He shelved his right ankle over his left knee, in a detached manner, looking completely laid-back. "You should smile more often; it suits you."

Knowing full well my hair was a mess, I darted fingertips to my head, quelling the rat's nest.

"Like I was saying before the storm," he prompted. "I tried calling you—"

"I lost my phone." Understanding, he raised his chin in a partial nod.

"After I dropped you at home, I meant to make a specific date for that cup of coffee, and it's been bothering me."

Becket knows where I live and he waited until after midnight to ask me out? Unless, he came by and I was with Henry at the Lucien mansion.

"If you really want that cup of coffee," I teased, "it's too late now."

"You're getting the sarcastic gist." He scratched his jaw, where there was a shadow of whiskers. "Tomorrow. After school." Embodied with self-confidence, he hadn't asked; he stated a fact.

He's assuming I'm one of his groupie, dreamy-eyed girls, which I am, but he doesn't need to know it!

"Can I let you know tomorrow?" I sucked at my puckish reply.

"Tomorrow?"

"Yes, tomorrow." *Hah… He thought I'd be all over it.* "I have second-period lunch. Can you meet me in front of the cafeteria around twelve? I have to check the cheerleading schedule. I might have practice."

His brow gathered in thought, then he said, "Sure. That can happen." He stood and slipped his arms into the sleeves of his leather jacket. "The rain is letting up. I'd better get out of here so you can get some sleep." He went toward the window and bending over slipped on his sneakers.

I joined him, keeping a fair space between us. Before I had a chance to grip the windowpane, he beat me to it and pushed it open. He then veered in my direction and tilted close, his beautiful eyes searching mine. "Sorry for this impromptu visit. But to tell you the truth, I kind of liked it," he whispered, his breath touching my cheek.

Mesmerized, I couldn't speak. He was my lodestone and my body wanted to lean into him. It was a mere second when I thought he was going to kiss me. Instead, he swerved to the window and was gone.

CHAPTER 10

I had to call Nona. *Becket Kane is juicy news.*

"Darnnit." I no longer have my phone. It had been a memorable evening, with the cherry on top being the random arrival of Becket. My body swiftly waned of energy. Rather than calling Nona on the landline, I funneled underneath the covers of my bed. My juicy news would have to hold until tomorrow.

A half-hour later, I was still tossing from one side of the mattress to the other, endeavoring to claim my comfort zone. From a fetal position, stretching onto my back, then my side to my stomach. The room became oppressive. Dragging myself to the window, I opened it a few inches, allowing the drizzling rain to pepper my face through the screen, and then watched my reflection smearing in the darkened panes of glass. I leveled the blinds to the sill and, thanks to Becket, double checked for any peepholes and hopped into bed. I conked out instantly.

I'm in Lucien Court. Across the street is the scorched cavity of the old Perkins house. Standing on my front porch. Sunshine sparkles on dollops of red.

In the kitchen. Carrot shavings. A pot on the stove furling steam.

"Mom?"

In the living room. A trail of red on the staircase. Apprehensive toe steps.

Stalling by their bedroom door. A storm of panic. It glides open. A body—fanning hair— blood—puddles and puddles of blood!

Arms band me. Thrashing. My nails claw flesh. Screaming. A sweaty palm filters my cries.

Oh my God, I know who it is.

"Leo." Dad rocked my thrashing body. "Leo. You're alright. It's just a dream."

I let loose a frenzied gasp, my eyes widened, sighting my bleak room. I was a ball of sweat and swept layers of hair off my cheeks and neck.

"Dad," I squeezed his name past the lump in my throat. "I'm okay."

"You haven't had one of these in months." He held me by the shoulders and examined my face.

"I know." My senses reeled because I could still smell the blood. "I walked by the house yesterday."

"Why?" His glum eyes were on the verge of watering. "I told you never to go there." Shadows filled in his face, making him look old. Skin sagged beneath each eye and his cheeks were sunken from lack of food and too much alcohol.

"I didn't go inside. But the side door was open."

"Open? It should've been locked." His hands dropped from my shoulders. "Maybe the realtor had been there. I'll have to call and find out." He agitatedly scraped his finger along the side of his collarbone. "I better get ready for work. Are you sure you're alright?"

"I'm good." I twisted to read the clock and groaned. Time to get up.

We arrived at school with minutes to spare. "Want to do some Halloween planning after school?" Henry inquired.

How should I break the news? An inner voice replied, *Blurt it out.* "Henry, I'm going out with a friend after school. So don't wait for me."

Removing his glasses, he squinted as if I were speaking alien or something. Then my words must've registered, and he said, "You going with Nona?"

"Er...no. A different friend." Why did I feel this was complicated? He put his glasses back on as we slogged into school with the rest of the herd.

"Who? Those cheer girl airheads? Marcy and Stephanie?"

I knew why it was complicated; Henry liked me more than just a friend. I went for it. "Becket Kane asked me to go out after school today."

"Kane? That quarterback dude?"

"That's the one."

"You've got to be joking?" He halted in the middle of the corridor and scrunched his nose as if he smelled something foul.

Guilt and anger stirred in my chest. "Why would I joke about it?" Students had to bypass our twosome, giving us peeved glances for blocking their way.

His head hung in dejection. "See ya..." He rounded the corner leaving me behind to feel... *What?*

An arm encircled my lower back. "Hey, Leo." Nona gifted me with a bubbly smile. "Did you tell your father about your phone yet? I didn't want to upset him with a late-night call and I was dying to talk to you."

"I wanted to talk to you, too." Forgetting about Henry, all guilt and anger dissolved. "You're never going to believe what happened—"

"Wait, girl—me first." Nona's brow heightened giving me a sidelong look, and I buttoned my lips. She glimpsed the crowded hallway, then summoned me to the side lockers. "I got some information from Reggie. Guess what he told me?" she said, riding high on her toes like an excited child. "C'mon, guess?"

"Reggie revealed…" I touched my fingers to my temples like I was reading her mind. "That Becket asked him for my cell phone number because he was going to ask me out after school today."

"How did you know that?" Her face knotted. "Reggie gave Becket your cell number before picking me up for the movies last night. But then I explained to Reg that you lost your cell. Reggie texted Becket your house phone num…" Her eyes lit up. "He called you at home?"

"Nope. He never called me." I grinned, liking this game.

"So, you're not going out, and he never called?" Her mouth puckered.

"We're definitely going out." I snickered at her look of befuddlement.

"Becket came to my house."

From befuddled to elated, she yelped, "Really!"

"Actually he came to my bedroom window."

"Tell me more; this is good stuff." Nona would not be so psyched if she knew Henry had been clambering through my bedroom window too. In her eyes, Becket was acceptable. "It was kind of awesome." I described my late-night visitor and how I made him wait, only to snub him. Nona ate it up.

"You're going to go?"

"I'm still thinking about it," I said, sounding smug, I gripped my chin and gazed toward the ceiling in thought.

"Oh, you'll go," she said, certain, adding a positive head shake. "You can't pull the wool over these honey browns. I know you better than you know yourself, hun."

Her mothering splintered my smart-aleck bravado. Turning somber, I related, "I had another one of those dreams last night." My best friend's cheerful features faded.

"I prayed you were over that hump." She embraced me, patting my back. "Leo, I wish I could help. Maybe you need to see the psychiatrist again."

"Hell, no. Psychotherapy and the anti-depressants didn't agree with me." On the brink of tears, I countered, "You're my psychiatrist."

She pulled back and I played with a loose strand of my hair. "Something's changed." *Don't get emotional; keep your head together.* "After I was grabbed from behind...I remember scratching his arms with my fingernails, trying to get away, and then...and then...I knew who it was."

Trepidation cut into Nona's face. "Who...who was it?" she said, her tone fretful.

"In my dream, I thought I knew who it was. When I woke up, I forgot. It's like I blacked it out all over again."

By lunchtime I was behind schedule and wondered if Becket had waited, or if he thought I stood him up. Turning the corner, I couldn't miss him. Tall and imposing, his back was leisurely fixed on the wall with a swarm of girls surrounding him. He was talking with Marcy, the captain of the cheerleading squad.

As if he sensed my approach, his eyes flickered down the corridor and pinned onto me. Making up for my tawdry appearance from the previous night, I primped especially for this occasion. He monitored my every move and the side of his mouth curved into a smile. I figured he liked what he saw. Confident in my form-fitting, red-knit dress and paisley print tights with my black ankle boots, I'd dressed to impress.

He shrugged from the wall, and the girls followed his gaze.

"Hey. Sorry, I'm late."

"No problem. I had company." Inquisitive girls glared at me and then dispersed.

Becket was quick to say, "You don't have cheerleading practice."

"I don't?"

"Marcy just informed me."

My eyes darted toward Marcy in the cafeteria, catching her intense gaze, targeting us. "Okay, then I wouldn't mind going out."

"I'll meet you at the gym."

"The gym?"

"Yes, the gym."

"Sounds wonderful," I voiced with the pretense of social etiquette and he sauntered off.

Wonderful? I said wonderful. *What a moron.*

CHAPTER 11

Becket turned, cruising onto Terrace Circle, and we'd barely said two words since I'd settled into the bucket seat of his car. I was battling a stomach of menacing butterflies, struggling for nonchalant. Nibbling my bottom lip, I brooded over the many girls that had sat on this exact seat. My so-called etiquette plunged into the pit. I plowed nervous hands into my hair, disturbing the layers. *Get a grip. Stop being a wimp.*

Star Hallow was in full autumn regalia. Haystacks, pumpkins, gourds, ghosts, witches, goblins, an assortment of paraphernalia-bedecked homes, and the main gazebo around Terrace Circle. Before Mom's murder, the season had been my favorite. Now it ranked lower than low.

He parked at Earl's, a homespun eatery. "You've misplaced your tongue." A smirk lifted his cheeks. "I've never bored a girl to death in the first ten minutes. I think it's a new record." He climbed out of the car and I followed suit.

Since last night's storm, standing groundwater had evaporated, permeating the atmosphere and making my skin feel sticky. It was unseasonably warm for the beginning of October, and if the splendid weather continued, the bleachers would be packed on Saturday for the football game.

I confined an errant piece of hair over my ear and hoped it didn't resemble a thicket of chaos. As we moseyed into Earl's, I wondered if Becket was staring at my scraggly hair or my butt, which looked decent in this outfit.

Becket was widely known as the high school's all-star quarterback, and as we entered Earl's, the hub for locals, his name came heralding from table to table. He waved and nodded hellos; it felt like a procession. Countless eyes sized me up for their approval. I had to quell my restless fingers from combing into my head of hair a second time, a nervous habit.

His hand pressed on my lower back, and the feeling was quite pleasant as he ushered me into a booth made for two. The waitress, Molly Schriven a classmate, was beside us before he had a chance to sit.

A broken grin showed off her braces. "What can I get you, Becket?" Her gaze tacked onto him, oozing fascination.

"Leo, what would you like?" he asked, peering at me.

He's polite. "Just coffee." I was falling faster than a shooting star.

"How about a doughnut or something to go with that?"

"Um..." My best tactical method was political. "I'll have whatever you're having."

"Two cheeseburgers, fries, a coke, and a coffee."

"Change that coffee into a coke too," I said, and observed Molly's blatant eye roll.

He set his arms on the table and sloped forward. "Leo, this isn't an easy topic to broach," he expressed, concern lacing his words. "But I need to tell you something."

Oh, no. I tensed. Whatever possessed me to think he'd been attracted to me?

He's giving me the friend talk like I gave Henry.

"I remember your mother. I had her for English as a sophomore. She was a cool teacher." His serious gaze caressed my face. "What I'm trying to say is—I'm sorry for your loss. Her murder devastated this village. She was beautiful and you look exactly like her."

Not what I expected. "Thank you..." I squeaked. "I think." It hit me like a wrecking ball—why I'd latched onto Henry. He hadn't known an inkling about my mom and never mentioned or even asked about her.

"I've been on a downer the past year." Unnerved, I tore my gaze from him and glanced at my fiddling fingers. "The anniversary of her death is coming up."

"I noticed you're getting your head together." His large hand covered mine, deterring my overanxious finger wrangling. "I didn't know if I should have mentioned it."

He noticed? When the heck did this happen?

"That's fine." I forced an imitation of a smile but, deep down, a lump was forming. I couldn't look at him. So instead, I stared at his long fingers covering my hand.

"She was very nice," he said. His gentle, sober tone drew my gaze to his face. Genuine and sincere. No joke. No sarcasm. His mouth bowed just right.

Time lapsed, gazing into each other's eyes. So perfect as if Mom were bringing us together. The magical ambiance was interrupted by a sloshing coke colliding into our hands.

"Your burgers will be up in a minute," Molly said, giving Becket goo-goo eyes.

He detached his warm hands from mine and then backed his spine into the booth. I wedged my hands between the cushioned seat and my thighs.

"Would you like to talk about your mom?" He again angled forward and crossed his arms on the table as if what I had to say was beyond a doubt imperative.

Not really. Unintentionally, he'd reminded me of the dream I had last night. "I kind of bottle things up and throw away the bottle."

"Understandable." He hit the two straws on the table, shedding their wrappers, sticking one in my coke and one into his. "Have a drink."

My throat was dry, and like a child being told what to do, I slurped the refreshing soda, quenching my thirst. I wondered why he decided to bring my mother into our date because fanning the flames wasn't a good idea. Wearing an empathetic expression, he cocked his head.

What was it about Becket that had me wanting to spew my darkness? I wiped the residue of coke from my lips and started talking. "It happened October twenty-fifth, close to Halloween, and I haven't stepped foot in that house since. I slept at Nona's until my father rented the place on Westgate, where we're living in now."

Drawing my interest, a wisp of wavy blond hair fell over Becket's brow. He had to have noted my shrinking voice because he said, "Leo, I'm sorry. You don't have to talk about it if you don't want to."

I rounded my lips on the straw and drew a liberal gulp, and then admitted, "I'm having a hard time living with the nightmares." I went on, chronicling the terror that had embedded into my soul. Disconnecting myself from the reality in the diner, I traveled back to the inescapable murder scene. Every minute, every facet of that day, describing the odor, the discovery of her torn body; the events unfolded. I confessed to him like a priest in a confessional. Somehow, I found myself in Becket's arms. During my heart-wrenching tale, he'd moved to sit beside me. I blinked away the haze as warm tears washed my face.

"I really can't remember," I said before a hiccup interrupted, "what happened," then another hiccup joined the conversation, "after I found her." I took in a deep breath. "The doctors call it retrograde amnesia."

I concluded by burying my head into his chest. He stroked my hair and cupped my trembling shoulders. I sniffled and restraining my imploding emotions, I reached for a napkin. He already had one in his hand and offered it to me.

I'd alerted Becket to my lunacy and complex nature.

When my vision cleared, the waitress, Molly, was gawking down her nose at me. Becket stood and flipped open his wallet. He thumbed dollar bills, letting them float to the table. "This will cover the check."

"But...but..." she stammered. "Want your burgers and fries to go?"

I scooched from the booth. What surprised me was when he nestled me beneath his arm as if hiding me from paparazzi. I didn't blame him for leaving without a bite to eat. I'd embarrassed the crap out of him. Like his reputation depended on it, he hustled us onto the sidewalk. I reckoned he wanted to get rid of the nutjob ASAP was on his mind.

I was crippled—in the head.

Becket settled into the driver's seat but didn't start the engine. His arm came forward and, with a bent finger, he caught a lone tear that had been suspended on my cheek. Why the compassion? He didn't know me and probably regretted asking me for this date.

"I'm an ass," he said. I peered at him through puffy eyelids. "I hope you can forgive me?"

Not trusting my voice, I could only stare at him and scrubbed the damp napkin under my leaky nose.

By the time he turned onto Westgate and drove into my driveway, I was somewhat composed. Ashamed of myself, I couldn't wait to flee the car. I pushed open the door, and while swinging my legs to the ground, his fingers ringed my forearm. I looked at his hand holding me in place and then my gaze skipped to his face.

"Do you feel better?"

"Yes." I fibbed and gave him a tragic grin. "I...I don't know why...sorry...um... That was awkward."

"My fault." Letting go of my arm, the pressure of his fingers remained. Spoken with regret, he repeated, "Totally my fault." He stepped out and crossed to my side of the car. I didn't move, wondering what he was doing. He opened the rear door and grabbed my messenger bag and slung it over his shoulder. I'd completely forgotten about it. Together, we walked to the side entrance of my house.

This was my first and last date with Becket Kane.

Schooling my humiliation that was bristling beneath my skin, I sensed his nearness. I slid my key into the lock and didn't have the foggiest what to say. "Thanks," I muttered and peeked at him from under my brow.

Unhurried, as if calming a skittish rabbit, his hands came up. He smoothed his fingertips on the sides of my neck. His feathery touch generated all kinds of delicious things. Becket perched his thumbs under my chin and raised my head. My breath held as his eyes browsed my face like he was bearing to mind every angle and curve.

He leaned down and the coolness of his lips brushed my cheekbone. Every nerve in my body spluttered and sparked. The fullness of his mouth skimmed to the corner of my lips. He retreated a meager inch to scrutinize my expression, our breath mingling. *Is he wondering if I am going to flake out on him?* He slowly closed the inch, molding his mouth perfectly to mine. An ambush of sensations detonated like the fourth of July.

I couldn't speak even if I wanted to, though I reminded myself to breathe. As he withdrew, a mute hum came from him. Then unhooking the messenger bag from his shoulder, he handed it off. He turned away from me, and there was a faint tug on the rim of his mouth.

He strode to his car and accelerated down the driveway, never glancing back.

CHAPTER 12

"Nona, guess what I'm calling you on?"

"Your father bought you a new cell. What did you tell him?"

"I didn't lie. I told him I was making a call and tripped. It fell out of my hands and I didn't realize it was missing until it was too late."

"And where did you trip and fall, hun? You've kind of left me out of the loop."

I didn't want to get Nona involved with the murder of Skipper Townsend and David Galbraith, but she'd badger me until I broke. "On the railroad tracks a few of nights ago."

"The tracks? What were you doing over in that part of town? You usually don't go there anymore."

"Just went for a hike."

"With who, not yourself?"

"I was with Henry."

"Oh, Lord, you weren't doing the naughty with that boy, were you?"

"We were drinking beers...and stuff."

"Leo, you're just getting clean. Don't let that boy drag you back to hell. See, that's why I don't trust him."

"He's not *that* bad." I'd been fooling myself and I was pretty sure Henry had a dark side, then again, *don't we all have a dark side?*

"Ahem..." She paused. "I've been waiting for some mouthwatering information. What happened with Becket? Was it so-so? C'mon, girl, I'm waiting here."

"Are you going to let me speak?" I reflected on what to say. "The truth—it was dreadful."

"Oh, nooo." She groaned. I noted her anguishing tone and then she was quick on the defensive. "Was he an arrogant prick? Did he treat you bad? If he did, I'm going to beat him to a pulp."

A snigger rumbled in my chest. "Nona. It wasn't him. It was me." Ousting a breath of air into the phone, I rolled over on the mattress of my bed from my stomach to my back.

"Leo, you're a sweet thing. How did you mess it up?"

"You remember how everyone in the Hallow was freaked when...my mom," I relayed haltingly, "with...with Mom and all—"

"My God, he threw that in your face? I'm going to kill him. Just wait until—"

"Please, Nona. Hear me out." I interrupted her prattling. "He said he was sorry about what happened a year ago. He thought Mom was very nice. She was his English teacher." I expounded on my bizarre desire to spill my guts at Earl's, and how I developed into a blathering, weepy dope. "He probably thinks I'm insane."

"You're beating yourself up for nothing," Nona reasoned. "Your crippled condition, as you call it, is understandable. The horribleness of what happened needs to be solved. It's that cold case that needs a solution so you can get on with your life. Don't you agree?"

"Ahh...Yes, that's exactly right." I propped myself up and brushed a shaky hand over my wrinkled dress. "After...

after seeing her and then being grabbed from behind, all I remember is waking up strapped to a gurney in the hospital. My throat was so swollen and sore from screaming and I was freaking me out that the killer was still in the house. I...I just couldn't see his face...I..."

"Stop it, girl. Now is not the time. Let's get back to Becket."

She flipped the conversation to get my mind off the murder. Then, sounding meek, I said into the cell, "He kissed me."

"What's that? I thought it went downhill at Earl's? Now you're saying Becket kissed you? You're holding back on me."

"I was as shocked as you are. He looked mad, like I ruined his afternoon. He called himself an ass." Nona yiked into the receiver. "He really did. I think he blamed himself for making me cry, bringing up my mother and all. He walked me to the door, and...and then kissed me."

"He kissed you. That's all you're giving me. No spicy details?"

"It was...it was sweet, gentle...perfect."

"Ooooo..." she cooed. "I knew it. I knew it! He knows how to reel in the ladies."

"That doesn't make me feel better; besides it won't happen again."

"What makes you say that?"

"He's done with me after my nuclear meltdown. He felt sorry for the nutcase, and that's why he kissed me."

"Leo, stop that nonsense. I'd come over there to straighten you out, but Reggie's taking me for ice cream." As an afterthought, she said, "Hey, you can come with us."

A *pat-pat* sounded on my window. "Nona, someone's knocking on my window."

"Do you think Becket's come back? Check it out."

I peeked through the levered blinds. "It's Henry."

"Shoot, why's that boy coming to your window?"

"I don't know." Drawing open the blinds, I gave Henry the wait-a-minute signal. He nodded. "I got to go. Enjoy your ice cream."

"Hey, don't forget," she sounded breathy as if she was moving around. "Mrs. Sweeny wants us at the school an hour before the game starts tomorrow to practice that new routine. I'll have Reggie pick you up at six o'clock, okay?"

"Sure, see you then." Before prying up the casement window, I tossed the cell on my bed. "Why don't you come to the door and ring the bell like a normal person?"

"'Cause your father hates me."

"He does not."

"Yes, he does. He practically told me." Gripping the casement with two hands, he scrambled up and over the sill, tumbling onto the floor. Not as athletic as Becket, so I tried not to snicker at his awkward, sprawling body.

"Did my father say he didn't like you?" Henry stretched his legs and readjusted the cockeyed glasses on his nose.

"He said it to my face over a week ago."

"No. My father wouldn't—"

"I'm not lying. Quote, I don't like you, kid. If you hurt my little girl, I'm gunning after you. End quote."

Pinching my lips, I squashed laughter. "He was being fatherly."

"You call that fatherly?" He unzipped his gray hoodie and I noticed his pockets were bulging with something. "I call it a threat." He checked to ensure the door was locked before making himself comfortable on the chair. "Hey, it's Friday night; let's go out."

Spotting muddy tracks on the floor, I scowled. "Your sneakers are filthy."

"What do you expect when your backyard is mucky?" He checked out his sneakers and hitched up his shoulders.

"Humph!" I bounced on the edge of my bed. "What's up? Where do you want to go?"

"I have a couple of beers and some weed." He submerged his hands into his pockets and extricated a goodie bag. "Let's go to the Lucien place. We can discuss strategy for a Halloween blast."

My brain couldn't handle much more of provoking the dead. Especially after the dream last night and then morphing into a raving berserko in front of Becket. I decided to go with my original plan. "Marcy and Blair invited me to Cheryl Ritter's for a party."

"Sounds decent. I'll go with you."

Not what I expected to hear. How can I get him off my tail without hurting his feelings? "I don't know if that's a good idea." His whole body wilted with my rejection.

"Why?" He sniffed and wiped a finger under the frame of his glasses. Henry needed someone to lean on, someone to love. I wasn't strong enough and I didn't love him. He surmised on his own. "Because Kane will be there and see us together?" He stowed the goodie bag in his pocket. "I saw Kane's car in the driveway. Your date ended rather quick."

"I really don't want to talk about it." He was probing for info that was raw at the moment.

"Kane's a self-centered jock." His shoulders slouched, looking scorned. "I know the type."

I got up from the bed and went toward my desk. "Sorry to burst your hopeful bubble, but he's not like that." I started piling up my books.

"Damn." His hand burrowed into his hair, giving it a thorough scratch job. "The Homecoming Dance is next weekend and you're going with me."

In the course of toting my history textbook, I stopped in mid-step. "I haven't made plans for the dance."

"Now you have a date. Me." He worked fretful fingers across his mouth.

"A group of us were supposed to be going together. No dates or anything like that." A complete lie. Worst. Friend. Ever. I crossed my arms in front of my waist. "Maybe you could find someone else to go with."

"No." Springing from the chair, he rubbed his hands on his jacket. "You're my date."

"Henry, I don't think so." He reached for my hand that was closest to him and caressed my palm with his thumb.

"I don't have anybody else." The lenses of his glasses extenuated his cow eyes. "You're the only one in this whole effing world that gets me."

"Henry, we're friends and that's not going to change. You need to stop assuming there's more going on between us." A mottling flush painted his face as his hand slowly released mine but stayed hovering in the air beside it. I pulled away and he seemed to shrivel.

He then threw his arms upward and let them fall on top of his head. Pacing my bedroom like a caged animal, he said, "I need a fix."

"Are you okay?"

His teeth clenched. "I just need a little something to help with my nerves. I'm balled up so tight that I'm going to—"

"What have you been using?"

"Oh...whatever." He scrubbed down his face, distorting his features. "Nobody will deal with me here. I'm so new."

"Who were you getting it from?" I knew the answer before he opened his mouth.

"That Skip guy. Now the pecker is dead."

"Did you deal with him the day he was killed?" Henry turned to stone, mouth quivering and face paling like he'd seen a ghost. I whispered, "What did you do?"

CHAPTER 13

"Nothing. I did nothing." He flapped his arms and lowered to my bed. Fixing his elbows on his thighs, he dropped his head into his hands. "The only reason they dealt with me was because of you."

"Me?"

"Yeah, I'd been looking for a dealer ever since I moved here." He ripped off his glasses and squeezed his nose. "Don't you remember? You told me who you got your shit from. So, in the beginning, I told them I was buying for you."

I cursed, "What the fuck, Henry!"

"It was the only way. Star Hallow is such a cow-poke village, and they suspect all newcomers like the friggin' plague." Repositioning his glasses onto his ears, he peered over the rims. "Like—do I really look like a nark, a cop?" His upper body stooped, folding in on itself.

His body posture said it all, and he knew his motives were wrong. "I guess dealers have to be careful," I alleged. "Look what happened. Someone took them out." I dropped into the chair and lodged my hands between my knees.

"It...it wasn't me," he muttered. "And, it was them in the graveyard—that night we were there."

My gaze flew to his face.

"They were early and why I acted like such an ass, making you run. I didn't want them to see us together." Mirroring me, he trapped his hands between his thighs. "I was meeting them at midnight—"

"Promise me you didn't do it. You were mad at the time and even threatened me."

"I never meant to threaten you. I just said that to…" His face hardened with the rest of his body. "Do…do you think I could actually kill somebody?" he said, voice sober.

"Relax. I believe you." I was sorry for him because he reminded me of myself. Could I help Henry like Nona helped me? "I didn't know you were so addicted."

"It's not exactly a…an addiction." He scraped his hands over his chest and began to settle down. "They help me to acclimate."

"You're acclimating yourself in Star Hallow by using drugs?" Shoving off the chair, I paced in front of him.

"I was pissed," he said, "when my father hauled me from the city to this one-horse town."

I spun toward him. "Why did he do that if you loved it so much?"

"He needed a job…and…I…I got in trouble." A guilty flush crept into his cheeks, and then he rolled his lips into his mouth as if he'd said too much.

"What kind of trouble?" Seconds passed as he rubbed his fingers across his jaw, reflecting. "Well?"

"Some slut got trashed," he murmured into his fingers.

"*Drunk?* And that relates to you—how?" I swirled my hands, wanting more.

His sneer twitched up his glasses. "She got what she deserved."

"*Deserved?* What kind of trouble are you in?"

"It's over. It's been taken care of. And, I'm not allowed to discuss it. So drop it."

Do I want to know? Yes and no. "You just don't want to tell me."

"Leo—truth." He crossed his fingers over his heart. "Someday I'll tell you all about it. But I can't right now. Okay?"

His pensive brow tugged on my sappy heart. "Fine. But you live in Star Hallow now, not the city. Be a big boy. Deal."

"Everybody knows everybody here. Have you seen how people look at me?" he whined and his forehead crinkled. "I'm an outsider. Some kind of fluke."

"No, that's not true. People like you." This was my stab at cheering him up. "I heard a few girls gushing over you the other day. You're more popular than you know. Newcomers, at least ones as cute as you, are like candy to those girls."

"Really?" he said, adding a wry curl to his lips. "Which girls?"

"I don't want to talk about them." I reclaimed my chair and fetched him back to the night in question. "I want to hear what happened that night in the graveyard."

Henry rose from the bed. "I was almost one of the casualties." This time, he paced while anxiously cracking his knuckles. "Gutted and shredded like lettuce and tossed into a ditch."

I grimaced, and my stomach flipped precariously. "Just tell me the facts."

"Skipper and Dave saw you run off. They were meeting somebody else, too. Waiting for a big deal. They told me to scram or they'd shoot a round of lead in my ass."

I could tell he was traveling back to that night as his eyes glazed and he stared straight ahead. "I saw this dude heading our way. Then Skipper told me to stay put. It was too late. The guy...he was...was..." Compressing his eyelids, he scrunched up his face, struggling to conjure every detail. "All in black," he said in a hushed tone, nodding because he'd remembered. "Yes, in black. He wore a ski mask. Skipper and Dave walked over to him like wearing a ski mask was normal. What dipshits." A terse snicker bumped his Adam's apple.

"I saw something shiny in the black dude's hand." Imitating the killer, he swished his arm and poked the air. "The dude jammed this dagger into Skipper's gut. Man, Skipper squealed like a pig until the dude sliced his throat. I can still hear him gurgling." Absorbed in recapping the murder, Henry blinked, coming down to Earth. "Dave took off and I ran home through the Lucien property. I guess the guy caught up with Dave, 'cause we both know what happened to him."

Nauseated and lightheaded, I crumpled in on myself. "Oh, God. What are we going to do?"

"Do?" he yipped. "I'm not going to *do* anything. Let it blow over."

"You have to go to the police."

"And say what?" he said, talking with his hands. "Hey, officer dick, I was taking a nighttime stroll through the cemetery and bumped into these drug dealers. I witnessed a big dude dressed in black who decided to play Jason and machete them to pieces." He chased his fingers into his short hair.

"We should do something." Peering at him, I disclosed, "I'm the one who dialed 911 that night. It was me, and then I lost my phone."

He gawked incredulously. "The call the police are talking about? That...that was you?" Like rigor mortis had set in, he turned rigid.

I wrung my hands in my lap. "I was worried about you. I..." A palpable frown carved his face, quieting my thoughts.

"What did you see?"

"I saw three people." He was frightening me as he breathed through his nose like a snorting bull. "I lost sight of them behind the tombstones and then the scream. That's all."

"Can you identify anyone?"

"They were too far away," I confessed. "It was dark and foggy, remember?"

"See, I told ya, there's nothing about our testimony that can help the cops. Nothing." The severe angles of his face softened and then he motioned a warning finger. "Keep your trap shut. Not one word about this or you'll get us both killed. Understand?"

This scenario felt off, instilling in me a full body tremor. "I'm scared." My breathy whisper misted over us, and I had stones in my gut being tossed into a frenzy.

Henry moored his hands under my armpits, and pressed me to his chest. His act of comforting didn't assuage my fear. Unraveling from his hold, I uttered, "I'll be right back. Don't make a sound. I don't want my dad coming in here and finding you."

Skulking into the bathroom, I spied Dad's prone form on the couch watching a football game, probably with his eyes closed. After rinsing my face with cold water, the ring of my cell sounded. I retreated hastily into my room, where Henry was dropping my phone on the end table.

"Did you answer it?"

"Becket," he said, screwing up his nose.

"What did you say?"

"I said you were busy."

Oh, dammit! "Why did you answer?"

"Because," he snipped. In an unanticipated, fluid motion, he twined his arms around my waist. "You're mine, Leo," he whispered huskily and leaned in. I turned my head before his lips found mine. His mouth brushed my cheek and then he drew me an arm's length away, holding firm, his brown eyes explored my face.

Sliding on a bland expression, I couldn't give him reason to hope because I wasn't into him. Didn't he see that?

"Go home, Henry," I said, sounding bored. A little boy pout slipped into his face and bowing his head, he departed through the window.

Not in the mood for more drama with Marcy and Blair, I dialed Marcy and begged off from going to Ritter's party. Afterward, I stared at my cell, wondering if I should return Becket's call? Calibrating an excuse as to why a boy answered was beyond me. *Maybe it'll be better if I explain in person.*

CHAPTER 14

Sleepless nights had been taking a toll, and I'd planned on staying in bed late on Saturday only to be awakened by my cell. I scrabbled for the chiming annoyance. "Hullo."

"You're my only friend." Henry commenced on a contrite spiel and finished with, "I can't lose you."

Muzzy headed, I registered half of what he'd said. After Mom had died, I recalled saying those exact words to Nona. An evocative memory of pleading with her, a remembrance that soothed my heart where Henry was concerned. "Okay. Okay. We're good."

"See you at the game then?"

"I'll be there."

Weatherwise, it developed into a beautiful October afternoon and a precursor to a great evening for the football game. Geared in my uniform and leggings, I draped a jacket over my arm and headed for the kitchen. "Hey Dad, are you coming to the game tonight?"

Seated at the table, he was reading the newspaper. "It appears like Detective Dyl isn't making any headway on his murder case. I wish he'd solve one before tackling another." He sighed and karate chopped the paper into a fold.

"Oh, Dad." My arms wound his shoulders, hugging him. "Maybe we should go on a trip. Visit Grandpa in California. What do you think?"

"We can't run away from our problems. They'll follow us wherever we go."

"I know. But..." I gazed into his grieving eyes and twiddled with the zipper of my jacket. "I just thought of getting away from here." My head lowered and I veered toward the door.

"Leo," he said, drawing my interest back to him. "Did your mother ever mention anything about moving to California?"

"Hmm...I remember her saying before..." My heart hurt, I couldn't say before she was murdered. "She wanted to visit Grandpa."

"I might come to the game later." He ingested a breath and his chest puffed out. "Do you need a ride home?"

"No, Nona will give me a ride. We might stop at Earl's for something to eat afterward, okay?"

"Yep." He eked out a smile. "Go Panthers."

Once outside in the diminishing daylight, I traipsed to the end of the driveway to wait for Nona and Reggie to pick me up. It'd been a long day of pondering. What was I going to tell Becket as to why Henry answered my phone? Nothing sounded logical.

Do I even need an explanation? It's not like Becket and I are together. Kneading my brow to repel my stinking headache, I felt miserable. Nona had phoned earlier, piqued about Henry's improper entrance, as she called it. Did she figure climbing into my window belonged exclusively to Becket? In Nona style, she sounded off in regard to Henry's adhesive-like attachment to me.

She'd continued her rant, "You know, Leo, Becket voiced his opinion to Reggie about that boy."

"When did Reggie tell you that? I thought he wasn't offering any info on Becket."

"That was before you went on that date. Reggie opened up a bit." She breathed into the phone. "With some subtle persuasion on my part."

"What else did Reggie tell you?" I prodded on a tenacious roll.

"For one thing, that boy needs to stop tagging you. Maybe we should start picking you up for school, or you should go back to taking the bus."

Neither concurring with her nor divulging Henry's erratic behavior, I'd promised to think about her offer.

I swiveled toward an approaching car. Expecting Reggie, I was flabbergasted to see Becket's car. My nerves twanged, accelerating my pulse. I nervously swept fingers over the sides of my head, taming any loose strands of hair into submission and into my ponytail.

Becket's car braked at the border of my driveway, and through his opened window, he said, "I heard you need a ride to the game. Hop in."

"What happened to Nona and Reggie?" Sensing Nona's hand in this stunt, I plopped onto the cold leather seat. The windows had to have been down for a while. His complexion shined blotchy red, even the tip of his nose was rosy from the wind smacking him in the face.

"Reggie just said to pick you up." He gave an apathetic shrug and forked his fingers into his wild mane of hair.

We shot along Westgate, the cool air stinging my eyeballs. Whether he noticed my watery eyes or my ponytail coming unglued, he pressed the button, rolling up the windows. Altering his choice of symphonic music from the preceding time I'd been in his car, today Led Zeppelin rocked. I love music, but not when it shattered my eardrums.

Wearing a stressed-out expression, Becket had one hand on the wheel and the other curled in a fist drumming his thigh in beat to the tempo. His jaw hardened as he continued to stare straight ahead. I wasn't about to compete with the blaring song and shifted in the seat.

When we were almost to Hallow High, I was more than annoyed by his cold-shoulder treatment. Taking the initiative, I lowered the volume. "I can't hear myself think."

He refused to glance in my direction and instead said, "I didn't want to think today."

"I'm sorry I missed your call last night." I wanted to divert the crisis and decided to break the ice.

He ceased his drumming action, spreading his fingers over his thigh. "Reggie texted your new number and I thought I should check on you. You were pretty messed up when I dropped you home."

"Thank you," I said amiably. "I feel miserable for ruining everything at Earl's." I needed to expand on my insanity. "Since my mom," tiny needles were pricking the lining of my throat, "I've been having these recurrent nightmares. It just so happened, the night before we went out, I had a bad one. When you asked about her, I lost it." Becket looked at me for the first time since I got in the car. A deadpan glance, I didn't know how to read him.

"I'm assuming that wasn't your father who answered your phone. I'm glad you had someone to keep you company then."

Is he being honest or flippant? "Henry James dropped by for a minute. He didn't stay long." I crunched down on my teeth. *Why did I say that?*

"No need to explain. It's not like we're dating or anything. You want to make out with that Henry guy, go for it."

My hackles spiked. "You're right. Henry's a..." I was going to say friend, but out of spite, I changed my mind. "He's nice."

"Nice, huh? Then why did Reggie ask me to pick you up?" He made the turn into the school. "Henry could've driven you in. I saw his car parked at his house."

"You didn't have to pick me up," I answered, disturbed. Then I realized Becket knew where Henry lived and the model car that he drove.

"I felt obligated," he said.

"Obligated? Why?" My temperature was on the rise.

"Because—I made you cry." Cocking his head sideways, solemn blue eyes peered into my face.

That extinguished my boiling temp. "I cry a lot nowadays. No big deal."

"Leo, if you have a thing with Henry, just tell me so I won't waste my time."

"You think I'm wasting your time?"

"No, not at all. You know that's not what I meant. Just tell me the truth."

Becket had spunk, a boy who didn't like playing mind games. He needed to know the facts and figures upfront before proceeding. So I lessened his concerns. "I like Henry. We're...we're friends."

"Friends with benefits? Or how-ya-doin' friends?"

Did he just ask that? Deceiving heat molested my neck and slithered into my face. I was suddenly plagued with thoughts of Henry pawing me in the graveyard, and then last night in my bedroom with him saying, I belonged to him.

"You answered my question," he rasped sullenly and shoved out the door before I had a chance to clarify.

Commotion hurried all around the car with chugging and squealing buses, cruising into Star Hallow High's parking lot. Football players were arriving along with a busload of their opponents—Sweet Home High. Spectators were lining the gates, going into the sports complex.

"Becket!" I sprang from the car and called after him. "It's...it's not what you think." Arresting in his tracks, he turned.

"I think I can read you fairly well, Leocadia."

"That's where you're wrong, Becket Kane," I barked in return.

CHAPTER 15

Cursing under my breath, I marched toward the football field where the cheerleaders would be warming up. Fingers bound my arm, spinning me around. My mouth parted in surprise as I peered into Becket's darkening eyes. He captured my lips, neither demanding nor abusive. Expertly caressing my mouth as his fingers slipped beneath my hair, igniting feelings I never knew existed. His kiss stole my breath and my heart.

"Meet me at my car after the game." As fast as he'd appeared, Becket was gone.

Enveloped in an elated trance, I ambled over to join the squad and stumbled on a group of girls blocking the path. The meddlesome ones, who spread vulgar gossip, leered at me.

"Leo Nelson," Becca said. "Are you screwing two guys?" Ignoring her snarky comment, I passed by their group only to hear, "It's not like Becket to scrape the bottom of the druggie cesspool."

I screeched to a halt. Their specialty to antagonize had me yearning to step into their ambush and start swinging. I'd done it before—that was the old me. *I'm clean. Don't listen to the trash.* Internally venting, I reinforced my steadfastness, lifting my head high, and pretending to act unfazed, I walked away from their withering stares.

Nona was on the lookout because as soon as I made an appearance, a giant smile shaped her face. "Hey, I was wondering if you were coming. You're late." She whispered in my ear, "Mrs. Sweeny's looking for you. Just say you couldn't find a ride or something." I nodded as she asked, "Becket drove you here, didn't he?"

"Thanks for the head's up," I scoffed and dumped my duffle bag on the bench. "Stop trying to set me up, okay?"

"Did something go wrong?" She looped her arm around mine as we walked shoulder to shoulder.

"Yes," I said, casting her a wicked eye, "and then everything went right." Her frown went from skewed to luminous in less than a second.

"So we're good?" Her head bobbed. "Are you and Becket coming with Reggie and me to Earl's?"

"I don't know, but he said to meet him by his car after the game."

"Ooo...that's good." She pranced up and down, taking my body with her. The incandescent field lights showered the turf, making it appear like daylight while the encompassing world was inky black. A blast of a whistle drew us to Mrs. Sweeny, and for the next half hour, we practiced routines while the bleachers on either side of the football field began to fill.

An hour into the game and out of habit, I scanned the bleachers, searching for Dad and Henry. It had been their custom to sit somewhere on the bottom bleachers so they could watch the squad cheering. Discovering Dad's face in the crowd, I waved. He offered a thumbs-up since the Panthers were winning seven to zip.

Henry was nowhere to be seen. For some dang reason, I felt responsible that he was missing the game. He had deserved to be booted out of my window last night, yet he made nice this morning. *What is that boy up to?* Was he spaced-out and trawling through the Lucien place, for God knows what?

A heaving groan milled around the spectators and I twirled toward the playing field. Two behemoth linebackers had sacked Becket. Gnawing my nails, I agonized along with the crowd, wondering if he was hurt. With the aid of a teammate, he staggered upright. The vast majority on both sides clapped and shouted.

I surveyed the events with the rest of the squad. Becket's head veered in our direction at the exact moment a pair of arms roped my shoulders from behind. A cool face snuggled into the crook of my neck. The tang of marijuana wafted in the air, offering me the potential of sniffing a buzz. Henry loosened his grasp enough that I could shift to face him.

"Hey," I said, "I didn't think you were coming." His prescription glasses were missing; although by the look of his soupy eyeballs, I doubted he saw much.

"I wouldn't miss watching you cheer."

My fingers clamped his wrists, and then I pulled him from eavesdroppers and curious eyes toward the chain-linked fence. "You're flying, Henry. Go home."

"You want me to drive like this?" He grinned and he kept squinting and blinking. I suspected he was trying to focus.

"How'd you get to the game?"

Unsteady on his feet, he poked his fingers through the linked fence to keep his balance. "I drove."

"Well, you'd better drive home—now." He looked over my shoulder toward the game being played on the field. "Kane got his head served on a platter." With his free hand, his fingertips stroked my cheek. "Kane deserves to get his head crunched for manhandling you."

I batted his hand away. "What the heck are you talking about?"

"I saw the way he kissed you." He placed a heavy hand on my shoulder, either to comfort me or to support himself.

He forced me to reference the breathtaking kiss. "What of it?"

He hiccupped and his complexion turned pukey. *I can't let him drive like this.* If something awful happened, I'd never live it down. I was a certifiable sap. "The game is almost over. Wait for me by the gate and I'll drive you and your car home."

His upper lip curled and his half-mast eyes were satisfied with my decision. He weebled forward expecting a hug or whatnot; instead, I turned and flew back to the sidelines and my team.

Nona appeared indignant. "What the hell was that about?"

"Henry needs a ride home." A group of girls inched closer, craving scandalous details.

She nabbed my arm and pulled me down to her height. Parting my hair with her chin, she said into my ear, "What about Becket? I thought we were going to Earl's after the game? Leo, you can't be juggling two boys at the same time. Not good, hun."

"But Henry can't drive in his condition."

"Find someone else to drive his butt home." She pointed to Grace Huffington. "Ask Grace; I think she likes Henry."

Fantastic idea. She'd be perfect for Henry. When I asked, Grace was ecstatic. She'd drive him home and tomorrow, I'd bring him back to pick up his car. It was all arranged. Now I could dream about the night ahead with Becket.

With seconds to spare, Star Hallow punted a field goal to squeak by and win the game with a ten-to-seven-point lead as the referee blew the final whistle. Dad waved goodbye with a happy smile, and turning my attention to Nona and the girls, we debated our plans for next week's homecoming dance.

"Actually, Paul asked me to go to the dance," Blair said, "and I said yes." Moans rolled around the minority of the girls, and she added, "I've been waiting for him to make a move. I wasn't going to blow it."

"Blair, I thought we were all going together?" Marcy complained, highlighting pouty lips. "We can have a good time without boys messing things up."

"Sorry, girls," Nona chimed in. "But I promised Reggie I'd go with him."

Marcy's expression turned sour as her knuckled fingers pinned her hips. "Jeez, thanks for being traitors Blair and Nona."

"If Becket asked you to go," Blair retorted, "you'd be the first to leave us in the dust and you know it."

Marcy sucked her lips into her mouth.

Nona's gaze darted to meet mine. All the girls shuffled their feet, not knowing where to look. It had been widely publicized that Marcy Cavanaugh, the treasure of Star Hallow High, had been trolling for Becket.

"Leo," Marcy targeted me, "Has Becket asked you to the dance?"

Jayne, a girl who was always two steps behind, broke in, "I heard Leo was going with Henry James."

Nona burst. "Where in the world did you hear that garbage?"

"Leo and Henry looked pretty involved tonight," Marcy stipulated. "But I heard she was kissing Becket before the game. What's up with that, Leo?" Wearing condescending brows, heads deviated from Marcy to me.

I was never one to play catty girl games. Let them gossip until their tongues turned blue and fell off. "I planned on going with y'all." I jerked my shoulders. "But if the group is splitting, I'll make other arrangements." So why did I feel like a two-timing wench? I pivoted on the balls of my feet to walk along the sidelines. I didn't care what they were cackling about behind my back.

My best friend came striding by my side. "Leo, you did good. Marcy's been a thorn in my ass since I made the team. Booya!" Nona raised her hand for a high-five. "Just 'cause they're seniors, Marcy and Blair think they run the squad."

By half-past ten, most of the congested parking lot had cleared when Reggie, full of pomp, danced from the field house. The wide receiver for the Panthers was pumped, and he swaggered while clapping his hands with his characteristic pearly whites shining. "Hey, Baby. Did you see my running catch into the zone? I was smoking toonight."

Nona took that as a directive to hop into his arms, wrapping her legs around his waist. "I sure did. But don't be so smug. You nearly lost the game with that fumble, sweetie."

He chuckled. "Figured you'd mention that." Reggie's eyes widened, seeing me leaning against Becket's car. "Hey, Leo. We thought you were going home with Henry."

"Who told you that?" Nona said severely and shimmied off Reggie.

"Marcy." He scratched behind his ear, confused. "Becket mentioned he'd seen Leo with Henry during the game."

"Why would you believe anything that girl has to say?" Nona was flaming. "You know Marcy is after Becket's balls."

"Hey," he recanted, holding his arms out to the side. "I'm just an innocent bystander."

The sound of girlish giggling flared through the empty lot as Becket and Marcy walked from the field house. Embarrassed by the miss-communication, I didn't know how to react, especially with Marcy clinging to his arm.

He'd hooked up with a replacement fast enough. The two of them were face-to-face chatting it up.

"Hey, Beck," Reggie hollered.

Becket swerved his head to the sound of his name and his body tweaked, noticing me. Marcy tightened her grip on him as she slit guarded eyes.

"Leo," he voiced, unsure. "I...I thought you were..."

"Nope, Beck. Wrong," Reggie countered for me. "Leo's been waiting for you, man."

"We're going to Earl's if you'd like to tag along," he said to Marcy. Becket tried to play it cool while unlacing his arm from her possessive hold.

"No thanks," she replied, heatedly. As if I had said the words tag along, she shed me a scathing scowl. "We'll get together another night, Becket."

Nona sneered at her departing back. "See y'all at Earl's," she said, tinged with mockery, rubbing it into Marcy.

Devoid of warmth or speech, Becket clicked the lock on his car. After I was seated, he slammed the door. I didn't know how to feel about the complex situation. But, he was quick to set the rules. "I don't do mind games." The engine roared to life. "I need to know if you're with Henry. Because I'm not playing tug-of-war." As he stared at me, his eyes gleamed from the falling rays of the streetlamp.

"Henry was wasted," I said and pocketed my cold hands. "I didn't want him driving, so I asked Grace to drive him home."

"You didn't answer my question, and this isn't the first time." He raked fingers into his damp hair, pushing it off his face and pressed on his baseball cap.

"I am not with Henry. He's a friend."

"Hmm... Good to know." A muscle tweaked in his jaw as he spun the wheel.

CHAPTER 16

When the four of us crammed into Earl's for victory eats, there were whooping shouts of jubilation—hailing the football players like reigning warriors.

"It wasn't me," Becket declared, foremost to dispute his hyped-up skills. "I had nothing to do with tonight's win. It was this guy here"—he buckled an arm over Reggie's shoulders—"Reggie flew like an eagle to catch my overthrown ball for the one touchdown; and Randy completed the punt to win the game." Everyone scoped out the joint for Randy, who was in the rear. He stood, flagging an arm.

Reggie went on, "And our defense rooocked."

Following a considerable amount of jockeying, Becket managed to claim a table by the large picture window in the corner. "This place is packed tonight," he said, escorting me past him with a hand on my shoulder to the chair in the corner.

"That's because the weather's cooperating." Nona lowered onto a seat in front of the window with Becket and Reggie on either side. "Next week, when it's drizzling and cold, this place will be deserted."

"Don't say that, young lady," Mrs. Torkelson said, overhearing the comment, with a pad in hand ready to take our order. "We love when you kids stop in. How else can we survive without your patronage?"

"We'll be here, Mrs. Torkelson," piped Reggie, beaming with his toothy smile. "Nothing can keep us away from your homemade fries."

"Spread the word, Reggie, and you might get five percent off your bill." Mrs. Torkelson gave him an insightful nod.

"How 'bout a free order of fries instead?"

Her fleshy eyes tapered. "Half price for you, just for today."

"Alright!" Reggie slapped the table, pleased with his haggling.

As the minutes elapsed, every taut muscle of mine had begun to slacken. Becket's charismatic laughter and twinkling glances had me swooning again. The boys conversed about the game, and Nona and I spoke in undertones concerning the drama happening with the squad. While he was in a discussion with Reggie, Becket's hand smoothed over mine and gently squeezed, as if it were a natural thing to do. A silly grin spread my lips. I was smitten.

Earl's hive of activity was buzzing down when I caught sight of Grace at the counter. She turned in my direction, blowing over the rim of a steamy mug. She met my gaze and then indicated a secretive finger gesture.

I excused myself from the table and went toward her. "What's up?"

"Henry wasn't by the gate."

"What?"

"After the game," she said. "Henry wasn't waiting by the gate. I didn't give him a ride home. He must've left."

"Oh." *I'm sure he made it home in one piece.* "He's probably sleeping it off by now. Thanks anyway," I said and squeezed back into the corner.

With her elbow on the table, Nona slanted toward me and quietly asked, "Everything alright?"

"Grace couldn't find Henry. She didn't give him a ride home."

"He's fine, hun." She patted my arm.

We were jabbering past midnight while the owner, Earl, was busy washing tables and chairs, getting ready to close shop.

"I guess that's a hint to vamoose," Reggie said.

Becket inclined toward me. Gliding his fingertips along my chin, it felt too good, and activated a rapid heatwave through my veins. Rather than kiss me, he gently veered my head to the side. "Henry is watching us through the window," he whispered, his breath tickling my ear. "His eyes are throwing daggers at me."

I didn't want to look and I didn't want Becket to stop touching me. He withdrew an inch and I moved forward an inch. Our foreheads came together, and I gazed into his velvety eyes that were devouring me. As soon as the tinkling of the diner's bell sounded, I knew Henry had walked in.

Earl also heard the bell. "Hey, buddy, I'm closing up," he said to the latecomer.

"I'll only be a minute. I need to talk to someone." Lacking any semblance of humility, he seized a chair from an adjacent table and parked it behind Becket and me. "Hey, how's it going? I'm Henry, by the way. We've never officially met."

"Henry." Becket modestly dipped his chin.

"Has Leo told you what we're going to do for Halloween?"

Nona, Reggie, and Becket gawked at me and I scowled at Henry.

Henry glanced around the eatery as if what he were about to say was confidential. "We're organizing an awesome frightfest at the old Lucien place. Cool, huh?"

"Really?" Becket's gaze flitted to meet mine.

"How are you going to pull that off?" Nona said.

"That'd be some feat," Reggie stated. "Especially since you don't own the property."

"It's hush, hush." Henry's brows rose over the rim of his glasses.

"Leo doesn't go to Lucien Court." Nona's narrowing eyes spoke volumes, ready to rip his throat out. "Or to that creepy mansion anymore."

"We were there a few nights ago making plans," Henry said. "It'll be awesome."

I dropped my head into my hands before Nona could spear me with her lancing gaze.

"You better hope the cops don't get wind of your plan," Reggie said. "But that would be righteous, man."

Henry snorted a grunt as if he'd forgotten to say something. "Oh, speaking of cops. Leo." I glared at him, wishing he'd evaporate. "There's a police car in your driveway."

"A police car?" I bolted upward. "Why are police at my house?" The table shook as everybody bounded to their feet. "Did something happen to my dad?"

"An ambulance would be there if your father were hurt. Not the police," Becket said reassuringly. Barring his arm in front of Henry, his hand sought mine. "I'll take you home."

"We'll meet y'all at Leo's," Nona prompted, pulling on her jacket.

"No. No. Go home. I'll call later." She gave me an understanding nod.

A tense silent ride ensued, with me biting my nails and Becket speeding faster than normal, rolling through stop signs. I squinted at the headlights in the side-view mirror. I presumed it was Henry and was correct when the car pulled into his driveway.

A dark sedan was located in my driveway. "It's not a police car."

"It's unmarked." Becket sounded sure as his car rolled to a stop.

I pushed out the door, but he cut me off on the sidewalk. "I don't want you to come in," I said.

"I thought you could use some support."

"It might be about my mom. I rather you didn't."

"Are you sure?"

"Yes."

"I'll call." He furnished heartening pressure to my arm.

I entered the kitchen on tenuous legs and found Detective Dyl and my father seated at the table, turning to look at me.

"Did you find Mom's murderer?" Dad peered through bloodshot eyes. He'd been imbibing heavily, and when he got to his feet, he held onto the chair to steady himself.

"Sit down, Leo," he said, slurry and strained.

Detective Dyl also stood, exposing black pieces of litter sprinkling the tabletop.

"Leo, I was hoping you'd come forth on your own." The detective's penetrating eyes were on me. "We know you're the one who called 911 on the night Skipper Townsend and David Galbraith were murdered."

CHAPTER 17

My sight was riveted to what was left of my cell phone. Approaching the table, I plopped into a chair.

"An officer recently found this on the railroad tracks behind Hallow Saint's Cemetery." Using his index finger, Detective Dyl tinkered with the remnants. "The train ran it over. It was effortless to trace the owner of the cell from that location. I was disappointed to discover you made the call or someone used your phone. I've been waiting for you to come forward." He hesitated. "Leo, did you make the call?"

Biting my lip, I nodded.

"I know how traumatized you've been this past year. But I have to inform you and your father, we believe your mother and these murders are somehow related."

"What do you mean related?" My father sunk into his seat with an audible thud. "How?"

"Purely speculation right now, Mr. Nelson." The detective appeared professional as his hand clipped the lapel of his trench coat. "I can't disclose any information, at least not at this time. We'd like to take Leo in for questioning."

"It's not possible there was a connection. Those guys were drug dealers." I tented my hands over my nose and mouth. "What does my mother have to do with them?"

"We don't know for sure, but we intend to find out." He then turned his sight onto my father. "Mr. Nelson, would you like to call a lawyer?"

"Why? Does she need a lawyer?" Dad argued. "Are you convicting her of murder?"

The detective's lips pressed together before responding. "Not yet. A lawyer is for Leo's protection. She's a minor."

"I don't need a lawyer," I cried. "I didn't do anything wrong."

"Mr. Nelson, you and Leo will have to come with me." The detective had realized my Dad wasn't in any condition to drive.

We rode in the backseat of his unmarked police car. Driving past Henry's house, a dark form hovered in the shadows, and looking over my shoulder, the form moved into a scrap of moonlight—Henry.

The municipal building consisted of the clerk's office, a courtroom, licensing department, and police headquarters. Since I was a witness in Mom's murder, I'd become acquainted with headquarters. The unit consisted of four desks and two offices.

"Leo," Detective Dyl instructed, "stay with Officer Simmons while I speak with your father for a moment."

A woman in a navy police uniform cast me a coddling grin. I parked my butt in the chair that adjoined her metal desk while Detective Dyl led my father into one of the offices.

"How you doing, Leocadia?" Officer Simmons wheeled her chair in front of me. Our knees touched. "You remember me?"

"Yes." She'd comforted me on several occasions during Mom's investigation. Heads veered in the direction of the detective's office as harsh voices rode through the room. I couldn't make out the words, and then all quieted.

"Don't look so worried, honey." She patted my knee. "We know you didn't do anything wrong."

"Then why am I here?"

"We have these two boys that were murdered, and you were the one who called us that night. Now we need to know what happened, what you saw. That's all."

"I...I didn't actually see anything. It was too dark."

"The coroner said the murders took place around midnight or so? Is that right, honey?"

"'Bout that time," I answered, coiling and uncoiling my finger in the hem of my shirt. "I was on the railroad tracks."

"Leo," she said protectively, "what were you doing on the tracks at that time of night?"

"I went for a walk." I wasn't going to implicate Henry. "It was a nice night, and...and I wanted to visit my mom."

"You always visit the cemetery by way of the tracks?" Officer Simmons questioned dubiously. "That's a risky route to make, past Tarpon Hill and onto the tracks. Isn't it kind of dark there?"

I didn't answer because she knew it was dark. Instead, I said, "When I was in the cemetery, I heard talking and got scared and ran toward the tracks."

"Then what happened?"

"I made out dark shapes. Three...no, two figures." I flubbed, not wanting Henry implicated.

"Honey, was it two or three people?"

"It was hard to tell with all the headstones and fog."

"Ahem..." She put her fingers to her cheek and leaned into her hand.

"They walked away and I lost sight of them."

"Is that when you called 911?"

"No, it was..." I dragged in a breath. "It was after a scream."

"Okay, honey, calm down."

I hadn't realized I was shaking uncontrollably. Officer Simmons took me into her arms. "You poor baby, going through this again." She patted my back and after a minute of solacing said, "Let me get your father."

My legs fidgeted as Officer Simmons headed toward Detective Dyl's office. Knuckling the door, she walked in. A second later, the three of them exited. Dad's body language, beet-red face, and hair spiked like a porcupine told me he wanted to throttle someone, presumably me.

I waited for the detective to call me in, but he never bothered to look my way. He said to Officer Simmons, "Drive them home." To Dad, he said, "I'll be in touch."

Didn't Detective Dyl want to interrogate me?

"Leo, thank you for cooperating," Office Simmons said as she pulled her squad car into our driveway. "Don't worry about a thing; try and get some sleep."

Once inside the house, I asked, "What did the detective ask you?"

"Same questions...after your mother." Dad strong-armed the countertop, and his body tensed.

"I kind of forgot. What were they?" I was horrible for giving him the third degree, but inquiring, idiotic minds wanted more. Weak-kneed, his face drained of color and he looked like he was going to pass out.

"Sit down, Dad." I shoved a chair toward him. "Forget I asked. We can talk in the morning if that'd be better."

"I'm okay, Leo." He brushed fingers over his forehead and wiped them on his trousers. "Dyl's a bastard, trying to trap me into something I didn't do."

"You were at work, right?"

"Yes, when the police called. I was in shock and couldn't drive. A friend drove me home, remember? The police were already at the house...and..." Fatigued eyes sought mine.

I shook my head because that was my problem—I couldn't remember. "What does this have to do with Skipper and Dave?"

"I don't know. The police are grasping for leads that aren't there."

Swinging open the cupboard, I took out two glasses, filled them with water, and handed one to him. After a generous glug, I wiped the back of my hand across my mouth and asked, "Why didn't the detective take me into his office to ask me his questions?"

"You talked to Officer Simmons, didn't you?" He set his glass on the table.

"Yes."

"I think Detective Dyl knew you'd open up to her." His lips mashed together, cheeks pinking, and then he snapped like a whip. "I specifically asked you if you were near Tarpon Hill that night." He blasted off the chair, ringing his fingers over my arms. "Why did you lie to me?"

"I...I didn't want to."

"You're buying drugs?" His nostril flared.

"No. I'm not, no."

"It's that new kid—Henry. He's a glassy-eyed space cadet. Toking in his car and wears weed like an aftershave. He's getting you hooked again, isn't he?" He thrust me away, hard. My backend thumped the cupboard. "He was with you that night—in the graveyard, wasn't he?"

"Stop it—no." I held back the tears. "I'm not using anymore."

"Leo..." He fell to his knees in front of me. "I can't let anything happen to you. I don't want to lose you, too." He hugged his arms around my waist and planted the side of his head on my stomach.

Awkward. "You're not going to lose me."

"I have to go to bed. My brain is fried." I shored up his elbow and helped to get sturdy legs under him. He trudged like the weight of the world was weighing him down.

When I switched on my bedroom light, I was not surprised to hear rapping on the windowsill. I lifted the frame for Henry. "My father just went to bed so be quiet."

"I'm not coming in." He slipped his fingers under the rim of his glasses and rubbed his eyes. "I just want to know what you told the police."

I knelt and rested my crossed arms on the sill, looking at him through the screen. "Henry, I'm tired."

"I need to know what you said. Will they be at my door any minute?"

"I didn't tell them you were with me." My voice sounded feeble. "I said I went for a walk to visit my mom. Alone." He seemed satisfied and shoved off without a word.

Peeling off my clothes, a vein of frigid thoughts flowed into my brain.

Was Detective Dyl still pursuing Dad as Mom's killer?

Am I a suspect?

CHAPTER 18

I glimpsed the clock on the bedside table and couldn't believe I'd slept till noon. Grinding sleep from my eyes, I stayed in bed and stared at the ceiling, willing myself not to think. When my cell rang, I suspected Nona was checking in. I crawled over the bed and snatched it. *Becket!*

"You sound groggy," he said. "Are you still sleeping?"

"Nah, just lying here," I conceded. "Didn't sleep much last night."

"Is everything alright?" he asked, his voice considerate.

Not giving it a second thought, I hastily enlightened him about the events at the graveyard, my ruined cell, my conversation with Officer Simmons, and omitting Henry's presence.

"Henry was with you that night in the graveyard, wasn't he?"

He'd surmised this on his own, yet I said, "What makes you say that?"

"Easy to figure out." He ejected an airy breath. "Last night at Earl's, he'd mentioned the two of you were scavenging in the Lucien mansion. It was that night, wasn't it?"

"Becket, I...I just woke up," I said, unsure of his intentions and myself. I didn't know who to trust. "Can we talk later?" He thought I was brushing him off and didn't speak for a few seconds.

"Fine," he said briefly. "I have football practice. I was just making sure you were alright."

"I'm good."

"Have a nice day." He hung up before I said goodbye.

Motivating myself, I climbed out of bed. An overcast afternoon darkened my room and my disposition. I chose a pair of baggy sweats and a knit sweater while I vegetated. Remembering midterm exams were cropping up, it was a good day to hit the books. I compiled a baloney and cheese sandwich and snagged water and a bag of chips before sequestering myself in my room.

Later, with a muddled head of knowledge, I decided enough was enough. I found Dad coffined into the seam of the couch watching football with one eye open. "Dad, how are you?"

"Relaxing," he mumbled. A half-empty bottle of bourbon was on the floor next to the couch. He'd be skunked by dinnertime.

I stepped away, then turned back. "Dad, I'm going to visit Mom. Would you like to come along?"

"Umm..." he hedged, rearranging his shoulders deeper into the couch. "I can't handle it today."

It was hard to digest his expected comment. It irked me like homework on a Friday night. "Dad, you can't handle it any day," I scoffed. "You haven't been there since the funeral."

Astonishingly, it looked like he was making an effort. He propped his elbows on the couch and tried pushing up. It appeared as if his body was too heavy for the task and he dropped back into the cushions. Dad grumped, "Leo, not today."

"Not today—not ever?" I griped, folding my arms. "Do you plan on drinking yourself into the spot next to her?"

"For crying out loud. Leave. Me. Alone."

"You got it." Trooping into my bedroom, I grabbed my fleece jacket. As a precautionary measure, I remembered the flashlight on my dresser, just where I'd left it. On my way out, I swiped two cans of beer and an apple from the refrigerator.

Once on the sidewalk, I tucked a can in each pocket and bit into the apple like a vampire in need of sustenance. My feet faltered as I peered across the street at Henry's house. His car wasn't in the driveway or on the street. *Where is he?* Daily he would call making a nuisance of himself, so why not today?

The dismal weather sullied my brain into a stage of sorry-ass melancholy. That was what I kept telling myself. The damp chill seeped into my bones and, zippering my fleece, I surveyed the thickening full-bellied clouds. I forgot an umbrella, a very important item by the look of the sky. It was too late to turn back now with Tarpon Hill around the corner.

I kept a swift pace and reached the junction between Lucien Court and Tarpon. I halted. The hour struck five and already murkiness cloaked the avenues. My toes pointed toward Lucien Court, which would be quicker. Then coming to my senses, I traveled down Tarpon to the gated entrance of Hallow Saint's Cemetery. Yellow police tape had been cordoning the perimeters where they'd discovered the bodies of Skip and Dave, and they had since removed them.

Plotting a course among the grave markers, my affinity to detour toward the monument that Henry and I had hidden behind that unfortunate night was no different today: An angel garbed in armor that was holding a sword with a mushrooming wingspan. The inscription on the foundation read: "Saint Michael, the Archangel."

"Hey, Mike. How's it going up there? Not so great down here. But you probably know that. Why do we continue to have these one-sided conversations? Tell Mom I'm coming."

Alternating to the left, I'd memorized the names on the headstones, another idiosyncrasy of mine. My destination was in sight and I noticed Nona with an umbrella standing at Mom's gravesite.

"Hi, Nona."

"Hey, Leo. Thought I'd join you. Been a while."

"You were smart and brought an umbrella." She elevated it higher for me to enter beneath its shelter.

"It's barely a drizzle," she said.

"How did you know I was coming here?"

"When you didn't answer your cell, I called the house." She pushed the collar of her jacket up to hug her neck. "Your father said you were coming here. He sounded blitzed, by the way."

I sat cross-legged on the moist ground.

"He's getting worse and I left my cell at home." Nona followed me to the ground. Digging the can of beer from my pocket, I corked the tab and handed it to her. She didn't have a derogatory word about the brew. Then I withdrew the second can from my opposite pocket.

"Love you, Mom." I saluted the beer toward her headstone and Nona copied me.

After a cursory stillness, she said, "I couldn't sleep all night. I was so worried about you. How are you coping?"

"I'm coping." I took a healthy swig and wiped my mouth. "I didn't tell you what happened a few nights ago when Henry and I were here. I didn't want to get you involved."

"You told me you went out with him. Does this have something to do with those two murders?"

"We were here. I saw it happen, kind of." I paused, hearing her gasp of breath. "I didn't actually see the murder. More like I heard it." For the umpteenth time, I described the night in question. This time I included Henry's association with Skipper and Dave. "That last part is for your ears alone."

"You didn't tell the police he was here with you?" Nona said, miffed.

"I told the truth, just omitted that little part."

"So you told the police you were alone?"

"Yeah," I said lowly.

"Aren't you compounding the problem in a murder investigation?"

"Henry doesn't know anything that would help them. Why get him in trouble?"

Nona contemplated as her brows pulled. "I don't like it." Then, tipping the can to her lips, she sipped the cold beer.

"Just pretend I didn't say anything. Keep it to yourself. I'm begging you not to tell Reggie."

"I'd never involve him." She locked her dark-brown eyes on me. "I won't perjure myself for that boy."

"I'm not asking you to. Just don't say a word." In total silence and engrossed in thought, my best friend reached over and held my hand. "Come on, I'll drive you home," she whispered as if we were in a church.

"I'd like to stay a little longer. I haven't had a chance to talk to my mom."

"Reggie's coming over for dinner tonight." Nona used my shoulder like a hitching post and clambered to her feet. "He's probably there watching football with my dad or I'd stay."

"Not to be mean, but I need some alone time anyway."

"I understand. But it's getting dark and I don't want you here much longer. Okay?"

"I'm good. Say hello to Reggie for me." She loomed over me, not moving.

"I know I'm interfering..." *Here it comes.* "Did Becket call you today?"

I kinked my head to peer up at her. "When have you ever apologized for interfering in my business?"

"It's this place. Makes me reverent or something." Fingering her necklace, she perused Hallow Saint's Cemetery. "Here, take my umbrella, just in case it begins to pour."

"Yeah, he called this morning," I said, taking the umbrella she was proffering.

"And?"

"And, nothing. He wanted to know how I was. He said he had practice."

"He didn't ask to see you, or...ask you to Homecoming?"

Her words had me vaulting to my feet. "What are you hatching? Please don't, Nona."

"I'm not hatching anything," she said, disgruntled. "I just thought he might ask."

"You don't have Reggie putting ideas in Becket's head, do you?"

"Not yet. But—"

"Don't, please, don't," I broke into her thoughts, even though she meant well.

Her mouth flattened against her teeth and her shoulders slouched. "I won't say a word."

"Thank you." I trusted her. "I'll bring your umbrella to school tomorrow."

"Speaking of school, you want Reggie to pick you up tomorrow?"

"Nah, I'm good."

"Hey, girl, after all that's happened, you're not riding with Henry, are you?"

"I don't know what I'm doing. Please, go home." A guise of dissatisfaction contorted her features as she hugged her arms over her waist and walked away.

I could still hear her footfalls hushing over the weedy grass as I diverted my sight from Nona to Mom's headstone. I read the epitaph aloud. "*Lillian Leocadia Nelson. Cherished Wife and Beloved Mother.*" Sinking back to the earth, I stared at the sculpted letters for the billionth time. "Well, Mom, it'll be a year. It feels like yesterday and at the same time—like forever."

My gaze drifted over the forlorn cemetery, wondering if I should tone it down. "Looks like you're the only one with company. I guess not too many people want to be here on a drab evening. Say hello to grandma for me. Tell her I promise to see grandpa during the holidays. I know how much she worries about him."

I bent near her headstone and plucked the expired bundle of daisies from the ground. "These are done. I'll bring more next week." The pitter-patter of raindrops sprinkled the umbrella's canvas. "The rain's coming. I'd better get home." I pushed off the ground. "Mom, if it's possible, could you help Dad? He's not handling this well, and while you're at it, maybe send a few prayers my way."

Water cascaded over the umbrella and, taking my initial step, my foot sunk into a lawn divot. It would be a wet walk home from here. I looked toward the railroad tracks, knowing the cut through the Lucien Estate would sever precious minutes.

CHAPTER 19

I plowed my sneakered toes into the ground and scaled the incline. As I held onto the umbrella with one hand, my free arm dragged through the muddy plane for leverage. I slipped and caught myself prior to face-planting; although, my hand was rooted in sludge. Slurping my fingers out of the impacted mudhole, I reached the tracks.

I used the wooden ties to scrape the gooey muck from my hands and smeared traces of mud on my jeans. I peered through a pane of rain to judge where the entrance was to the Lucien property. After walking a few yards, I dug my heels into the hill leading down to the Estate. I hiked through quite a menagerie of undergrowth and spied an outline of a gazebo nearby. Wandering under the deteriorating gazebo with a sagging roofline, I lowered the umbrella.

It rendered me a brief reprieve from the downpour. The moldy floorboard groaned under my weight as I went to the outer border to see the Lucien monstrosity, bleak and foreboding in the encapsulating shadows. In the uppermost window, I snared a passing light. It wasn't hard to miss in the gloom. Adhering my sight on that one particular window, it then blackened. Minutes ticked by and a dim light shone in the fourth window. Someone was inside the mansion.

Henry?

Protected from the elements under the umbrella, I snaked between tangles of shrubbery, over the slate path to the mansion's wraparound porch. Upon finding the opening where Henry had pried a weathered plank from the window frame last week, I set the umbrella down and squirmed through the hole.

Landing on my hands and knees, I stood and dusted the dirt from my jeans. Adapting to the dreariness, thoughts of kicking myself in the ass crossed my mind at this harebrained enterprise. First things first: turn on my flashlight. I advanced through the mansion like a covert spy and winced at the noise of my squishing sneakers. Wet footprints trailed behind me on the crusty floorboards. My leg batted something hard.

"Ooaf...stupid couch." The couch was again covered with what was at one time a white sheet, fading to a grubby yellow. The last time I was here, Henry had discarded the sheet, so he must have recovered it. If he still imagined a Halloween spookfest, the sheathed furniture provided the room with a haunted atmosphere.

Reaching for the newel post of the banister, I called up the staircase. "Henry, are you here?" My body recoiled at a strident bang. Whether it were Henry giving me a signal or a burglar was house squatting, I wasn't sure. If my latter scenario held true, then I was shit out of luck.

Not dawdling but clinging to the banister, I breezed up the stairs to the second-floor landing. Adjusting to the dimness, I gazed into the extended hallway. A billowing shape floated by with long, silvery hair.

My tone quavered, "Is that you, Henry?" Either he was wearing a wig to scare me, or Monique Baskerville's ghost decided to make an appearance.

"Up here..." My head jerked to the distinct words coming from above.

"Henry, I just peed myself," I said, singing the words, "just in case you're wondering." I veered around the banister to take the third set of stairs. Footsteps came from behind me and my skin chilled into mounds of gooseflesh. *Is someone following me?* I stopped and chafed the freeze from my arms. Whoever or whatever had also stopped.

Resembling a motorized robot, I took one stair, waited and listened, another stair, waited and listened. I heard rustling, and sensing a presence I twisted on the spot. White misty flecks evaporated into thin air leaving behind a lingering scent. An extremely familiar perfume.

"Mom? Is that you?" Stifling my inhalations, I half expected her to respond. With nothing forthcoming, the thoughts of witnessing a ghost loosened my vocal cords. "Henry. I need you!" I chugged up the staircase faster than a locomotive. "Henry! Hennnry!"

The velocity of my running legs was astronomical and, panting like a thirsty dog, he called me again. "Up here." I looped the banister and sprinted to the top story. The staircase had narrowed considerably as I arrived at a slender six-panel door.

The attic.

As I went through the door a slew of memories unfolded: I was twelve and holding Mom's hand, exploring the mansion. Still daylight and we were trespassing. Mom had said, "Consider this a unique history lesson."

"He-hen-ry..." my voice warbled like a horror-struck little girl. Breathing in scads of dust, I sneezed.

"Bless you..." intoned a small, willowy voice.

"Henry, are you here?" Approximately thirty feet in front of me was the mammoth, circular stained-glass window.

Another recollection came to life: Mom and I performing pirouettes and dancing as a spectrum of colors painted our bodies.

It wasn't as prismatic at night but considerably grimier than the last time I was up here. The window centered the main gable that faced the facade of the mansion. Lower, on either side of the stained glass, were two rectangular windows. Which one Monique Baskerville dived out of was a source of conjecture.

Jagged holes and pieces of glass were now scattered over the hardwood floor. The windows let in delicate night light as my sneakers crackled on the broken glass. Extending my hand, I touched the cooled stained glass. Leaning my face close to a broken gap, I peered into the night. Across the cul-de-sac, my old house came into view. I was a bit shaken to see someone standing on the sidewalk. A draft caught the hem of an unforgettable flowery sundress. The woman stretched her neck and looked up. Our eyes connected—Mom.

I blinked and she was gone. My overactive imagination was taunting me.

I orbited to the left, and the huge ornate-framed photograph remained where Mom and I had dragged it years ago from a stockpile of junk. Lightly, so as not to damage the photo, I administered the sleeve of my jacket and dusted the black and white print. An attractive man with a head of curly, dark hair and a handlebar mustache was staunchly posing next to a high-backed Victorian chair. In the chair was an exquisite young woman, dressed in a lacy wedding gown, with poufy, silvery blond hair.

I swore Lucien and Monique were watching me through those unplumbed eyes.

My bone marrow turned to ice as I gazed at their thinning smiles that were decorating their faces. When that photograph had been taken, little had they fathomed what impending tragedy awaited them.

I wheeled around at the sound of a minuscule squeak, and my flashlight splashed upon cobweb central and loads of stuff: an armoire, bureaus, antiquated lampstands, a mountain of junk from ages past.

As I rotated, a partially opened doorway came into view. It was the constructed addendum to the attic, the room of Louisa Alcott, housemaid and mother of Lucien's bastard son.

I tiptoed toward the door. Shining my beam into the room, it bypassed a lone casement window and alighted on a bed. A disheveled modern-day comforter and sheets covered the mattress as if someone had just risen, and next to the bed was a small table with a vase.

What stumped me was a flowering lily exuding a zesty fragrance.

CHAPTER 20

Transfixed on the trumpeting white lily, I stepped inside.

I touched the milky petals and brought my fingers to my nose, inhaling its rich scent. Above the table, someone had tacked a picture frame to the wall. Transferring the beam from the lily to the frame, I gaped in dazed alarm.

My mother. So vivacious in life, a waterfall of blond hair gushed over her shoulders, and her eyes glittered like blue diamonds. *Why is her picture hanging in the Lucien attic?*

Averse to leaving her beauty, I sheared the light toward the disorderly bed. On closer inspection, russet splotches dappled the sheets. Deducing the stains to be dried blood, I found the inability to blink or to avert my eyes from the splotches. My heart thrashed against my ribcage, a warning gong. What happened in this room?

Arms belted my waist from behind. "H-h-hennry!" My primal scream reverberated throughout the mansion.

"For chrissakes. Shut the hell up." Henry detached his arms, and I turned into his laughter splashing me in the face. "It's only me."

"I hate you, Henry James," I balked with a patent catch to my voice. His arms strapped my body, drawing me to the bed. "Noooo!"

If this were his ploy of alleviating my turmoil, he had another thing coming. I was nearing that point of no return. Disentangling myself from him, I sprinted toward the open door.

"I need to get out of here. There are too many emotions, memories getting jumbled in my head. I can't think straight. And with you constantly scaring me doesn't help."

"I'm sorry, Leo. I guess I like scaring you because you're an easy target."

"You what…?" Shaking my head, I rushed from the attic and sailed down the stairs like a sword-swinging Lucien Baskerville was chasing me. Bungling my footing, I tumbled down a flight of stairs. Grimacing and scrambling upright, I somehow achieved supernatural adrenaline.

"Leo, don't go. I was just messing with you." Emerging from behind me was Henry, pounding swiftly down the stairs.

"Leave me alone, Henry," I hollered. "I'm out of here. I had enough fun for one night." I slowed to finagle my dive out of the living room window and onto the porch. My feet finally skittered to a stop on the bordering walkway of the Lucien Estate.

Henry jogged up beside me, then bent over to grip his knees, catching his breath. "Phew, you sure can run fast."

On the downside of catatonic, I gazed upward at the stained-glass window. Dust mites had impaled my body and I was itchy all over. I scrubbed my hand over my nose as if I were trying to separate it from my face.

"What's the matter with you?" he harassed, fixing his glasses. "My intentions were somewhat honorable. Raping you never crossed my mind, figured I'd wait."

Cutting my gaze from the window to Henry, I hissed, "Not in the least bit funny." My scathing rebuke wasn't strong enough. I had thoughts of pulverizing him in the mouth.

"See, I helped. You went from fainting to enraged. My tactic worked."

I whacked him twice in the arm and essentially felt better. "Did you see the blood on the sheets?"

"You mean those stains?"

"It's dried blood." I scoured my hands over my shirt and jeans, ridding the feeling of creeping bugs.

"Cool. Ancient blood."

"It's not ancient blood." My adrenaline exhausted, the frantic feat zapped my oomph. I slumped to the sidewalk. "The room looked like it'd been cleaned, and those sheets and comforter were modern. "Did you see that fresh lily?"

He squatted to his haunches. "Yes, and I doubt the ghost took up a broom and picked flowers to add atmosphere to the attic."

"You saw the ghost too?"

A grin carved his zealous face. "Haaaunted," he said, while making silly eyebrow lifts, and then placed his hand on my knee. "Think—Epic. Halloween. Party."

I needed to ask, "Did you see the picture hanging on the wall?" Making sure I didn't imagine things.

"Yes. I've seen her before. In your bedroom." He shed his glasses and scratched his eyebrow. "A picture of you and that woman is on your desk. I assume it's your mom."

I sniffed and scaled to my feet. "Why would there a picture of her in the attic?" I looked to him, seeking answers that I knew he couldn't supply.

"I dunno."

Clicking the button on the flashlight, I stuffed it into my pocket. "I forgot my umbrella on the porch. Go get it, Henry."

"Me?" His brow heightened, insulted. "I'm not your indentured servant. You go get it."

"Please, pretty please."

A lopsided grin crawled over his face. "I'll get it if you go to the dance with me."

"How about…" I thought for a moment. "I consider your invite?"

"It's better than an eff-off." Tilting his head, he said, "I'm not totally against a pity date." He jaunted into the yard and retrieved Nona's umbrella.

Commencing at a vigorous pace, we made it to Westgate Road by ten, and the rains had reduced to a tolerable sprinkle. I waved goodbye and Henry continued further down the road to his house.

As I moved along my driveway, Henry had raised his voice. I faltered and swerved toward him. "Be ready by seven fifteen tomorrow. I forgot my homework in my locker, and I want to get it done in homeroom."

"I'll be ready." My natural retort, then I recalled Nona's advice. *Don't drive to school with him.*

When I entered the house my ears were assaulted by Dad's snoring. The noise was similar to a finicky lawnmower. An empty whiskey bottle was on the cupboard. He was wasted. I scrounged around in the refrigerator and then scarfed down a leftover piece of pizza and poured a glass of milk.

In the meantime, I phoned Nona to convey the catastrophic events. "That's freaky," she said. "I don't know what I can say to make you feel better. But, you know what I think, girlfriend? How long have I been telling you not to go onto Lucien Court? Don't go there. Leo, it's not a good place for you. You know that!"

"Henry wants to have a Halloween party there. He's thinking up all sorts of frightening things."

She grunted into her cell. "I remember sneaking into the Lucien place with you years ago, and it scared me even in the daylight. That oddball Henry is right, though; it'd make for one hell of a party. But, I repeat, don't go there!"

Concluding my conversation with Nona, I went into my bedroom and disrobed, slinging my damp clothes over the chair. My gaze instantly sought the photo of my mother. Sliding my fingers along the frame, I picked it up and lay on my bed.

"Why is your picture in the Lucien mansion? You were there tonight, weren't you? I wish you could tell me what happened." I waited for her to speak.

"Who killed you?"

CHAPTER 21

"Nona, it's Monday. Who goes out on a Monday?" The lunchroom was jamming.

Subsequent to the weekends, ambiguous scandals had the habit of flaring through the school faster than a forest fire. I shifted on the hard chair, experiencing every pang and cramp due to my stumble down the Lucien staircase.

"We do, hun." She was lost in space, fiddling with a short strand of hair. "It's girl's night out."

"Where are we going?" I concentrated on winding spaghetti noodles on my fork tines. "Not that I'm agreeing to this."

"Marcy wants to go to that new club on Dumont Street."

"What kind of club?" I forked saucy noodles into my mouth and spoke around the noodles. "Don't you have to be eighteen to get into those places?"

Nona picked at her food. "Why would she ask us to go there if you have to be eighteen?"

"Because, Marcy's eighteen and we're not." Nabbing a paper napkin, I blotted my mouth. It came away with red sauce. "She'd love to make us look ridiculous."

"You're probably right." Nona's lips ruffled to the side. "But I need to go, and I want my best friend with me."

"What's going on?" I knew her well enough to know that something was bothering her. "Why is it so important that you go out tonight?"

Her brow stiffened. "Reggie's getting too comfortable in our relationship. He's taking me for granted."

"What's that supposed to mean?" Using the side of my fork, I cut the one meatball in half.

Nona was upset, shoving her food around her tray. "I usually don't walk down by the art rooms, but Mr. Cleaver asked me to drop a message to room 110, and I saw Reggie talking to Missy Charles."

I was hungry and crammed the meatball into my mouth while listening to her sob story. "What's the big deal?" Sauce leaked over my lips and I swiped it away with my finger. "You flirt with all the boys too."

In slow motion, she dramatically shook her head. "My flirting is not serious. It's funny, good-natured."

"Okay, I'll give you that."

"You can read body language, can't you?"

"Sometimes."

"Missy had her back on the locker looking up at Reggie. He leaned over her with his arm next to her head. You know, close talking." Enhancing a single eyebrow lift, she said, "Looks bad, doesn't it?"

I was far from a dating guru. "It's probably nothing. Reggie loves you."

"I thought he did, but now." Depositing her elbow on the table, she positioned her chin on the palm of her hand.

"I guess we're going out."

She raised her head, dropping her arm. Her glum expression evolved into a lovely poignant smile.

Sniggering, she said, "Yeah, baby, we're going dancing tonight."

I fussed with my hair and makeup before rummaging through my closet. Nona insisted we dress hotter than hot, and my clothes were moderate and tempered at mild. I chose a vintage dress that hugged my paltry curves and then wedged my feet into a pair of black spiked heels. Scrutinizing my reflection in the mirror, I was amply outfitted.

Nona and I were meeting Marcy, Blair, and Grace at Club Seven and, for once, Dad let me borrow his car. After Mom's death, he thought I'd drive myself off a cliff or smash into a building, so he'd guarded his immaculate Ford against my grubby, little fingers.

"You can use the car tonight," he punctuated with caution. "I have to work late for the rest of the week. No hanky-panky. I want to trust you."

"I'll be fine. You can trust me." I was steaming after his remark, knowing it was about my short-lived drug abuse. "You haven't had to work late in a while." Dad wasn't comatose yet, perhaps nursing a hangover from yesterday's all-dayer.

"Always gets busier the closer we get to the holidays. People moving their money around." Dad had spread out envelopes all over the kitchen table in random order where he was writing checks, paying bills. "I just paid the car insurance. No fender benders, okay?"

"Got it." I went to the hall closet and searched for my raincoat. "See you later." I pinched the keys from the peg.

"What, no kiss goodbye for your old man?" He tapped his cheek with his finger. I pecked his cheek and headed out the door.

133

Nona strutted out of her house before the wheels stopped rolling. Her chin was poised elegantly, polished ebony hair, poker straight, riding an inch off her shoulders, and her multihued dress dazzled her voluptuousness. As she got into the car, her demeanor seemed slightly off-kilter.

"Is everything cool?"

"I just had a blowout with Reggie."

"Oh, not cool." I steered for Club Seven on Dumont Street. "What'd he say?"

"He's mad because I'm going out with the girls."

"Really? The guy doesn't own you." I noted her dark eyes were swimming in tears. "It only goes to prove, he loves you."

"I used to think so, but now I'm wondering if he thinks of me as his personal property."

Deflecting the sore subject, I said, "You look hot, girl. I love that dress. Let's have fun."

"Absolutely." A preoccupied smile pulled her mouth sideways.

The bouncer raked his eyes over us, and said, "Gimme your hand, sweet thing." He printed an X on my hand with a magic marker, and then on Nona's. "That X means no alcohol, girls."

"We figured that out," Nona retorted.

The *clickety-clack* of our heels vibrated against the floor in the long entrance to Club Seven.

"Have you heard anything from Becket?"

"Not since yesterday morning," I said. "I saw him in the hallway after sixth period talking to Marcy. Kind of in the same way you saw Reggie talking to Missy."

She harrumphed.

We straight-armed the double doors into a surplus of bodies grinding to a definitive beat of music. A kaleidoscope of neon lights blasted the room and smoke whorled over the floor.

"Freakin' gnarly," I chirped. "There's the girls." We wended through the diverse crowd, touting a semblance of pure hotness.

"Hey, there. Glad you could make it," Marcy said like she really meant it. "Here, have a drink."

"Ah..." I wavered and showed her my hand. "I thought this stylish X marked us like the plague."

"There's a couple of guys that buy our drinks," Blair said. "We give them a little tip."

"Sounds good to me," said Nona. In a provocative gesture, she glided her hands down the side of her hips. "Keep 'em coming."

Nona and I had switched roles. She'd been the mother figure, keeping me grounded, and now it was my turn to watch over her. My only hope was—there'd be no regrets in the morning.

The evening was a nice diversion, whittling away my deep-rooted anxiety. My chest pumped with the rhythmic tempo as we united our bodies to the dancing throng. Moving and grooving until my arms and neck were clammy. I didn't want to take a break even when nature called.

"I'll be right back," I told Nona. Since I was the designated driver, I had to sober up.

In the restroom, I learned what the name Club Seven insinuated. The seven deadly sins were depicted on an elaborate lithograph. Wrath. Greed. Sloth. Pride. Lust. Envy, and Gluttony. It was the devil's den and we were having a helluva good time.

Tearing a piece of a paper towel, I swabbed my sweaty face and neck and tended to my makeup before heading back into the main room. I temporarily stalled, studying the obnoxious representation of lust. At that moment, Marcy burst through the door.

"That's a real eye-catcher, isn't it?" she said.

Oddly, she searched the room, making sure the stalls were unoccupied. "I wanted to speak to you in private. Do you mind?" And she gestured me toward the sinks.

Passing the mirrors, Marcy admired herself. She licked her fingertip and slathered it over her eyebrow. "I wanted to let you know before you found out the hard way."

I hated her uppity tone and anticipated the worse from her.

"Becket and I are going to the Homecoming dance together. I thought you ought to know before getting your hopes up."

CHAPTER 22

Marcy's admission felt like a wallop to my gut and caused damage to my heart. I wrestled with a mulish grin, masking the sting. "Why did you feel it was necessary to tell me in private?"

"Because you've been out with him a few times, and I could tell you were falling." Her flighty eyebrows winged upward. "But, that's how Becket is." She reeked of confidence. Gazing into the mirror, she dabbed her pinkie by the corner of her mouth, fixing her smudged lipstick. "He's not the type to stick with one girl. You should be thankful. I'm taking him off your hands before you get hurt."

I fancied smearing that pretentious grin off her jungle red lips. "Alrighty then, thanks for the heads-up." Then, with my voice laced with mocked sincerity, I retaliated, "I'm going with Henry James anyway, but thanks for taking Becket off my hands. Mighty big of you."

Thrusting open the door, I stomped toward our table until a hand clipped my arm, detaining me.

"Wanna dance?" It was a man, possibly in his twenties, sporting a goatee and a head of black hair.

"Sure."

Still clipping my arm, he pulled me onto the dance floor. Our bodies sandwiched together, undulating in sync to the tune, thanks to the horde of individuals. His penchant to roam his hands rather freely over my body upped my exasperation. I was on the defensive with this guy. As the song's final stanza dwindled, I mouthed *"Thanks and See-ya."*

The music segued into a mellow tune, and the jackass linked an arm over my receding body, winching my back into his chest, gyrating his hips against me. I felt his breath on my shoulder, and he had the audacity to suck my neck. Furious, I whirled on him.

The guy backpedaled and peered over my head. A deep cadence said, "I'm cutting in."

I smirked, hearing my savior's voice, totally rescued. The guy bowed out gracefully and I tucked myself into the secure embrace of Becket Kane.

"That was uncomfortable," I admitted.

"You don't mind that I took you away from him?"

"Hardly, I owe you."

"I'll take you up on that someday." He offered me a devilishly handsome smile. "The girls are having a night out at Club Seven?"

"Yes, the girls. Why are you here?"

"Reggie's spying on Nona. Can't keep the girl out of his sight for long. He's hooked and tied."

"You think?"

"He's applying to a local college to be near her. He received an offer from Syracuse to play ball and he turned it down."

I peeked through clutching couples and saw Reggie and Nona dancing to the slow melody. "How sweet."

"That's ludicrous. A free ride to a great college is a dream."

"C'est la vie," I quipped. He applied pressure, hugging me into him. My eyes drifted closed and I laid my head on his chest, whiffing his intoxicating scent.

"Why didn't you tell me you were going to the Homecoming dance with Henry?" My clumsy foot tripped over his, but he held me tight. "Everyone knew except me. Marcy told me today in school."

"Then you quickly asked Marcy?"

"No. After I heard you were going with Henry, I decided not to go at all."

"That's not how I was informed." His fingers kneaded the small of my back. The stimulation created promising sensations. He brushed the hair from my shoulder, baring the column of my neck. He angled low, his breath spreading over me like warm honey. Becket's cheek wasn't quite touching my skin, and I was tempted to turn and possess his mouth.

His deep, rich voice said, "What did you hear, Leo?"

Speechless, his lips traced a titillating path across my chin, spurring a jumble of emotions. The song petered to a conclusion and I clung to his broad shoulders for support, feeling perfect and right in his arms.

"I wanted to take you to the dance," he acknowledged and pressed me all the more into his hard body.

Suddenly feeling encumbered, I pulled away, giving myself room to breathe. "Then next time," I said, fortified, "ask me instead of waiting until the last minute." Freckled pink patches beautified his cheekbones and I left him standing alone.

I passed Marcy. Her eyes were following me, dispensing a fatal glower. Unswervingly, I made a beeline to where Nona and Reggie were tongue thrusting. "Nona," I dashed in, "I'm going home." Sticking my hands on my hips, I clicked my heel on the floor. "Do you want a ride or are you going home with Reggie?"

"I'm with you, girl."

That's my Nona. She'll play him for all it's worth. Reggie was heartbroken by her announcement.

"Sorry, babe, but I came with Leo and I'm going to leave with Leo."

After a fleeting glance at my petulant stance, she reckoned I was in a hurry. Saying goodbye with a peck on Reggie's lips, we threaded through bodies. I never looked back; though, I felt Becket's piercing gaze.

A frigid draft ripped through the fibers of my dress, and jogging in heels was absurd, but we managed to make it to the car in one piece. I cranked the heat.

"Can you believe those boys?" Her attempt at sounding irate failed radically. "Imposing on our girls' night?"

"Give it up, Nona. You loved it." Her stretching mouth told me what I already knew.

"Soo...what happened with Becket? Did he finally ask you to Homecoming?"

"Marcy cornered me in the restroom before the boys arrived." I swallowed my anger while making a right turn during a red light. "Becket and Marcy are going to Homecoming, together."

Nona jerked in her seat. "No way!"

"That's what Marcy said." My skin burned, and not from the car's wafting heat. "When I danced with Becket, he made it sound like I'd planned on going with Henry all along."

"Where did he get that notion?" She yanked on the collar of her coat, uncovering her neck. "I can guess. Bitch Marcy is at it again. Twisting words to get what she wants."

"I don't understand how Becket could be that naive."

Driving past a couple of neighborhoods, I spun into Nona's driveway. "He denied asking Marcy to the dance."

"Then why did she tell you that?"

"I said it didn't matter because I was going with Henry."

"What the hell is wrong with you?" Nona banged her knuckles on the seat. "You didn't?"

"I did."

CHAPTER 23

The morning after Club Seven, I massaged the kinks out of my feet; a night of dancing in heels was excruciating. Nonetheless, I'd do it again in a heartbeat. Today was a sneaker day and I pulled on my washed-out jeans and cable-knit sweater.

When I strolled into the kitchen, Dad was prepped for work in his navy blue, button-down shirt and trousers. "You're looking good," I flattered. It had been a while since I'd seen him somewhat respectable. I suspected it would not be the best time to broach the subject of Mom's picture and fresh flowers in the Lucien attic.

"I had a decent night's sleep. Feeling good." He downed a glass of orange juice and then said, "Do you have cheerleading tonight?"

"Oh, shoot. I think so." I'd forgotten that Mrs. Sweeny had broadcast the un- scheduled practice during Monday morning's school announcements.

"I won't be able to give you a ride home. I'm working late the rest of the week."

"Don't worry 'bout me."

Reaching for his coat from the back of the chair, he pushed his arms into the sleeves. "Do you have something you'd like to tell me?"

My eyes flickered up to his. "What makes you ask that?"

"You look like you have something to say."

"Ah...no. I have to get my cheerleading uniform from the dryer; that's all."

"Make sure you eat something for dinner," he suggested, making his way toward the side door. "You're wasting away to skin and bones."

His words were a reminder as my stomach grumbled. Selecting a granola bar, I ran to the basement to unload my uniform and stashed it in my messenger bag. Then I darted out the door expecting Henry's car, but the driveway was empty. I crossed the sidewalk seeing that his car was still parked at the curb. As I continued walking, he came loping from the house.

When he saw me, his mouth bent. "I'm running late," he said loud enough for the neighbors to hear.

Star Hallow's temperature had dipped below freezing during the night. A hoary frost adorned the lawns, shimmering like crystals in the rising sun. In haste I parked my butt on the sub-zero seat. Henry tucked himself behind the wheel, the lenses of his glasses fogging.

"How was Club Seven?"

"It was fun." He stopped the car at the light and whipped off his glasses to clean the lenses. "I've been wondering if you had the nerve to ask your father about your mom's picture."

"Not yet."

"What are you waiting for?"

"It's difficult."

"Why?"

"Do you even know what happened to my mother?" I swerved, raising my leg to balance on the edge of the seat, giving him my full attention. "All these months, you never once asked about her."

"I didn't want to pry." He threw me a shifty, sidelong glance. "Figuring if you wanted to talk about her, you would have."

"You're lying." My brows pinched, astounded. "Someone must've told you."

"Wait!" He made a display of slapping his palm to my face. "She died, right? That's why you go to the cemetery a lot."

"You're yanking my chain," I grumbled like my elderly grandfather. It was hard to believe that Henry hadn't heard the gruesome details by now.

"Okay, okay, okay," he relented, bobbling his head. "I know. I know. I'm playing dumb so you'll confide in me. I've heard all kinds of bullshit."

"Well, guess what? I don't want to talk about it now." My lungs decompressed, ousting a breath.

"After all that, you're not going to tell me?"

"Maybe later—tonight."

His eyes brightened. "Great, we'll go out."

Oh, dear, I stepped right into that. "By the way," I said. "Do you still want to take me to Homecoming?"

"I was planning on it."

"Kind of sure of yourself." Rearranging myself, shifting frontward, I pressed my messenger bag over my lap. "I haven't made up my mind yet."

Henry glided his hands on the steering wheel before admitting, "I told that ass-wipe Kane you were going to the dance with me."

"You said that to Becket!" I had a sinking feeling, dropping down the center of my chest, it ached.

"Yeah, he had the nerve to come up to me after class. He wanted to know if the rumors were true—If I was taking Leo to Homecoming? I told him, 'That's no rumor, pal.'"

Henry's head flung backward, laughing, and then he added, "It was huge to watch Kane squirm."

I moaned and pressed my hands to my eyes.

"You feeling okay?"

I wanted to cry—*I like Becket.* Henry ruined everything. Stifling my anger and tears, I growled between my teeth, "I'll go to the dance, but I have one very important stipulation."

"Huh?" His mouth hung open.

"I will go to the dance with you—as friends, nothing more." I reiterated, "Purely on friendship."

"Friends. I can live with that." In an inaudible undertone, he emitted, "For now."

I benefited from Mr. Slepe's praise in English class. He peddled my short story as if it were the second coming. Regardless of deriding sneers, I planned to dig myself out of a failing funk. Last year, I'd flunked every subject, plummeting from honor roll to barely making it.

After English, I rumbaed into the third-floor bathroom and stumbled on a gaggle of girls voicing heated opinions, destroying my great mood. Nona was livid, embroiled in a debate with Marcy. They were discussing me. The concept of exiting undetected wasn't going to work. Nona caught sight of me.

My gaze strayed from Nona to Marcy. "What's going on?" I queried, coming forward.

Nona parted her lips to speak, but it was Marcy who chimed, "Henry James told me he was taking you to the dance," she snapped with an insolent glint in her eyes. "I wasn't lying to Becket."

Nodding heads confirmed Marcy's statement. Evidently, Henry had perpetuated quite a coup.

"Leo never said yes to Henry," my friend admonished. "She was waiting for Becket to ask her, and he would've if you hadn't screwed it up. You knew they just started going out."

"Leo, forgive me. I didn't know." Marcy's insolence morphed into an apologetic facade, a master of disguise. "Henry bragged how he stole you from Kane."

"Yeah," Becca trumpeted. "That's what Leo gets for scamming two guys."

"Shut your grungy cakehole, Becca Pinarski." Nona clasped my wrist and carted me from the lavatory into the hall. "I'm so mad. Miss Bitch acting so innocent makes me puke."

"I came in a little late."

"Marcy insists that Becket is taking her to the dance," Nona illuminated. "I don't know what transpired after we left Club Seven last night. She definitely got her talons into him, somehow, someway."

"Becket must've been willing." My heart wept.

Nona commenced to speed walk and I kept pace. Her method of dealing with her rage. "When I walked in, Marcy was gloating, telling the girls how Becket dumped you to take her to Homecoming. That he was getting his rocks off with your skinny ass."

"She said that?"

"She said Becket's been hounding her for a year and she finally gave in," Nona seethed, baring teeth. "I wanted to drown her face in the toilet bowl. I still might."

"I might beat you to the punch." Coping with a lipless grin, I looked at her and said, "Thanks for having my back."

"Oh, jeez." Nona rolled her eyes. "We have cheerleading with them after school. That stinks."

"Could get dicey."

"She better not get close to a toilet bowl." Our harmonious laughter bounced along the corridor.

***

The morning frost had frittered away during the afternoon shine; although the temp scarcely hit fifty degrees when Coach Sweeny led us outside. Instantly, the cheerleading squad zeroed in on the boys dressed in gear and practicing for the rival game against Kensington High. It took willpower not to search the players for one specific boy, Becket.

It had turned into an irritable practice with Mrs. Sweeny's constant whistle-blowing and brash commentary on our unsynchronized routines. "You girls should have this routine down pat by now."

I also had to contend with the evil glowering of Marcy and Blair.

During the pyramid stacking, my gaze wandered to the bleachers. It was customary for Henry to wait on the bench to drive me home. Off to the side, a man in a trench coat was heading toward Henry. He said something and Henry nodded. The man lowered onto the bench next to him and looked out onto the field. I recognized him immediately—Detective Dyl.

Coach Sweeny terminated the practice with criticism. "Today was the pits. You girls better show some stamina on Friday."

Straightaway, I went toward the bleachers because the detective coming to the school could only mean bad news, and a horrible prickling infected my body. Detective Dyl was conversing with Henry, and his face flooded with color. I was a few feet from them when I tripped on the walkway and went down onto my knees.

Henry leaped to his feet and charged at me, snarling, "You lied. You said you didn't tell them I was with you the night Dave and Skip were murdered."

"Henry," I said, breathing heavy, "I didn't tell them."

CHAPTER 24

"Come with me," Detective Dyl ordered.

"I...I have to get my stuff. It's over there, on the bench."

"Henry and I will wait for you by the gate." A calculating frown engraved his face. "Leo, no messing around."

I hurried along the walkway onto the grassy field.

Nona zipped to my side and asked, "What's going on?"

I fixed my gaze on my sneakers, not wishing to see a bunch of gawking girls. "I have to go to the police station with the detective. It has something to do with that night I told you about."

"Why?" For my sake, she maintained a quiet volume. "You had nothing to do with those murders."

"I...I lied to the police." Fingering the handle of my messenger bag, I then peered toward the field. My eyes hooked onto Becket. He pulled off his helmet and stared at me. Despite my distress, or maybe due to my distress, I couldn't take my sights off him. A light wind sent his pale-golden hair billowing about his head.

"I warned you," Nona said quietly, breaking the spell. "You should have told them about Henry being there. The police always seem to find these things out."

Either it was so we couldn't pool our resources on the night in question, or he didn't trust us, the detective put me in the front of the police car, and Henry rode in the back.

"I phoned your parents," the detective said during the short drive. "They'll be meeting us at headquarters."

Trailing Detective Dyl into the station, my legs were noodley and uncooperative, and I clumsily slipped over my own two feet.

"Take a seat," he ordered. Leaving us alone, he walked away. Seated on wooden chairs against the wall in the police headquarters, Henry and I looked at each other for support.

He whispered, "I'm fucked."

The detective returned, holding a folder in his hand. His no-nonsense gaze deviated from me and slid to Henry. "Henry, come with me."

"My dad's not here yet."

"You're eighteen, right?" Henry nodded. "You want a lawyer?"

"Do I need one?"

"I have a few minor questions. But you have the right if you want one," he said, gaging Henry from beneath his inflexible brow. I couldn't interpret the hardnosed detective's expression.

"I don't need one," he said, a cantankerous lilt to his voice.

"Then follow me."

Henry swerved toward me. "I don't like this shit. He's trying to trap us." His eyes were enormous behind his glasses.

I angled into him and clasped his arm. "Just tell them what happened. The truth."

"Leo, you really don't know what's happening." His body shuddered. "You'll never understand."

"I understand, you should tell the truth." I thought he was panicking. Instead, his features developed into a mien of pure aggression.

"C'mon, Henry," Detective Dyl repeated.

Henry was easing off the chair when his father, causing quite a commotion, stormed in. Fiery eyes full of contempt, and his lips nonexistent in his bloated, controversial face.

"How dare you," he cussed, "bring my son in without my consent." Mr. James cropped his hands on Henry's shoulders. Henry's mouth tightened, and he made a point of stripping off his dad's fingers.

"I'm glad you're here, Mr. Ethan James," the detective said. "You can both follow me."

Did I imagine it? Detective Dyl's gotcha-mouth quirk?

After they departed into the detective's office, I squished both hands between my knees and concentrated on my grass-stained sneakers. Henry had never told me he was eighteen. He must've failed a grade.

"I'd like to say, nice to see you again, Leo, but not under these circumstances." I yanked my head up as Officer Simmons offered a Styrofoam cup. "I brought you some coffee. I just made this batch, so it shouldn't taste like tar." She carried a benevolent smile on her face.

"Thanks." I rounded the hot cup with my hands.

"Would you like to sit over here, keep me company?" She indicated her desk with a sideways head tweak.

I remembered the last time I talked to her. She'd tricked me into telling her about my plight on the tracks. "No thanks. I'm good." Her mouth crunched and she moved to her desk.

I hovered over the steaming cup of coffee like a vagrant in a cheerleader's uniform. I shut my eyes, letting the steam warmed my face. At various intervals, I tipped the Styrofoam to my lips and sipped, not relishing the taste, just for something to occupy my blistering thoughts.

It felt like forever when the office door clacked open. Henry and Ethan James emerged. Disconcerting was how Henry scowled at me as if I were the criminal. He evaded my questioning gape and thumped into the chair.

"Leo, would you come in, please?" My gaze went from Henry to the crafty-eyed detective, overawed by his ability to creep me out. "Your father called. He's still in the city. He's finding it hard to get out of a business meeting. I told him what I planned on asking you, and he gave me parental permission. He might stop by later, or I'll speak to him on the phone."

My legs were full of nuts and bolts as I labored into a stark room with a metal table and chairs.

"Sit here." The detective designated a chair for me. A yawning folder lay on the table; however, he didn't touch it.

"You and Henry we're having a late-night picnic at Hallow Saint's." He watched me like a hawk. "Drinking booze and smoking some weed." He didn't question, so it was a statement. "Leo, why did you lie?"

"I...I didn't actually lie." I balled my overwrought hands in my lap.

The detective angled his head. "What exactly do you mean by that?"

Drifting from his judgmental gaze, I stared at my fingers. "When I saw those dark figures in the graveyard, there was no way of knowing for sure if one of them was Henry."

"Do you realize Henry's life could be in danger?"

"What?" My eyes flitted to his face.

"The perp is still at large. He might have seen Henry and could be tracking him down as we speak. On the other hand, the murderer might already know where the boy lives."

"I...I never thought..."

"That's the problem with kids; you don't think." His knuckles rapped the surface of the table. "We have little to go on."

"You said my mom's murder and these were," I cleared the sludge, hindering my voice, "connected?"

"As I said before, I can't divulge the—"

"Why not," I sobbed, coming apart. "It's been a year... My mom..."

Arranging his arms on the metal table, he leaned into them. His features changed to granite and he peered like a man-eating tiger.

"I'll give you a clue. Promise me not to say a word. Not one word."

I sucked in my lips and bit down and issued him a slight head nod.

"The murder weapon."

CHAPTER 25

Ethan James drove past the village toward the high school to pick up Henry's SUV. The peculiar part was that his father turned on the charisma, like the previous hour never happened. I knew the man had a temper; at least that was the general impression I got from Henry's bruises.

"Leo, I've watched you grow into a real beauty," he articulated. "Just like your mother. She could charm a rattlesnake."

"Stop it, Dad." Henry sounded scornful.

But I wanted to hear more. "You knew my mother, Mr. James?" I asked from the backseat. He watched me in the rearview mirror. Uncomfortable was putting it mildly, more like creepster, and amplified the queasies attacking my stomach.

"I met Lily a couple of years ago at a teacher's convention in New York City." He smirked and a starburst of crinkles lined his eyes. "We became close friends."

"She doesn't want to hear your lame-ass shit, Dad. Knock it off." Henry swiveled to look at me from the passenger seat. "Can't you see it's upsetting her?"

Disregarding his son's wishes, Ethan said, "You're just like Lily, am I right?"

"I don't know," I replied, not getting the gist of his question, and my restless-leg syndrome kicked in. "I...I guess so."

"She was so clever, so beautiful. She—"

Henry had bolted from the car, opening the back door. "Let's go. Get out, Leo."

"Thanks for the ride, Mr. James."

"My pleasure, Leo. See you soon and—"

Henry slammed the door, hacking his father's voice. Then, seizing my arm, he tugged me across the asphalt. Evening had fallen and the school was abandoned as we climbed into Henry's SUV. He didn't ignite the engine until his father's taillights were driving along the avenue.

"Your Dad knew my mother and you never mentioned it?"

"This blows." He smacked the steering wheel as he turned toward home. "He ordered me to stay away from you."

Puzzled, I said, "Your Dad?"

"Dyl!" Henry enunciated the detective's name like a threat. "Does that cop think I'm going to listen to him?" A snort whisked through his nose. "What did he ask you?"

My fingers toyed with the button on my jacket. "He asked me why I lied. I should've told the police about you being there." Henry clenched his teeth. "I was kind of surprised that you told him everything. About us drinking and smoking in the graveyard."

He hit the brakes. The inertia sent me flying; luckily, my seatbelt restricted my face from colliding into the dashboard.

"I didn't tell him that." Taking his hands off the wheel, he flexed them into fists. "I said I took you on a picnic date and we ate cheese and crackers; that's all. We had a disagreement and you ran off, and then those guys showed up. I said nadda about the drugs."

"Oh..." I winced. "A date in the graveyard. Like that's not weird."

"Son of a bitch. You told him we were drinking and smoking weed?"

"Not precisely, he told me. So, I thought you—"

"No. He's playing you like a fish on a hook. Did you admit it?"

"I didn't deny it if that's what you mean." I was duped. "He said you might be in danger. That the murderer knows who you are."

Henry braced his hands on the wheel, arms trembling. A horn beeped, and headlights flooded into the rear window refracting off the mirror. He stepped on the gas.

"The guy was covered from head to toe." His voice vibrated. "There's no way in Hades I could identify him."

"Did you tell that to the detective?"

"He wanted a description." Henry palmed his forehead and moved down to rub the nape of his neck. "I told him what I told you. He was all in black with a knit black cap covering his face. The guy was taller than me. His clothes were baggy and he was wearing black boots, like combat boots or something."

"That's something to go on. The police maybe have plaster imprints of the boot indentations in the graveyard." Keeping my promise to Detective Dyl about the murder weapon would be challenging.

"Come on, Leo, Star Hallow isn't CSI." He released a bitter huff. "Besides, the ground wasn't drenched like it is now from the rainstorm. It'd be tough to find the exact prints with people coming and going in the cemetery."

Dwelling on the scene, Henry was dead-on. It would be near to impossible.

The SUV turned into my driveway and Henry blew an exasperated breath. "My father's not… He's not…" Henry coughed, clearing his throat, but then he didn't expound as if he'd changed his mind about what he was going to say.

"You never talk about your parents." I remembered the gash on his lip where his dad had hit him and more than likely not the first time.

"Sore subject." He kept the car running. "See you tomorrow."

That was my cue to remove my body from his car. I lugged my messenger bag and walked to the side door to find it locked. *Dad isn't home yet.* That was much appreciated because I wasn't ready to deal with him. I rummaged in my bag for the key and went in.

Since going to the police station, I had silenced my cell. Scrolling, I saw a missed call from Becket, no message. Nona texted three times. Blair and Marcy texted the identical message: *Hope everything's alright.* The latter two were ridiculous. They just wanted the scoop before anybody else. Spinning the device on the kitchen table, I wasn't in the right state of mind to talk.

I jumped in the shower, washed my hair, and then was too lazy to dry it. Since taking scissors to it last year, it had been growing like a weed. Either I had to revamp my layers or let it grow out. It was simpler to let it be. Tying the damp mane on top of my head, I climbed into my favorite pair of sweats. After a disastrous phone call with Nona, I switched on the television. Neglecting my homework, I lay on the living room carpet peeling the crust off of a peanut butter and jelly sandwich.

It was going on ten o'clock and Dad still wasn't home. Perhaps he went for dinner with a colleague and a drink, which was good and bad: bad because he'd been boozing like a fiend, and good because he needed to chill with people his age.

A dreaded pang rippled through my chest when a car pulled into the driveway. I'd been curbing my anguish all night, afraid a sloshed Dad would take my head off for lying to the police.

Bell chimes.

I hadn't locked the door. *It's not him.* Did Henry cough up the nerve to come to the door for a change. Comparable to a neurotic-nilly, I fingered the side curtain to have a peek. On the threshold, looking tremendously attractive, was Becket. My hands flew to my fountain of hair and then grumbled, eyeing my ratty sweats.

"Leo, I know you're on the other side of the door. Open up."

Crap, he saw me. Grappling to unravel the hair tie with one hand, I opened the door with the other. The outside sconce spilled light into his dazzling blue eyes. Spellbound, I lost my equilibrium. If it weren't for his excellent reflexes, I'd be sprawled on the floor.

Performing a classical backbend with Becket leaning over me, onlookers would have thought he was seducing me, old-fashion style. He smelled of leather and soap and I felt like an unmitigated klutz. He towed me upright and steadied my stocking feet on the linoleum.

"You're falling for me pretty hard, eh?"

Blazing heat bombarded my body after the combination of my near fall and his teasing wit. One last yank and the hair tie ripped from my head, launching my mutinous strands to my shoulders and veiling my face. His fingers parted the mess like a curtain and hooked my hair over my ears.

"There, that's better," he said.

"Thanks, have a seat. I'll be right back." My goal of sneaking to the bathroom to right my wronged hair was impeded by fingers confiscating my hand.

"You look fine," he said, voice guileless. "I like that tousled look." Rather than releasing my hand, his fingers intertwined with mine.

Satirizing myself, I said, "And my ensemble meets with your approval?" Elevating our conjoined hands in the air, I posed so he could get a gander at my sweats.

"Lovely." He wasn't looking at my sweats. His sapphire-blue eyes took their time, wandering over my face like a titillating facial. Then, concentrating on my lips, he lifted a suggestive eyebrow.

Surviving his suggestive brow, I tried to uncouple our hands without luck as he held tighter. "Why are you here?" I asked rudeness tracing my words.

"I was worried. It's not every day I see someone I like being carted away by the police."

"How did you know he was with the police?"

"I know." He didn't offer further details. "Mind if I take off my jacket?"

"My father should be home any minute."

"I thought he was home." Becket glanced around the kitchen for the first time. "Are you saying that to get rid of me?"

"Not really." My voice pitched into an unnatural level. I was apprehensive about Dad staggering into the house like a buffoon. "He's with friends, um...having a few drinks."

A faint snort sounded in his throat. "You mean he might be toasted."

"Something like that."

"I'll leave if you want me to."

Leave. No. Never. "You're here. You may as well come in." His fingers loosened from mine and slipped from my hand.

Shrugging out of his leather jacket, he draped it on the back of the kitchen chair. While he looked away, I inspected his windswept hair and the fine knit sweater that impeccably molded to his body like a glove.

"What's the verdict?"

Admiring his snug jeans, my eyes snapped to his face. A cocky grin pulled his lips when he caught me in the act of ogling.

"Your boyfriend will see my car in front of the house." He slid one hand into his front pocket. "You sure he won't take it out on my hide tomorrow?"

He didn't buy the line that Henry and I were simply friends. I wasn't about to beat a dead horse; besides, Becket could wipe the floor with Henry. I wasn't concerned and headed into the living room.

"I can have a friend over if I want."

His hands came down on my shoulders and he whirled me into his chest. "Leo, I'm not your friend."

CHAPTER 26

"Do you know how long I waited for you to get your shit together?" Becket's dreamy eyes chased over me. "Nine months ago, I drove you home from a party. You were so smashed and passed out in my car."

"No. That's not true. I'd remember." My brain searched into my druggy archives. Zilch.

"You didn't remember a damn thing because a few days later, I tried talking to you and you snubbed me."

Thunderstruck and mortified. Those months had melded together, a surreal daymare of sorts. *What did I say to him nine months ago? What did I do with him?*

"Nona would've told me," I said ruefully.

"Nona wasn't there. It was a party in Getzville, and I was surprised to see you walk in with Skipper Townsend. One look at you and I knew I had to get you out of there. I never said a word to anyone."

"What happened… exactly?"

"I can never be just a friend." His hand skimmed the length of my arm, and with the other, he cupped the side of my neck and guided me to meet his mouth in a scorching kiss. I wanted more, much more. My fingers traveled over his chest, feeling the strength beneath his sweater. Smoothing them around to his back, I closed the space between us.

Becket slipped his lean fingers into my hair, and his other hand dipped lower, pressing the small of my back into him. My body melted in his arms, responding to his touch and yearning for more. His tongue teased my lips, my mouth, teaching me the art of seduction. A wave of unfathomable sensations rocked me to my core. My shirt rode up and his palm sizzled across my bare skin. My blood boiled like molten lava. I quivered as he wrapped his arms around me while I teetered on my toes until he drew me up, putting pressure where our hips met. Quivering, boiling blood erupted in my veins.

Following his lead, I found the hem of his sweater and slipped my hand underneath. I explored his firm skin and bunching muscles. He groaned, intensifying his kiss. Succumbing to meet his need, I vowed to throw all inhibitions to the wind. His throbbing demand was evident, and I greedily held onto a bit of heaven.

Unpredictably, Becket shoved me away. His chest heaved in choppy breaths, and his eyes darkened to limpid pools of desire. Camouflaging his obvious hunger and in a sultry inflection, he said, "That's why we can't be just friends."

My unfulfilled hunger sputtered and diminished. No cool retort came to mind.

"You're back to the silent treatment?" His biceps bulged while he stabbed fingers through his golden hair. "I should go," he said, looking out of his element.

"No, stay."

"Ah...she speaks."

"You just got here. Um...sit down." I turned toward the couch, then choose the recliner.

Don't Forget to Breathe

"Smart move," he said. "But, if I really wanted to ravage your body, I'd take you into the bedroom without the picture window for everybody to watch."

The curtains had been drawn to their outer frames. Becket and I had been on display, making out for the neighbors. Hurdling from the recliner, I raced to draw the curtains closed. Across the street, prehistoric Mr. Jankowiak was probably wetting his pants, and then there was Henry. He hadn't called since coming home from the police station.

Our small living room shrunk when Becket walked in. Now seated on the couch, he leaned forward, propping his arms on his parted legs. "I am going to the dance with Marcy. I thought you should know."

I picked at the fabric on the couch and said, "She already informed me and everyone else."

His lips thinned into a taut line. "Marcy said she talked with you about it."

"Talked what with me?"

"Marcy thought—you and I had a thing." Tentative, his gaze clung to my face waiting for my reaction. Rather than take the bait, I turned into a stone-faced lump. "She begged me to take her to Homecoming because you'd planned on going with Henry James the whole time."

"That's a lie," I declared.

"I confirmed it with Henry."

Tamping the heels of my palms into my eye sockets, I growled. "Let's not talk about the dance or Henry. I already told you how I feel about him."

"Okay." He straightened, easing into the couch and lengthening his arms on top of the cushions. "You'll be at the game on Friday?"

I was so screwed. All I could think about was the feel of him, and his large hands touching me, those kissable lips, the delicious taste of him. A credible, competent conversation fell apart the moment Becket took me in his arms.

I thought, small talk was better than no talk, and since I didn't want him to leave, I obliged. "Mrs. Sweeny said she'll kick me off the squad if I miss another game."

"The season's almost over," he said.

I managed to form another sentence, "Do you think you'll beat Kensington?"

Becket's fingertips kept moving back and forth on the top of the couch cushion while frisking me with his appealingly wicked eyes. Observing his fingers doing their thing, I wished they were moving over me. The corner of his mouth quirked. *Can he guess what I'm thinking?*

"It'll be rough." He cleared his thickening voice, then furled and unfurled his long fingers. "We're tied for games won and lost."

I licked my tongue across my mouth, tasting him still. Finally, I labored for an exchange of dialogue and said, "Have you gotten an offer like Reggie to play football for college?"

He reflected for a moment. "A couple, yes."

I didn't like to think about him going away to college. Not yet, not now. "Since Mom died, my grades have been in the dumps. I'm trying to rectify that." When I referred to my mother, his eye twitched. He'd retained my asinine blubbering at Earl's and was cringing on the inside. I refrained from saying more.

He remedied my blunder by switching topics. "Is it true that you and Henry are putting together this Halloween party at the Lucien Estate?"

"Who said that?"

"Henry did at Earl's. Rumor has it, he's recruiting people to help."

"What? I told Henry the police would find out. It's a bad idea."

"It'd be brilliant in that haunted house. Don't you think?"

"It's beyond a doubt haunted."

"I figured as much."

He didn't appear astounded; although, most people in the Hallow knew the stories. "It's Star Hallow's claim to fame," he said. "I'm just surprised after all these years the village hasn't made the Estate into a tourist attraction."

"I remember my parents discussing whether the village was going to demolish the site since they couldn't find a developer. Then rumors spread about it becoming a draw for out-of-towners. Maybe, Star Hallow would prefer to be a quaint village in rural American, rather than notorious for heinous murders."

"Or the tills have run dry," he added. "The grounds and the mansion require tons of work to pass state inspection codes."

"I wish they'd tear it down." I scraped my fingernails over my knee, not that it itched, an antsy problem.

"It sounds like you and Henry have been in there quite a bit." He intoned friendly-like, though there was a razor's edge to his voice. "Have you seen things?"

"Yeah, I think I saw Monique Baskerville floating down the hallway, and there was this vaporous mist that smelled like..." I was going to unburden myself again about my mother, her perfumed scent, and seeing her through the Lucien's stain-glass window, standing in front of our home. I had an uncanny sensation, like icicle fingers enclosing my heart, caging it in. I stuttered, "I...I don't want to...party there." Where had Becket received his information? Was Henry spreading tales in school?

"I understand, being so close to your old house and all."

An arcane aroma of a lily passed under my nose, a reminder of Mom's picture hanging in the Lucien attic. Which presented me with this inexplicable urge to unload, telling him what I'd seen.

"I visited my mother on Sunday and cut through the Estate because it started to rain. I saw a light in the mansion. I figured it was Henry...so I went in."

Becket curled forward, intrigued. Void of emotion, he didn't squinch when I mentioned the ghostly figure until I came to the part of my mom's picture in the attic. His spine uncurled, sitting erect.

My cell started vibrating on the kitchen table; I'd forgotten to unmute it. "I better get that. It might be my dad." Leaving the recliner, I snagged the cell to see that Henry was calling. I pressed the mute button and felt Becket looming over me.

"I'd better be going," he grumbled, brow furrowed. In one swoop, his jacket was off the chair and over his shoulders. "We never did talk about the police dragging you and Henry in."

"Long story."

"I have time. If you want to talk about it."

Unwillingly, I recounted, "I told you that I was on the railroad tracks when I heard that God-awful scream when Skipper was murdered." Becket dug his hands into his jacket pockets. "I lied to the police. Said I was alone. Somehow they figured out that Henry and I were in the cemetery together." I sensed the steam building in him. "It's a great place to down a few beers." I declined bringing up the weed, then said, "Detective Dyl is concerned that Henry might be in danger."

"In what way? Why would Henry be in danger?"

"He was there when that guy slaughtered Skipper and Dave. As soon as the guy knifed him, Henry ran away."

"I knew Dave and Skipper from school. Got into dealing some pretty lethal stuff. Of course, you knew that, right?"

"Kind of." I frowned, he was aware of my drug reputation. "After Mom…"

He pulled his hands from his pockets and clutched the high-backed chair. "How did you end up on the tracks, alone, with Henry still in the graveyard? Was he making a deal for the two of you?"

"No. Not at all. I don't use… I haven't… A little weed, that's all." Becket's inquisition felt like a stab in my heart. I strived for honesty, yet, Henry's botched make-out session and his behavior should remain my secret.

"Henry saw some people and…and he told me to run. By the time I got to the tracks, I felt bad leaving him behind. I went back and—"

"Why did he want you to run?" Becket interrupted me. "Your story isn't meshing."

"Because…Henry knew who they were. He didn't want me there." I read the denial in his face and stressed, "Stop hassling me. You're worse than the police." I crushed the tears welling in my eyes, adamant that he couldn't make me cry.

Becket squared his shoulders. "Henry was meeting them, wasn't he?" He looked down at me, eyes guarded, and said, "Henry could be the murderer."

CHAPTER 27

"Not Henry." A quiver wiggled down my backbone. "He told me what happened."

"Could be lying to save his criminal ass."

"The police would've found evidence and arrested him by now." I thought of Henry's temper, but he didn't strike me as a homicidal murderer. "Detective Dyl said there might be a connection between my mother and these murders, and Henry didn't live here a year ago. Besides, why would the detective tell me Henry might be in danger?"

"How are the murders connected, did he say?"

Becket had the power to unharness my thoughts. I spewed, "The murder weapon." Slapping my hand over my mouth, I threw my promise to the detective out the window. "Don't repeat that. I wasn't supposed to tell."

"The police are probably tailing Henry." Becket turned toward to door, then looked over his shoulder. "If you're with him, be careful of what you're smoking and drinking."

"What's that supposed to imply? You still think I'm a junkie?"

"I never said that." He twisted the doorknob. "I don't want you to get hurt in the crossfire, that's all." The door breezed shut behind him.

Eliciting a shuttering breath, the thought of Henry murdering Dave and Skip hadn't crossed my mind—until now. He didn't have a motive for killing them, did he? I glanced at the clock before heading into my bedroom. Dad had yet to return home, and I was getting paranoid. *If he's not home in an hour, I'll call him.*

I scrabbled my fingers on the wall reaching for the light switch in my dark room. Fingers manacled my arm, yanking me forward to whack into a rigid body, and another hand covered my mouth. My eyes widened; although I couldn't see my assailant. Muffled screams rang in my ears. Instinctively, I jabbed my knee upward, hoping to maim.

"Arrgh! Sonofabitch. You caved in my balls."

The intruder shoved me toward my bed. I'd acclimated to the duskiness and saw a hunching figure massaging his crotch. A pair of lenses sparkled, catching an exterior glow from the open window. "My God, Henry. Why are you always so frigging off the wall?" I clicked on my bedside lamp. "What are you doing in my house, in my room?"

"You were with that jock, making out for the whole neighborhood to see," his voice quaked. "What the fuck—why was Becket here? I told him we were together now, to back off."

"Why would you tell him that?" I had to nip his inventive thinking, pronto. "We are not going out." Beneath the frame of his glasses, Henry had somewhat concealed an angry black-and-blue swelling .

"Leo," he said, voice warbling, "I love you." His body deflated, sinking to the floor, and he linked his arms around my legs. "I love you."

"Henry, don't say that. We hardly know each other." I lowered to my bed and, bending over, pulled his arms off me. "Are you okay?"

"Not really." He laid his forehead on my knee. "In two months, I know you better than anybody else. You and I are good together. We're the same."

He weirded me out. "I don't love you, Henry. We're friends, that's all." His fingers dug into my sweats and into my shins.

"You don't have to love me." Relaxing his hold, he moved back, sitting on the floor. "I'm such a loser."

I had thoughts of cuffing him across the head, knocking sense into him. "Stop feeling sorry for yourself. It's unbecoming, Henry. Did you know Grace Huffington likes you? You should ask her to the dance?"

His head jerked. "I'd rather take you. But if you force me, I'll ask Grace."

"What happened to your face?" Henry inspected his newly acquired shiner and the inflamed swelling thawed my pent-up anger.

He touched the inflammation and said, "I walked into a door?"

"Are you asking or telling me?"

Henry garbled, "Don't worry 'bout it."

"Did your dad hit you again?"

"Pretend you don't see it."

Is he joking? "Your father was mad about us breaking into the Lucien place, wasn't he, and Detective Dyl hauling us into the police station?"

He lowered his eyes. "I'm not getting into this with you." A few beats later, and slinging his gaze to my face, he breathed, "Go with me to the Homecoming Dance."

It was probably too late for him to ask Grace, and feeling like a hurtful human being, I said, "I will go with you. But do me a favor and quit telling everyone that we're an item, or whatever it is that you're saying."

He snuffled and asked, "You like Becket Kane, don't you?"

Was it sane to tell him how I felt about Becket? Opting to stray from that question, I said, "I want to know why you were meeting Dave and Skip that night in the cemetery?"

"You know why." He climbed from the floor and sat next to me on the bed. He dropped back on the mattress and nested his head in his arms. The smell of marijuana exuded off his clothes like a spicy perfume. No wonder Dad despised Henry, his essence had him believing I'd be converted back into my junkie days.

"You were making a drug deal?" I guessed.

"Small-time shit."

"You told them it was for me, didn't you?" I had to get far away from his attachment. Getting off the bed, I went toward the window, then turned. "That's why you wanted me to run so that I couldn't deny it?"

"We were cool by then." His eyes followed me. "I hooked them up with someone I knew from the city."

"Hooked them up?"

"Dave and Skip were leaving Star Hallow." Henry snickered, though it stuck in his throat. "They certainly left the Hallow alright—in body bags."

"Don't do that, Henry. It's not amusing."

"They were douche bags. You know that."

I brushed my knuckles along my brow; a headache was stirring. "Neither of them were prime role models, but they didn't deserve to be gutted like that. Ugh." As I kneaded the tension from my temples, there was a grateful temporary silence.

Henry cut into the quiet saying, "Does it remind you of your mom's murder?"

Did the room tip underneath my feet or was the Earth rotating faster than normal? Feeling lightheaded, I eased onto the chair and said, "You didn't have anything to do with it...did you?"

"Me? I wasn't living here when your mom was offed." He moved from laying over the bed into a sitting position.

"Not my mom. Dave and Skip. Did you... did you?"

"Are you asking if I hacked them to death?" he patronized me. "You think I'm a serial killer like the dude that murdered your mother?"

Piece by piece, I was disintegrating. "I can't handle any more reminders of that day." I dropped my face into my hands.

"I shouldn't have said that. It was harsh." The mattress heaved as he stood.

"Just leave, Henry."

He kissed the crown of my head. "I never meant to hurt you." And departed through the open window.

I sighed, saying, "You could've used the door."

Completely drained of energy, body and mind, I lumbered to the bathroom's medicine cabinet and downed a sleeping pill. I didn't want to feel. I didn't want to think. I wanted to blackout. Channeling beneath my blankets, I closed my eyes...

Again and again. Over and over, I searched for Mom.

Red splotches.

Bright orange carrot shaving. Boiling water.

My heart pounding.

Fearing the outcome.

Can't stop.

Standing at her bedroom.

Door opens.

Blood—Mom watching me.

Dagger.

Arms tie me and a clammy hand covered my mouth.

I scream, doubling over.

I see his feet—black combat boots!

CHAPTER 28

"Leo...Leo..."

I dragged open my eyelids to see Dad shaking the daylights out of my shoulder. "Dad?"

"Kiddo, another bad one?" He stripped hair from my sweaty cheeks. My throat was raw, and I swallowed, then smacked my tongue on the roof of my mouth. "Maybe, we need to make an appointment with the psychiatrist."

I croaked, echoing him. "Maybe."

"I stopped by the police station to see the detective, but he was gone. So what did he want?"

I glanced at the time on my digital clock: 3:10 in the morning. "Are you just getting home?"

He wiped the lid of his eye. "Was a late one."

"Can we talk in the morning?" I said, with a jaw-wrenching yawn.

"Sure, get some sleep." He got up from the side of the bed and offered, "Do you want me to sleep in the chair?"

"No, Dad. Go to bed. I'm fine." He leaned over and stroked the side of my temple and I was happy he didn't smell of booze.

"Goodnight."

As soon as Dad clicked the bedroom door, I swiped my cell and keyed in Nona's number. I crammed my head beneath the pillow to mute my voice. *Pickup. Pickup. Pickup.* She answered on the fifth ring. "I had another dream."

"Leo? What time is it?"

"It's after three. I have to talk to you."

"Uhum…go ahead."

"The person who grabbed me from behind was wearing black boots." I plucked a hair from my mouth. "Henry said the guy who murdered Dave and Skipper had on black combat boots." There wasn't life on the line and I wondered if she fell back asleep.

"You dreamt it," she finally hushed into the cell. "Could've been osmosis. Maybe the black boots got caught up into your psyche after Henry told you."

"The doctor said I might start to remember bits and pieces as time goes by."

"It seems like a coincidence; don't you think?"

"I thought you didn't believe in coincidences." I puffed into the phone. "It's fate. My memory's beginning to heal."

Lethargic, she mumbled, "It was a dream."

"The psychiatrist said my brain is still working during my sleep cycle. It can bring things forward that I don't want to remember when I'm awake. Kind of like I have those memories caged in the nether region of my brain. Or something like that."

Nona wasn't responding. *I hear her breathing.*

"Don't tell a soul," she said, sounding pensive. "At least not yet."

"I have to tell the detective. Finding the bastard is my priority."

"Absolutely. Telling Detective Dyl is a smart move," Nona said. "Just him and no one else. Got it?"

"Got it." There was promise at the end of a dark tunnel.

※

Lounging in bed at six o'clock in the morning, I should have been bone tired after spending hours devising my day. Nonetheless, I was invigorated. I phoned Henry. "Don't pick me up. I'm staying home from school."

"Are you sick?"

"I didn't sleep. We'll talk later." I severed the connection before he gave me the third degree.

Dad was bumping through the house. Coming home so late, he had to be exhausted. Although, padding into the kitchen, he was full of vim and vigor.

"Hey, kiddo, feeling better this morning?" He poured his customary juice into a glass.

"Not so much." I waited for the inquest concerning Detective Dyl. It was bound to get sticky.

"I'll be late again tonight," he said and downed his ritual morning drink like a two-ounce shot of bourbon. "I have a backlog of paperwork that needs to get done." I speculated he was preoccupied because he hadn't broached the subject or he wasn't in the mood for more drama.

Relaxing coiled nerves, I said, "You're pretty chipper this morning." I wasn't mentioning his late hour, but he finally looked at me since I came into the kitchen. He lifted a definitive eyebrow. *Uh oh, here comes the sermon concerning the inefficient police department.*

"Why aren't you dressed for school?" he asked, rather than discussing my visit with the police.

"I'm taking a mental health day."

"When I was a kid, we called it skipping school. Mental health day sounds better." Breezing his coat around his shoulders, he waltzed out the door, but turned back to say, "Your brain could use a day of rest. See you tonight."

Who is that man? Two days ago, he was a floundering drunkard. When had he ever chuckled when I skipped school? Even during the anarchy of Mom's murder investigation and my psychosis, he hired an aging tutor to keep me standardized. Perhaps Dad was over the proverbial hump. Great for him, but not for me. Until the police solved Mom's murder case, I'd never be well.

Even though my brain was sleep-deprived and mangled in cobwebs, I showered and dressed in record time. I tied my hair into a ponytail and then downed a bowl of cereal, which curdled in my stomach.

Slinging on my jacket, I eyed the gold-tone key hanging innocently from the peg—the key to our house on Lucien Court. The metal felt cool in the palm of my hand as I split through the side door into the October morning. Perusing the unwelcoming atmosphere, I went back into the house for an umbrella. I fingered the penlight and the key in my jacket pocket. I'd formulated a systematic schedule.

Star Hallow's police headquarters was approximately two miles from home, and I longed for Mom's car parked in the garage. Dad had removed the license plates months ago, alluding he couldn't afford the insurance. I knew better; he was iffy of my instability.

Besides being tired, I felt more than fit and ready to battle my demons.

The clock struck nine when I walked into the police station. Inquisitive heads revolved in my direction. The person I searched for—medium build, shouldering a tawny suit coat, graying at the temples and a rugged face—was leaning on the wall with a mug in his hand speaking to a uniformed officer. Detective Dyl's gaze pinpointed me and he straightened his spine. Then, neither smiling nor seeming to have a pleasant attitude, he headed toward me.

"Leo? You have something for me?"

It's like the man could read my mind. "Yes."

"Come with me." He set the mug on the counter and went along a hallway. Stepping into an office room, a placard on the door read: Detective Mark Dyl. Papers scattered the desktop, a computer, and file cabinets lined the walls.

"Have a seat." He took the chair adjacent to mine and appeared relaxed. "I've been waiting for you."

"Waiting for me?" His words caught me off guard.

"You have something to tell me?" His eyes deepened from light to dark gray in a matter of seconds. Like he knew what I was going to say.

"It was the same man. The guy that murdered my mother is the same man who murdered Dave and Skipper," I told him in confidence. His mouth moved from side to side, chewing over what I had to say.

"Not what I was expecting. How did you come to that conclusion?"

"You know how I've had this amnesia since…you know?" I held my hands in my lap to stop them from shaking. "The psychiatrist said I might never regain the memory or, in time, random pieces to the puzzle might begin to break through. I've had the dream a million times of finding my mother."

His daunting eyes stared at me, and nodding sympathetically, his mouth pinched. He'd been well informed of my nightmares, rehashing them for months devoid of recourse.

"Each time more details enter the dream. Last night I had another one. After the guy grabbed me, I remember clawing the heck out of him until he tightened his arms around me, but I pushed forward and my body bent over his strangling hold. That's when I saw he was wearing black combat boots."

"Black boots?" His eyelids contracted. "Are you sure?"

"Positive. I heeled one of them, trying to get loose. There was a divot on the toe of the right boot like he'd scraped it on something or kicked something sharp."

He steepled his fingers over his mouth. "You know Henry's description of Dave and Skipper's killer?"

"I do. He was dressed in black wearing a black face mask and wearing black combat boots."

"Could be possible the mention of the boots uncovered a vital statistic you had buried. Or, your mind used the description in your mother's case."

"You said the murders might be connected. Now you have proof."

"Not the kind of proof that'd be admissible in a court of law. A dream rarely is grounds for a conviction."

"We have to find the boots," I said.

"Leo, the weapon involved is a unique dagger."

"I saw the dagger."

His eyes tapered in thought. "What I haven't revealed remains confidential. A select few on the case know this detail." Indecision marred his rugged features; something was weighing heavily on his mind. Whether to tell me or to keep me out of the loop. He shifted on the chair and tinkered his fingers on the armrest. His fingers stilled, coming to a decision. Inclining forward, he said, "The bloody boot prints at the crime scene in your house and the boot prints at the cemetery are a match."

CHAPTER 29

"I knew it. I just knew." My pulse ratcheted a notch.

"Young lady," he said with an influx of caution, "we are going to keep this confidential."

"Yes—I mean, of course. Now what? If we find the boots, we find the killer."

"Sounds easy, doesn't it?" He slipped a hand into the front of his suit coat and withdrew a pack of gum. "What makes you think the murderer hasn't discarded or destroyed those incriminating boots?"

"Because the dude's a nutcase and keeps them as a memento along with the murder weapon," I hastily said.

Deep in thought, a rut formed between his eyes. He unhurriedly breached the plastic wrap on the pack of gum. His intimidating gaze flitted to my face and extended the pack of gum. "Take one."

My tongue felt icky. "Thanks." I teethed the sweet wintergreen flavoring, relishing its juiciness. "But if you did find them," I said while chewing, "they'd be sufficient evidence, right? Enough for a conviction?"

"Depends."

"Depends on what?" I pondered and solved my own question. "The murder weapon?"

"That would help tremendously. You dream that up yet?" His cynicism put quite a damper on my day.

"No." My intentions were to tell him about Mom's picture in the Lucien mansion, but after his remark, I decided to check things out. *The entire police department already thinks I'm loony, so it'll be better if I can prove it.*

Standing, like our meeting was terminated, he tossed the pack of gum onto his desk and then fingered a business card.

"Here." He held it like a cigarette between his fingers. "I gave you my private cell number after your mother died. I doubt you still have it."

"Nope. I don't remember that at all."

"Take it." He waved the card in my face. "Call me any time of day or night. I'm here for you."

I slid the business card from his fingers. "What did you expect me to say when I walked in here today? You said you were waiting for me."

"I can read people fairly well." He buttoned his suit coat. "I misread you."

"Misread me in what way?"

"I expected you to recant your story on the night that you and Henry James were in Hallow Saint's. It didn't mesh."

Becket had said that.

"Leo, you've had a traumatic year. I don't blame you for going off the deep end. I would've done the same if I were in your shoes. I know about the drug deals with Dave and Skipper."

It didn't surprise me that the detective knew of my breakdown; just about everyone in Star Hallow had been privy to my psychosis.

He righted his necktie. Changing the theme, he probed, "How well do you know Henry James?"

"Henry? He moved here in August. If I were to take a wild guess, his parents suspected he was dealing illegal drugs and thought by moving here, he'd get away from it all." I harvested an uncouth grunt. How wrong could they be?

"Legally, I can't divulge Henry James' rap sheet. My best advice is to cut any ties you have with the boy. He's a ticking time bomb."

"Is Henry a murder suspect in Dave and Skipper's case?" I drew together my eyebrows in dismay. "I don't remember what he had on his feet. At least I don't think he had on boots."

"Until we find the killer, everyone is a suspect."

"Even me?"

"Even you."

I persisted in my next assignment: Hallow Saint's Cemetery. Like usual, I'd been meditating on memories of Mom's life before her demise. She was well-liked, even loved by her students as a teacher. Recently, I recalled her asking, "Leo, I miss your Grandpa. Would you like to spend the holidays with him? Maybe we can purchase a little bungalow for ourselves."

"You mean like a second home?" I'd replied.

"Something like that. Grandpa's getting fragile. He's going to need round-the-clock care and I'd like to be there for him."

"I can't leave Nona and all my friends."

She'd smiled and tapped her finger on my nose. "I thought you'd say that. But I need to get away from...from here. Think about it."

I had blown it off as one of Mom's hankerings, and that was the first and last time she discussed it.

Mom and Dad had been fighting a lot, more than normal. Dad was staying late at the office and Mom acquired a part-time job at night, tutoring. That was it in a nutshell and that was all my brain could conjure at the moment.

I walked into the cemetery. "Oh, darn it, I forgot to bring flowers." My voice deadened over the graveyard. I glimpsed the memorial stones, not much action today, or any day for that matter.

Spotting flowers bordering Mom's headstone, I slowed. Pink lilies. Had Dad finally mustered the nerve to visit? How strange, lilies like the ones in the Lucien attic.

"Hi, Mom. Did Dad visit you?" I steadied on bended knee in the damp soil to finger the petals. "Just passing through. I'm going to the Homecoming Dance with Henry but we're just friends. You know my heart belongs to Becket. I'll be back on Sunday to tell you everything."

Standing tall, I browsed the network of oak trees flanking the perimeter of the railroad tracks. I scrabbled up and over the ties and into the Baskerville Estate with purpose. By midmorning, the unpromising skies had dispelled into a finicky shine as voyaging clouds played hide and seek with rays of sunshine. The umbrella was an absurd burden.

The lofty mansion eclipsed me in shadows as I approached. Hopping onto the porch, I dropped the umbrella and crawled through our hole. I landed on the grimy floor and cleaned my hands on my jeans.

Precisely what I'd anticipated, gloomy, but no need for the flashlight, yet.

Functioning on autopilot, I ascended the towering flights of stairs. The mansion creaked and wailed, protesting my intrusion. My objective hadn't been to linger in the bowels of a haunted mansion, simply to investigate and accumulate evidence. I just about flew out of my sneakers when my cell chimed. "Thanks for waking the ghosts."

I retrieved my phone and checked the screen. Nona. She was wondering why I wasn't in school. I muted the ring and stuffed it in my pocket.

A wink of mist floated in front of me and then I felt as if I'd stepped into a freezer. Instantly cold to the bone, I catapulted the final flight of stairs, barged through the attic door, and slammed it shut. *Like that door will deter a ghost.* A rainbow of prismatic colors radiated from the massive stained-glass window; although the confines of the attic were dingy.

"Monique and Lucien, let me be for today." I wasn't alone, or ghosts had concrete footsteps. My head whisked to the side to monitor the hoarding debris. I whipped out the flashlight, my finger fumbling for the button, and aimed the beam into the junk pile, scanning for anyone or anything.

When I was a child and cried about hearing footsteps during the night, Mom said it was the house settling. I veered right and tiptoed to my destination. The door was yawning open. Was that how I had left it? I didn't need the flashlight, but I refused to turn it off, just in case. Sunlight leaked from the one window into the room.

I gawked at the bed, immaculately made, with no mussed sheets. The place was spotless and I expected to find a wilted lily under Mom's picture. Not a wilted lily, but three new pink lilies, perfuming the room.

My legs moved on their own accord and stalled at her picture. "Mom, what happened here?" Pivoting to the bed, I gathered the comforter in my hand and ballooned it onto the floor. Same sheets. Russet stains bled into the threads in a disorganized pattern. The police could get a DNA sample from the stains and establish who belonged to the droplets. "Mom, is this your blood? Is this where it all began and ended in our house?" I gripped the edge of the sheet and tugged, dislodging it.

My strategy: Give it to Detective Dyl.

The far corner was stuck on something. I crawled onto the mattress and was in the process of yanking the sheet when there was a definite footstep and a swish of a door.

CHAPTER 30

In the course of turning, a solid body flattened me to the bed. Whoever it was planted a hand on the back of my skull and mashed my face into the mattress, making it hard to breathe. I screamed into the sheets while his hands restrained my arms, jerking them behind me. A zip-tie or some kind of cording tied my wrists. A body weighed heavily over me. I grunted, catching a hint of oxygen.

I was held captive and his legs bracketed my body, pressing my bound arms into my spine. It hurt like hell and when I lifted my head he was there to batter it back down. A cloth was then wound around my eyes, blinding me. Something was jammed into my mouth, muffling my screams.

His weight shifted. Relieved, I attained a dose of air. Screeching and sounding like a ghostly wail, drool saturated my gag. Two arms dug beneath my waistline, fingers seeking the zipper of my jeans. *Oh my God, he's going to rape me!*

To foil the pervert, I forcefully thwacked my legs every which way. In retaliation, I received a boring knuckle into my shoulder blade. He lay on top of me, sinking my body farther into the mattress, impeding my feverish squirming. A chin dug into my shoulder. "Stop fighting me. Or you're going to get hurt," said an abrasive voice. He climbed off. Again, fingers scraped into my skin at my hips as he yanked off my jeans.

I felt the strength of his hands on my ankles, slapping my legs together, and then something was bound around my kneecaps. The mattress buckled under the weight of his body as he lay beside me. A large hand cupped the back of my skull and slowly nudged my face into the mattress. He was suffocating me.

"Don't follow me. Don't look for me. Don't talk to the police. I know where you live."

I can't breathe…

My eyelashes fluttered, brushing the blindfold. My arms were free and achy, lying by my sides. Spitting the gag from my mouth, I then slid off the blindfold. Rope still bound my knees so I rolled sideways, only to realize, not rope, but he'd used my jeans. Feeling woozy, I untied my jeans and massaged my numb legs. My body trembled like a bowl of gelatin as I climbed into my jeans and spied a pair of woman's nylons and a sock. My gag and bondage. Ugh!

Had the guy found them in a bureau drawer? He hadn't expected company and hid in the rubble of junk when he heard me clomping up the stairs. Perhaps it wasn't Dad, but this guy who put the lilies on Mom's graveside?

My cell booped in my pocket. Two texts. One from Nona and Henry. It was nearing three o'clock. The unknown man had knocked me out for a while. The flashlight was under the tiny table, broken. I felt the need to take it, leave no evidence behind. Packing it in my pocket, I came in contact with Detective Dyl's business card. My fingers itched to make the call. An abrasive voice resonated through my aching head: *"Don't follow me. Don't look for me. Don't talk to the police. I know where you live."*

I left the blood stained sheet, figuring the detective's forensic team could collect it, and made a slap-dash sprint down the staircase, not stopping for a breather. Once outside, I surveyed the cul-de-sac, wondering if the guy might be hiding somewhere, waiting and watching. It was clear and I doubted he'd take a chance of being recognized.

My plans had been final: to be gone from Lucien Court before sunset. Scrutinizing the pewter skies, I estimated I had an hour before the street darkened. So I headed to my next task.

Since Mom's murder, my toe hadn't touched the inside of the house. A total recall of that day had been torturous. Nightmarish dreams, significant and insignificant aspects of the crime scene had been plaguing me. I realized it was vital, for my sanity, to remember.

Dedicated to my undertaking, I charged the porch steps of our old home and wedged the gold-toned key into the front door's lock. It had always been tricky to operate, and the procedure came to me like it was second nature. Left, right, and a jiggle.

Dormant musty air engulfed me from the start. My sneakers polished the hardwood floor, slinking in like a wary snail. With the furniture and area rugs removed, it was a hollow shell. A furtive pull had me rotating toward the staircase. I wasn't prepared for that venture, not yet. Instead I stepped into the kitchen, and like the living room, the countertops were empty. I approached the rear windows, my footsteps echoing in the room. Mom's perennial gardens had deteriorated. Overgrown, unkempt, and in the midst of decomposing.

"Mom...?"

It was again, October twenty-fifth. I called and couldn't find her. My legs carried me into the living room toward the staircase. I tried not to disturb the reddish-brown wetness.

Too quiet.

"Mom—where are you? Are you home?" I walked through a mirage and came upon the second-story hallway. I squinted, trying to focus through the vision. I didn't remember moving, but found myself standing in front of my parent's bedroom door. A stinging pain cut into my heart like a sliver of glass, shredding it to pieces.

The door inched open.

I had known and didn't know what sight awaited me.

My breath clutched on a scream.

Caged by strong arms. Flogging my legs like an untamed ninja, thrashing in vain. My eyes caught sight of the black boot with a rent in the toe.

"I'm not going to kill you. Not yet."

"You killed my mother! You killed my mother!"

A clammy hand squeezed my nose and mouth, then the words, "Stop fighting me."

My world blackened.

I was laying on the hardwood floor. Someone said, "Are you hurt?" An image receded in and out like a broken picture, and I focused on Mom, still staring at me from her disjointed vantage point.

"Leo?" A hand soaked in blood pushed hair from my forehead.

CHAPTER 31

My back arched off the floor, gagging on my tongue, gasping, and coughing. Foul acid trampled up my esophagus. I rolled to my side, enabling me to choke it down. Fluid was trickling down my neck, I was burning up. Mopping the contours of my face, I examined my fingers, expecting blood, but it was sweat. A lightning bolt of realization hit me—it was the same man. The guy who assaulted me in the attic. *Is it Mom's killer?*

Similar voice. Same words. Same pressure to make me faint.

A sudden illumination encased me in a golden halo. My sight skipped toward the bedroom where the atrocious memory of the murder scene churned and dispersed. Replaced by a hailstorm of glorious colors, a coalescing radiance that formed into her spitting image.

I mouthed, *"Mom."*

Angelic and wearing a heartfelt smile, Mom beckoned me and then crossed her arms over her heart. "Leo, I love you. Be careful." Her translucent form floated toward me before evaporating into a wisp of a breeze.

Afterward, I lay there, recreating her ethereal image. I crept to my hands and knees.

Spent of fortitude, I tottered toward the stairwell. My quivering fingers clasped the railing, and my shoulder braced the wall, scraping downward until I reached the first floor. Fumbling for the handle of the front door, I lurched onto the porch. Drinking in fresh air, and somewhat stable, I canvassed the Court for a man wearing combat boots. I reckoned he'd be long gone by now. The road was abandoned and I headed for Westgate.

Once I hit the main drag, vehicles swooshed by, going home from a day of work. Weak and broken, my brain was piecemeal; nevertheless, I replayed Mom's beatific apparition like a skipping record.

Bumbling into the kitchen, I hung the key on the peg where it belonged. Then I hurled the broken penlight into the trash and unloaded my pockets, including Detective Dyl's business card. My eyes adhered to his name: Detective Mark Dyl. Should I call him? A bold, imperious gurgling belly interrupted my thoughts. Foodies first. Lots of foodies.

I stuffed whatever was eatable into my grub hole: cold chicken, a banana, and cookies. Whether from being physically beaten or reliving the worst day of my life, I was ravenous. Following a resounding burp, I plodded into the basement.

I hadn't rifled through the boxes since our move. There had to be some sort of clue the police had overlooked. Mom had been an English teacher, and I remember journals, lots of journals.

This house had a crawlspace where Dad stored the boxes. I pulled on a drawstring, and fluorescent light showered the area. There, stowed to be forgotten, Mom's life on Earth, four corrugated boxes. I climbed into the crawlspace and flipped open one of the box flaps. Her sweet perfume invaded the small enclosure. I shoveled my arms into her clothing and squashed them to my face, drinking in her essence.

I went to the next box and then the next, looking for something—anything that would bring me closer to the truth. After accumulating extensive clutter, I hit paydirt—composition notebooks.

Carting an armload, I stacked them on the basement's concrete floor. Most of the notebooks were from students. These must have been special to her. I paged through, looking for what? I didn't know. Frustration gripped my innards at the grueling, tedious job of riffling through pages. The tower of books seemed to multiply and scrawling passages were an eyesore. Reading these would take forever, I moaned.

"Leo, are you in the basement?"

Dad. What should I tell him? Everything?

He stomped on the stairs, finding me in the middle of bedlam. "What's going on? Why are your mother's things all over the floor?" The fluorescent light emphasized the fine lines in his perplexing expression.

"I'm looking for clues."

"Clues for what?"

"Evidence. Clues. Something the police must've overlooked." I placed my hand on the pile of notebooks. "There has to be—"

"Stop it, Leo." His fingers curled. "You'll only be disappointed."

"Her killer is out there. I need to try." I itched the side of my nose and then told him, "Dad, there's a picture of Mom in the Lucien mansion. In the attic."

"What did you say?" His head tilted as if he misunderstood.

"Henry and I were in the Baskerville mansion. In their attic is a photograph of Mom hanging on the wall, and someone is putting flowers there."

Ashen faced, his body weaved. I shot to my feet, afraid I might have to catch him.

"C'mon, let's go upstairs." Clasping his arm, together we shouldered into the kitchen. I thought of telling him about the boots, though I reconsidered.

Resembling an automaton, he reached for the cupboard where he stored his liquor and poured a healthy draft into a glass. Carrying the bottle, he settled onto a chair. He took a swig, swallowed, and said, "What the hell are you and that idiot boy doing trespassing in that place?"

"Dad, did you hear what I said?" I rinsed my dirty hands under the faucet. "Mom's picture is in the attic. Why would there be a picture of her there?"

"How the hell do I know? Maybe Lucien's ghost put it there." He guzzled the remnants of the honey-colored bourbon.

"And the flowers, too?"

He reiterated, "You shouldn't be trespassing."

"We need to tell the police," I stressed.

His empty glass clunked on the table. "What will I tell them? My daughter and her dickwad boyfriend broke into the Baskerville mansion for a little hanky-panky and—"

"Dad, stop—Oh my God!" I clung to the back rail of the kitchen chair. "It's not like that at all."

"What the hell am I supposed to think?" He poured another hefty dose and set the bottle next to him. "Are you still taking your meds?"

"What's that got to do with anything?"

"Answer me."

"No."

"Then you're using again, aren't you? It's that boy. He's no damn good."

"No, Dad, no. Please, listen." I was desperate and competing for my sanity. "Everything I told you is true and there's something else. I don't want you to go ballistic." I buffed the heels of my palms over my hips. "A guy attacked me in the attic this afternoon. I think it was the man who killed Mom. He's still around. Then I went into our old house and…and I'm starting to remember what happened after I found her."

A conflict of emotions skittered over his face. "How could you do this to me? To me!" He hammered his hand against his chest, looking unhinged. "After all I've done for you. I can't go through this again."

"Let's go. Right now," I begged because he didn't believe me. "You can see for yourself. The picture is there. I'm not hallucinating." I wanted to say Henry saw it too, but it'd only summon filthy notions in his misconstrued brain.

His gaze sliced to the window and blackness stared back. "I wouldn't step one foot into that hellhole when it's dark."

"We can use a flashlight."

He ingested a mouthful of booze and then swished the liquor in his glass. It appeared to have a calming effect. "I have a better idea," he posed. "We'll call Detective Dyl in the morning." He poured another round and raised the glass like a salute. "Your ass is on the line with this one, kid."

CHAPTER 32

"Get dressed." Dad prodded me awake. "We're meeting the police on Lucien Court in fifteen minutes."

"Huh?" My head was a throbbing fuzzy globe. "In the middle of the night?"

"It's morning. I said get up and get dressed." He toggled on the light switch. The glare stung my eyeballs.

We were in the car and heading to Lucien Court by six. Streetlights washed the avenues, viable in the dusky dawn. An aura of tension bristled around my father; his breathing clipped. I had hoped that throughout the night he just might start to believe me, and offer a tad of credence to my story.

A grumpy noise rattled his throat when he made the right-hand turn onto the Court. A squad car and the detective's unmarked vehicle were parked on the street. Two uniformed police officers and the detective were already on the wraparound porch. Utilizing heavy-duty metal snips, they were in the process of cutting through the rusted chain links that someone had attached to the dual main doors long ago.

Detective Dyl turned, his speculating gaze tacked onto me, and then glanced over my shoulder. He gave Dad a curt nod.

Dad addressed the police, "This could've waited until it got lighter."

"We'll talk later, Mr. Nelson." The detective signaled with a dismissive hand. Again, he looked at me, eyes narrowing. "It's good to check every lead."

"We're in," said one of the policemen. Their flashlights skimmed the once-grandiose foyer.

"Leo, you saw something in the attic?" Detective Dyl asked, businesslike.

"Yes," I said meekly.

The two policemen proceeded up the staircase with Dad, me, and then Detective Dyl trailing. A parade in motion that arrested when they heard a baby crying. The officer flashed his light along the second-story hallway. "Is everyone hearing what I'm hearing?" he asked.

"Keep going, Murphy; it's only a figment of your imagination," the detective said.

"Some figment." Officer Murphy's eyes broadened, peering at his partner.

"You hear it, don't you?"

His partner jerked his shoulder and then protruded his chin, a gesture to keep moving.

Everyone crossed the threshold into the attic, and the ancient floorboards squawked at their excessive weight. I pointed. "Over there." Striding toward the room, a hand descended on my shoulder.

"Wait here." Detective Dyl borrowed the officer's flashlight and started for the closed doorway. The door was locked when he turned the knob. "Are you sure this is the room?"

"It was never locked before."

"You got this, boys?" He waved over the policemen who appeared to be in their late twenties.

First one and then the other administered a kick to the door, shattering hinges.

"Good work."

Summoning a sense of complacency, I waited to hear confirmation, that I hadn't been hallucinating.

"What the frig," Officer Murphy said. "Is this some kind of a prank?"

"Leo, come in here," Detective Dyl ordered. My heart jump-started.

I was positive I'd see a bed, stained sheets, Mom's picture, and flowers. I skidded to a stop. "No...no...that wasn't here." Hanging from the rafter was Henry's mannequin with dried duck's blood. "He put that here last night. He knew I'd be back with the police," I cried.

Going to where Mom's photograph had once hung, I ironed my palm over the wood. I wanted to feel a nail or something to prove it was there. I veered to where the bed had abutted the wall. All gone.

Detective Dyl knelt on the floor, closely observing, what? I didn't know. "Hand me your light, Murphy," he said to the officer, outstretching his arm.

"Leo, Leo..." Dad shambled over and embraced my shoulders. "Are you alright?"

"A freaky kid's prank," Officer Dobbs said. "That's all."

"When are they going to demolish this haunted house anyway?" Officer Murphy studied the dummy with fascination. "That thing looks real. Whoever made it did a good job."

"Dad, you have to believe me. It was here. Mom's picture and the flowers. "Yesterday the guy—"

"Leo, that's enough." Dad gave me a firm shake. "You must've imagined everything. Another one of your realistic dreams."

"No." *I'm not schizophrenic.* "Everything I said is true, not a delusion."

Certain that Henry could confirm my story, I was ready to throw him into the fire when the detective said, "What did you say about a guy?"

"It's nothing." Dad flaunted a trivial hand.

Dad didn't believe or want to listen to anything I had to say. That's when I snared Officer Murphy's awry glance, judging me as a juvenile delinquent or in need of a psych ward. I scraped Dad's comforting arms off my shoulders.

Detective Dyl went to the wall where I'd been feeling around. He shined the light over the area, reading the wood with his fingertips like Braille. "You're off the clock now, right, guys? Why don't you head out?" he said to the officers.

Officer Dobb's flashlight spliced through the room, a final check before heading out behind Officer Murphy.

I stepped over splinters of broken wood as we all exited from the room. The sound of the policemen tramping down the stairs resonated into the attic, and Murphy said, "You did hear that baby crying, didn't you?"

"Probably two cats getting it on," Officer Dobbs replied.

Detective Dyl chuckled, then looked at my father. "Do you want to talk here or headquarters?"

"I'd rather get this over with here." Dad seemed to look anywhere but at the detective. "I have to get to work." He shifted his feet and cast me a hard-hearted stare down.

Detective Dyl sauntered toward the stained-glass window. His shoes crunched on remnants of glass, and then he inspected the floor. Swerving, he leaned on the window frame, crossing his arms. "Leo, what happened yesterday when you were here?"

"You're making this worse," Dad said. "Leo's not well, so stop placating her."

"I'm fine." My jaw ached from clenching. "I wasn't seeing things." I went on and described in detail my spontaneous undertaking and what I had wished to accomplish yesterday. I neglected the part of witnessing the angelic image of Mom because, they *definitely* would be locking me into the psych ward. But then there was Henry who I decided would have to be tossed under the bus. "If you don't believe me, ask Henry James. He saw everything."

"Oh my God," Dad belted out. "Don't you have a shred of decency? Are you shacking up here with that kid?"

I gasped in disbelief. My dad had just ruptured my heart. On the verge of thawing into a puddle, my eyes and throat burned. I wrestled to hide my unstable emotions.

"If we get an anonymous tip about any murder," Detective Dyl sighted Dad, eyes flinty, "it's my duty to check it out. But, Paul, why don't you believe your daughter?"

Dad's chest expanded and his mouth twitched. "Didn't you just prove her story to be somewhat preposterous? This is a prank for attention. Leo has these...dreams. We've been suffering through them since...her mom."

"Leo, your father has a point," the detective said with hardened resolve. "We haven't been able to substantiate your claims and you haven't given us any credible proof. Let's ride this out for a while."

My bones shattered into agonizing fragments. "What's wrong with you people?" I cried. "Ride what out? Another year?" Turning, I sprinted from the attic.

CHAPTER 33

"Dad, I can't believe you said that." Endeavoring to get my scrambled egg of a brain functioning, I scoffed, "Thanks for throwing me to the wolves."

"If we would've uncovered your mother's picture and flowers, then I'd be in your corner." He took his eyes off the road to give me a passing glimpse. "After Lily died—"

"Murdered," I corrected. "She didn't just die. She was murdered—in our home."

"May I continue?" He wiped a hand across his mouth. "After your mother was murdered, I thought you'd have to be placed in a sanatorium. Your delusional nightmares were relentless, and when you were well enough to go to school, you started taking those mind-altering drugs."

"But—"

He threw his arm up, preventing me from speaking. "I know what you were doing—trying to break away from reality. I do the same thing with my drinking. But whatever drove you back into our old house...to...to relive that day is beyond me."

"I confronted my fears and it worked; I remembered something new."

Dad grumbled under his breath. It was apparent he wasn't interested in my exploits nor equipped to handle anything I had to say. Adopting his belligerent attitude, I also grumbled and crossed my arms over my chest.

The Westgate sign smeared past my vision. "Where we going?"

"I'm taking you to school."

"I don't want to go to school."

"You skipped yesterday, and all that did was cause problems."

"My messenger bag is still at home with my books and homework."

He made a ham-fisted U-turn. "I'll stop at the house. Run in and get your things."

"But I look terrible. I can't go to school looking like this." I gaped at my mismatched clothes.

"Tough. You already had your mental health day." He pulled into the driveway, leaving the engine idling.

I charged into the house, simultaneously whisking off my grody T-shirt. Like a quick-change artist, I dressed in a jiffy, wolfed down a piece of bread, and grabbed a handful of cookies.

Hurrying out of the house, I lobbed my messenger bag on the floor of the car and hopped in. After stuffing a cookie into my mouth, I worked my fingers into detangling my hair.

"Healthy breakfast," Dad said, reversing down the drive.

"I'm starved," I said, spitting crumbs from my mouth.

"I was thinking about that wormy new kid. Ever since he moved here, the trouble started. I don't like him. I don't want you near him. I don't want you to talk to him. Do you understand?"

Motoring through Star Hallow, the quaint village was stirring. People were walking into Earl's for their morning brew and breakfast, and local shop windows were brightening. I couldn't set foot in the village without people feeling sorry for me; I'd seen a year of melancholy expressions. Residents of the Hallow were coming to terms with Mom's unsolved murder, whereas I was just getting started.

"That'll be kind of hard since I'm going to the Homecoming Dance with him on Saturday." Dad was blaming Henry for our problems, the one person who could verify my story.

He drummed his hand on the wheel. "When were you planning on telling me?"

"The dance is no big deal. Henry needs a friend." On the horizon was Star Hallow High and I gathered the strap of the messenger bag over my shoulder. "I don't understand why you dislike him."

"I already told you why." Dad decelerated into the school's main thoroughfare. "It's not just Henry," he said, tone simmering. "His father is a slimy weasel."

"You know his father?" News to me. Dad stalled the car near the school's main entrance.

"We need to sit down and hash this out. I might be late again. Leo—" He waited until I made eye contact. "In light of this morning's incident, think about revisiting Dr. Mathias. I'll make an appointment for you today."

It would be useless to bicker with him. The shrink route helped to an extent. The side effects of the antidepressants had caused havoc. The tremors had increased instead of decreasing, insomnia escalated my headaches, and I suffered from grave stomach issues. It wasn't worth it. That was when I discovered Dave Galbraith. Dave and Skip had hooked me up, a prodigious rollercoaster ride.

Star Hallow High frowned upon tardiness, although for me, the girl whose mother had been brutally murdered, I was given a pardon from punishment. The bell clanged for a change of classes, and the amassing bodies choked the corridors in clamoring mayhem. I joined the herd toward the stairwell where it would lead to the second level of the school. Next year a locker would be assigned to me on the main floor, a privilege for seniors.

Before hightailing upward, it had been my custom to locate Becket's senior locker in hopes of catching sight of him. Sure enough, I couldn't miss that head of hair spilling over his shoulders as he was reaching into his locker.

At that moment, Marcy strolled around the corner; her skanky shirt should have been outlawed in school. It was comedy central as girls and boys craned their necks to gawk at her impressive rack. She diverged straight to Becket and extended her arm to ring a piece of his satiny hair behind his ear. His back was to me, and reading lips wasn't my forte, but he shook his head at whatever she'd said, and her cutesy smile turned into a frown. She had to have seen me hovering in the background because her gaze slung right to me. Her mouth slanted into a hard-edged smirk.

Becket began to turn, but Marcy hampered his roundabout by winding her arms around his neck, drawing him to her mouth. My heart fractured as his hands gripped onto her shoulders. Nevertheless, I didn't linger and whooshed up the stairs, bumping through kids.

This day can't get any worse.

That was when a perturbed Nona was hastily advancing toward me. Her mocha glow waned, lips meshing together. "Where have you been? You don't return my calls. I even stopped by your house yesterday and no one was home. I don't know what's going on with you."

Wading through curious onlookers, I rounded an arm over her petite shoulders, shepherding her to the side wall.

"I'm sorry, Nona. I have so much to tell you, but it'll have to wait until later."

"When?" she said, not being put off.

"Can you manage a night without Reggie? Dad's been working late, and you can help me go through some things of my mother's."

Her expression distorted as if she'd sucked a lemon. "No offense, Leo. That sounds creepy, and no disrespect to your mother, I mean that in only the nicest of terms."

"No offense taken." I repositioned the messenger bag on my shoulder. "I'll explain tonight. Can you come over after school? We'll order a pizza."

"Did you get my text? We have cheerleading practice tonight."

"Oh, cripes." I angled my head onto the wall, closing my eyes. "My uniform is at home. Then there's Marcy." I pictured her lips on Becket, and snarled.

"I have news about Becket and Marcy that'll interest you." Nona squeezed my arm. "And I wouldn't beat yourself up. Mrs. Sweeny surprised us with this practice during yesterday's announcements. You weren't in school."

"I read your text last night but still forgot. You'll understand why when I tell you what happened."

Her eyebrows hiked up her forehead. "You're going to make me wait all day. I'll explode."

Delving into Mom's treasure trove of boxes pissed Dad off to no end. So prior to investing energy into carting the composition notebooks from the basement, I dialed his cell to double-check on his imminent arrival. When it went straight to voice mail, I keyed his office number.

"Mr. Nelson's office," answered an unfamiliar voice.

"Is Mr. Nelson in?"

"May I ask whose calling?"

"This is his daughter, Leo."

"Hello, Leo. We're done for today. He just left. You can try him on his cell."

"Is this Regina?"

"My name is Ellen."

"Dad didn't tell me he had a new secretary. What happened to Regina? Did she get a promotion?"

"Ahem…" She sounded tentative, "You should ask your father."

Four minutes later my cell rang. *Dad.* "Leo. I missed your call."

"Just wondering when you were coming home."

"It'll be a late one. I'm getting something to eat and then back to work. Are you home?"

His remark struck a nerve, especially since his new secretary mentioned they were done for the day. "Yes, I'm home. Nona's coming over."

"I like Nona. I don't want that James boy in my house, understand?" His comment left a sour taste in my mouth.

"Yep, see you later."

Nona promised she'd be here by six, and I ordered the pizza to be delivered. I'd finished transporting the last of the composition notebooks onto the kitchen table when my cell buzzed. "Hey, Henry, we need to talk."

"Yes, we do," he said, voice agitated. "Want to go out?"

"I can't right now. Nona's coming over." Dead silence met my comment. "Henry, are you there?"

"Detective Dyl just left. He paid my family a little visit."

"I think I know why."

"Duh, you could have warned me."

"I searched for you in school, and you weren't at my cheerleading practice."

"Upset that I wasn't there to chauffeur you home?"

Whoa, he is grouchy. "I took the late bus home."

"You played hooky yesterday," he said, "and I stayed home today."

"Are you ill or loafing?"

"Loafing. I went to the mansion and guess what I found?"

"I already know," I cut him to the quick. "Isn't that why the detective came to talk to you?"

"Yep. My father tore into me, big time. You really should have given me a heads up."

"Oh, no. I am so sorry," I said and thought of his father's abuse. "Did he beat you up again?" There was a temporary silence and I gnawed on a hangnail waiting for his answer.

"He wasn't happy. I'll live."

"Henry, Nona just walked in." I felt wretched for having to put him on standby. "Can I call you later?"

"Whatever," he complained, then hung up.

Nona stood in the middle of the kitchen looking like a beautiful drill sergeant, knuckling her hips. "I still can't believe you blew Becket off to go with that boy."

"C'mon, you know the whole story."

"Yeah." She flapped her hands, commiserating with my debacle. "Marcy's a sleazeball."

"Did you hear what she was saying at practice?" I opened the fridge and doled out cans of soda.

"I heard." Nona's tongue spiked from her mouth, and then copycatting Marcy's voice, she said, "We're planning an all-nighter."

"I wanted to pluck the black roots out of her head," I added. "Did you notice how she tried to be buddy-buddy, asking me how I'm feeling today? Arrrgg!"

"She thinks she has Becket by the curlicues."

"That's a visual I didn't need."

Expressing a mischievous wink, she motioned me into the living room. "C'mere, girl. I've been dying to tell you something." She bounced on the couch, patting the spot next to her. Because I had to be right next to her to appreciate whatever news she'd been saving.

"We both know that Marcy basically lied to get Becket to go to the dance, right? Well, it seems that he's having second thoughts. He's been trying to break it off and Marcy won't hear of it. She's a clinging vine that needs to be removed."

"Marcy kissed him in school today."

Nona cursed, and I tipped the cold can of soda to my mouth.

"Reggie said he's not into her as much as she's into him," she enlightened. "Becket's been down lately."

"Reggie's filling you in on Becket's love life now?"

"Only when I ask real sweet like." She grinned and rounded a manicured eyebrow. "You're not going to believe what else slipped from Reg's mouth. Becket's been wanting to ask you out for a lot longer than we thought."

CHAPTER 34

Following the arrival of cheesy pizza, Nona and I parked at the kitchen table and began sorting through an avalanche of notebooks.

"What am I looking for?" she said, biting into her slice of pizza and fingering through pages.

"Anything that mentions my mom." I crumpled a paper napkin, cleaning grease from my hands. "What I'm really searching for is my mother's journal. I'll know her handwriting when I see it."

"Why would she keep her personal journal with her students?"

"I don't know. I'm looking for a needle in a haystack, okay?"

"You got that right." Her head waggled. "When did you become Nancy Drew? It'll be impossible to uncover something the police overlooked. I can only imagine what's eating your brain."

I updated her on the events of the past two days, comprising of Henry's recent call and the detective's unannounced visit to his family.

"You could be dead right now, girl." Fuchsia bloomed across her face, eyes blistering. "Do you know that?"

"I could've been killed with my mother, and sometimes I wish I were."

"Stop talking like that. They'll put you away in a straitjacket."

"Do they still use straitjackets?"

"Why, you want to find out?"

"Not really," I said abstracted, picking at the cheese of my crusty pizza. "C'mon, let's try to put a dent in these."

"Leo, some of these are old. Why would your mom keep them?"

"Just go through the ones from the last two years. Mom was sentimental. Maybe she thought if one of her students became a well-known author or politician or even an actor, she'd have something of theirs to remember them by."

Forty-five minutes ticked by and the monotonous shuffling of pages and reading became frustrating. I slammed my back into the chair and scrubbed my eyes. "This isn't getting us anywhere. What was I thinking?"

"I'm thinking we need some music," Nona said, pushing back her chair, and getting to her feet.

"That might work. I wish I had one of those wireless speakers." I rushed into my bedroom and returned with my iPod and dock. "Anything special you want to listen to?"

"Something that'll keep me awake."

I turned up the volume when a popular tune drifted through the speakers and Nona began to move. "Good one, hun." She spread her arms over her head, swaying like a lock of hair in a breeze. "Girl, loosen up."

Letting the music strip away the angsts from our bodies, we were again carefree, dancing, yakking, and giggling through three songs. It was Nona who lowered the music and said, "Let's get back to work. I have to leave soon."

The prolonged drudgery concluded when Nona whooped. "I found Becket Kane's!" She held up the composition notebook, pointing to his scribbled name. "His journal when he was a sophomore in your mom's class."

Taking my chair with me, I darted over to her side of the table. Together we thumbed through the pages. We read a few essays and poetry. "These aren't too bad. I'd never guess him for a prolific writer."

"Listen to this one." In an overdramatic voice, Nona read,

> *"Her moon-spun locks glisten in the rays of day*
> *Eyes like blue sapphires turn to me*
> *I shudder*
> *Feasting upon her lusciousness*
> *She has bewitched me with her beauty*
> *I am but a boy*
> *Her maturity is titillating*
> *She wiled her way into my heart*
> *She laughs and jests and pierces me through*
> *My teacher in body and soul*
> *I will love her until the end of days.*

"Wow, this is so corny."

Nona and I giggled, putting our heads together.

"Look what your mother wrote on the page." She indicated Mom's legible cursive. *Nice poem. You're selling yourself short, Becket. Tell the girl how you feel.* Underneath she had drawn a smiley face in the shape of a heart.

"It doesn't sound like him, does it?" I said.

"It sounds like he's writing about your mom. Moon-spun locks, eyes like blue sapphires. Then this line, my teacher in body and soul. Freaky shit. Your mom had blue eyes, right?"

"Yes, she was beautiful."

"It's evident she bewitched Becket."

"That day at Earl's, he said I looked like her, but I don't. My natural hair color is reddish-blonde, and I have green eyes."

"He didn't mean her twin, but beautiful like your mom." Nona's honey-brown eyes were ringed with white, clear and chilling. "You don't think—No! It's not possible—is it?"

"What do you think?" I breathed.

"Becket and your mom?"

I didn't like the sound of that. "That's a definite no. Oh my gosh, Nona. You make me wanna barf."

"It's on the news all the time," she warned. "A teacher falling for their student. Or a student falling for their teacher."

"No way, not my mother," I uttered, adamant, with a negative head shake. "She—No—Never."

"You're probably right. That kind of heat would've hotwired gossip channels in less than a second."

I blew a long-winded sigh.

"I'm not writing Becket off, hun. This poem makes him look guilty as sin." Her brow tweaked. "And I remember the police were ruthless in cross-examining your Dad. They always blame the husband first."

"Nona, you're killing me here. First, you have Becket as Mom's young lover and now you're accusing my dad."

She shrugged. "I'm just saying."

"Dad had an iron-clad alibi. His secretary attested that he was in his office all day. He never left except to go to the men's room. You see how he's become unglued, drinking himself into oblivion."

"Yeah, he's a mess. Well." She sighed. "I guess my job here is done." She pushed back the chair.

"Do you have to leave?" I whined, tracking her to the side door. "Can't you stay for another hour?"

"I have to finish a lab for Mr. Denton's class. It'll take me the rest of the night."

I hugged her and said, "Thanks for your help."

"See you tomorrow." Nona went into the night, and minutes later, her car motored down the road.

Henry had to have been watching the house because the side door squealed open. "Man, I thought she'd never leave," he said, creeping into the kitchen.

"Henry, you shouldn't walk in like that. What if my dad were here?"

"I knew he wasn't home."

"It still isn't right. What if I was taking a shower or something?" I frowned at his expressive lewd grin.

Making himself at home, he unzipped his jacket and filched a bottle of beer from the fridge. In doing so, I checked out his face for any signs of abuse, none showed, at least none that I could see.

He brought the brew to his mouth and, after a vigorous glug, swiped his hand over his lips. "So what gives? I want to hear it from you." He pulled out the chair and sat, then teetered backward on the rear two legs.

Taking the seat opposite him and for the hundredth time, I described the previous day.

"What do we think?" he asked. "Some low-life setting up a home in the Lucien attic or what?"

"I don't know," I said and pulled on my earlobe. "We don't see many homeless guys loitering around the Hallow."

"Could've hopped off one of the train cars passing through," Henry tried to justify, "needing a place to cozy up for a while."

"If that were the case, then he'd probably be long gone after the police were in there searching around."

"I wouldn't count on that. The mansion's huge. The dude could've been hiding someplace."

"It still doesn't answer why my mother's picture was hanging there, or the flowers, or the bed with bloodstains." I jiggled my can of soda, sloshing the fluid around inside.

"Kind of being farfetched, aren't you? You don't know for sure if it's blood."

"Maybe, maybe not. Where did the picture, the bed, and flowers disappear to?" I glared at him, wanting an answer. "The guy who attacked me must've removed everything and replaced it with your dummy."

"Pretty clever of the dude."

"Everything is still in the mansion. I know it," I said with conviction and rubbed my hands across my chin. "Detective Dyl must've figured that out, now that you confirmed I'm not a total basket case." Henry was focused on peeling the label on the bottle of beer. Not responding or corroborating my statement, I felt a sudden qualm. "You did tell him, right? About seeing the bed and my mother's picture, didn't you?"

He squeezed his eyes behind his lenses and a smudge of blushing pink touched his cheeks. "Not precisely."

CHAPTER 35

"Even before that Dyl dude came to my house, my father found out I'd been hanging at the Baskerville Estate."

"Did you tell him?"

"No, not at first." He kept arranging and rearranging his glasses on his nose. "My dad noticed his tools were missing and that I used his credit card to buy the duck blood and a few other things. Then, I forgot his drill at the mansion when I was rigging up the mannequin. He spazzed and threatened to take away the car if I stepped foot in there again." He took a drink of beer before continuing. "When the detective came ringing our doorbell, my dad played it cool, but I could tell he was ready to combust. Dyl interrogated me like I were a crime suspect. He wanted to know what I was doing in there and what I saw in the attic. He never mentioned you once."

"What did you tell him about the attic?"

"I told him I saw a mannequin hanging from the rafters. I wasn't lying, 'cause I went in after you and after the police left this morning."

"You...you're not going to back me up?" I blinked back the sting happening in my eyes. "Everyone already thinks I'm delusional. I can't believe you did this to me."

"It's better this way. Let's forget about that haunted house."

"You can forget about it, but I can't. My mother was murdered. I have to know why and who put her picture in the mansion." Slouching over the table of composition notebooks, I forcefully swiped the tears tripping over my lids. "I can't forget. I want her killer to burn in hell."

Henry jumped to his feet and took me in his arms. "Sorry, Leo. I'm sorry. After school tomorrow, I'll go to the police station and tell the detective about your mom's picture in the attic, without my dad being around." His petting my shoulder was soothingly awkward. "Will that help?"

"Yes, that will help, a lot." I snuffled and wiped my cheeks on his sleeve.

After Henry left, I cleared the kitchen table in a hurry and stashed the notebooks under my bed when the side door opened. Jaunting into the living room, I divebombed onto the couch just as Dad wandered in.

"It's getting late. You should be in bed instead of watching television." He stepped over and kissed my forehead. "How you feeling?" he asked, pulling off of his coat.

"Good." I yawned. "What happened to your old secretary?"

His brow knotted. "What did you say?"

"Regina. What happened to her?"

"She's on the ninth floor now. The receptionist for the trust department."

"Did you ride her too hard?"

Dad frowned. "Something like that." Ending the conversation, he turned and went into the bathroom.

Before nestling beneath my comforter for the night, I made an impractical decision and called Nona to join my subterfuge. Afterward, I didn't even remember falling asleep.

Blood ribboned Mom's arms and fingers. The rancid smell roiled in my belly like a trapped typhoon.

"Leo?"

I tried to speak. I moved my jaw, lacking sound, frayed vocal cords. My retinas focused on Mom, drowning in a sea of red.

"Dad," I gasped through my burning throat, "is that you?" I closed my eyes, making the bloody sight and Mom vanish. There were blaring sirens and pandemonium thundering on the stairs. Light touches of hands. On my shoulders, my neck, my chest.

"She's alive," someone said, holding my wrist. My body declined to oblige my brain so that I couldn't move. "She's in shock. We better get her out of here."

"Not yet," said an insensitive voice. "Have my men take the pictures first. Get the hell out of there, Murphy. You're contaminating the scene with your boots."

Again, I opened my mouth. "She's trying to say something."

Someone loomed over me, and a thread of breath touched my cheek. The same voice, but this time compassionate. "Did you see what happened? Do you remember anything? Shake your head or blink if you understand me."

"Mom..." I murmured on the brink of unconsciousness. Involuntarily my body started thumping around like a dying fish.

"We're losing her. We're losing her!"

Roused by a grueling heartbeat, I thought I was having a coronary. I gobbled a deep breath and held it, then again and again until the jackhammer in my chest subsided.

I jostled into an upright position and looked around my bedroom. My clock blinked six-ten, time to get up. I'd slept through the night. Although, my muscles ached as if I'd been performing a strenuous workout for the past six hours. I massaged my head and moaned, remembering.

We're losing her! Then nothingness. I had woken in the hospital on a gurney. A flurry of nurses and doctors coming and going, taking my vitals, my temp, administering intravenous drugs. I'd lain there like a limp dishrag. I was in and out. When did Dad come to see me?

Detective Dyl had made an appearance. After conferring with the doctor on duty, he'd walked over to my gurney. His lined face was overwrought as if fearful I might go into cardiac arrest. "How are you, Leo?"

I had stared at a bug on the ceiling.

"Are you up to a few questions?" The bug hadn't moved. *It's dead.* "Do you remember seeing anyone out of the ordinary?"

I'd shut out the world and sunk into a bottomless chasm.

"When you got off the bus and walked down the street, anything?" His fingers had circled the rail of the gurney. Was it me, or was his body trembling? "When you went into the house. Did you hear or see anything unusual? Anything at all?" Nailing me with his dark eyes, he growled, "Goddammit! What did you see?"

A hyperactive machine had beeped and everything swam like an abstract Picasso. Nurses rushed into the room, yelling at the detective, and I launched into a much-appreciated coma.

※

Dad was showering and I ransacked my closet for something to wear. This sleuthing business wrecked my brain, bringing to life the past year in vivid Technicolor. It was infrequent that I beat him into the kitchen and poured his glass of juice. Then, I waited.

Donned in a charcoal woolen suit, he smiled and kissed my cheek. "Thanks, Leo."

"How come you didn't come to the hospital right away to see me?" I asked out of the blue.

His arm holding the glass stopped in midair. "What are you talking about?"

"You were at the house when I found Mom. How come you didn't come to the hospital? I really needed you."

His mouth moved like a wiggly worm. "Leo, I wasn't there."

"Yes, you were. I remember you leaning over me. You said my name."

"No, you're imagining things again." He shook his head. "I wasn't in the house. I was at work when the police called."

"That's not possible." I lowered onto a chair and, lifting my legs, I balanced my heels on the edge. "Then who called the police?"

"You did."

CHAPTER 36

"I didn't call the police."

"The police said the call came from your cell phone and it was a girl's voice. Kiddo, it had to be you."

"I was so out of it. How could I call?"

"You must have intuitively dialed 911. You have more stamina than you realize." He went to the closet to fetch his coat. "I'll be home early tonight. We'll talk then if you want. I'll bring home supper. How about chicken?"

"O-okay," I said, distracted. For the life of me, I racked my brain, wondering how could I have dialed when I was practically comatose.

It was another dingy morning which enhanced my doldrums as Henry drove us to school. "Leo, stop with the unhappy face." His lenses were crystal clear, glancing my way. "I promise, right after school, I'm going to see the detective." A chuckle rumbled up his esophagus. "Now turn that frown upside down."

"Cute, Henry," I said, dripping with sarcasm. "Your father is going to find out you lied last night."

"Ah-ha," he said, shooting an index finger in the air. "I didn't lie. Just neglected the whole truthisms."

"Is there such a word?"

"There is now." I indulged him with a flat grin. "I can drop you at home after school first, before heading over to the police station," he suggested.

"That's alright. I'll take the bus." I didn't include him in my scheme. "I might stay after. I need help with calc."

His head rocked up and down. "Then you can teach me. I'd like to shoot whoever invented Calculus. I'll never use that bullcrap in my lifetime, and it's lowering my average."

"Mine too."

Groans milled around Mr. Slepe's English class due to his next assignment, a book review. I sympathized with the majority because I was neck-deep in homework.

Increasing my day of misery, Nona disclosed, "My mom wouldn't let me take the car today." My shoulders wilted, moping. "But I got the next best thing." A brilliant smile shaped her face. "Becket is taking us."

That jerked me into alertness. "How did he get involved?"

We quieted for a moment while Mr. Slepe's gaze swept the classroom before going back to his book. We were supposed to be reading, as he called it, fifteen minutes of expanding our brains. I called it teacher's break.

With her elbow cocked on the desk and a hand cupping her mouth, Nona angled toward me and whispered, "Reggie's car wouldn't start this morning, so Becket picked us up. I mentioned you needed a ride into the city and he offered." Her rich brown eyes sparkled.

"Sweet." My doldrums squander into joy. "You didn't say why, did you?" Guilt plastered Nona's face. "You did, didn't you?"

"Not specifically." She squinched. "Just that it had something to do with your mom."

Irritated, I slumped over my desk and nested my head in my arms. That was when Mr. Slepe said, "Leo and Nona, is there something you wish to share with the class?" His standard reprimand. We shook our heads. "This is reading day, girls. Not conversing time."

※

I tumbled from the school with the rest of the flock, and my gaze slew to the right. I couldn't miss his tall physique. Riding low on Becket's head was a Panther's baseball cap, the rim jutting downward. He was talking to Marcy.

Marcy's chin jutted in my direction and Becket turned. The cap shaded his expression, and I quickly began fake-searching for something in my messenger bag. When I looked up, Nona was summoning me. I headed her way while Becket sauntered in a diagonal pattern toward his car. The locks popped; he'd used his key fob. Reggie and Nona cuddled into the rear seats. I was riding shotgun.

"Hey, how's it going?" he said, depositing himself behind the wheel.

"I'm good." But, when it came to him, I wasn't the ultimate conversationalist.

"She speaks today. That's a good thing." Flashing a stellar smile, he removed the baseball cap, pronged fingers through his hair, and replaced it on his head. Like it wasn't perfect the first time.

Becket followed a string of vehicles from the school's lot, and I spotted a snub-nosed Marcy sneering from the window of her car. This time I could read her lips—naughty word Marcy.

"Where to, Leo?"

"Ellicott Street, downtown," I informed him. "Are you sure you don't mind driving all the way into the city?" I looked over my shoulder at Nona, who shrugged, and then to Becket.

"It's a good day for a ride."

"I'll give you gas money." It was the least I could do.

"Keep it," he said, his tone crisp. He switched on the radio, silencing me.

"Leo, what's the address on Ellicott Street?" Nona expressed from the back seat. "I'll key it into my phone so he knows what ramp to get off on."

"4545 Ellicott."

I relaxed into the bucket seat as we merged onto the highway, setting sights for the metropolis. By three o'clock in the afternoon, skyscrapers and opulent high-rises poked the cerulean skies. The city was alive and thriving, with people hustling from building to building.

Becket negotiated amidst a convoy of taxis, trucks, and cars before parallel parking less than a block from my father's building. I was slightly startled when everyone got out. I had planned on handling this part by myself.

"How about I meet everyone in a half-hour?" I said. "This won't take long."

"I'd love to shop a few stores while we're here," Nona said. Her appetite to shop the posh, up-scale boutiques had Reggie looking less than enthused.

"We'll meet across the street at Sharf's," I recommended, checking my cell.

"At four, okay?" I took a step toward my father's place of employment with Becket stepping in line. "Um...aren't you going with them?" I glanced over my shoulder at the backsides of Nona and Reggie.

"I'll stick with you."

"I can handle myself." A nervous compulsion of fingering my hair ensued. "I've been here before."

"Your hair looks like it's on fire when the sun hits it just right. Did you know that?"

"Is that a good thing?"

"Brilliant." A compliment from Becket, I liked.

"I saw Henry leaving school today," he said, offhandedly. "He must've had an appointment or he would've driven you in."

"Henry doesn't know I'm here." Lowering my gaze, I sighted Becket's lean legs and a pair of grey and orange sneakers, keeping stride with my smaller steps. "How tall are you anyway?" Peering up into his face, I squinted from the sunshine.

"Too tall or too short?" His fingers rounded the nape of my neck and gently shunted me aside to avoid rear-ending a lady pushing a wire cart. "Last time we checked, I was six-three."

"Think you're done growing?"

"Beats me." After a brief minute, he said, "I was told not to ask questions, so I won't. After we get inside, would you like me to wait in the foyer?"

Nona probably cautioned him not to say anything. He held open the heavy glass door for me to enter, and nearing the elevators, insecurity washed over me. *What am I trying to prove?* I knew and didn't know where this chronic impulse was coming from, but I needed information.

"You can come with me." I sounded unsure. "If you don't mind."

Becket's height drew people to branch apart into the packed elevator. When we hit the ninth floor, the doors shimmied open. Directly centered was a mahogany receptionist desk, and there was Regina, my father's old secretary.

"Why hello, Leo." She recognized me immediately. "What brings you here?"

Regina appeared regal; brunette hair flowed in ringlets over her shoulders. On the tip of her slim nose perched her reading glasses, and she peered over the rims approvingly at Becket. I hadn't seen or talked to her since Mom's death, and I wanted to hear it from her mouth.

"Regina, mind if I ask you a question?"

"Not at all, dear. Is something wrong with your father?" She detached her gaze from Becket and looked at me.

Abruptly, I blurted, "Is it true that my father was in his office the day my mom was murdered? All day?"

Her chin knocked backward, astonished. "Er...ummm..." She shifted on the chair. "That's what I told the police, honey. You came all this way just to ask me that. What is going on in that teeny-tiny brain of yours?"

"At that time, you answered my father's calls, correct?" I didn't pause because I knew the answer. "You weren't the one who took the call from the police, were you?"

A prickly redness crawled between the folds of her white button-down shirt toward her neck. She fixed her eyes on the desktop, where her fingers fidgeted with her pencil and pen collection, stabbing them into a small canister. "We were in a private business meeting in your father's office when the call came in. The police know this."

"In his office—just the two of you? Or were you somewhere else when the call was forwarded to your phone? I've been in his office. I'm aware of the outlet leading to the stairwell in case of fire." Her head wrenched up.

"You have a lot of nerve coming in here accusing me of perjury."

"I didn't accuse you of perjury yet. Was my father here when the call came in?"

She sniffed, twitching her nose and mouth. Regina's gaze skipped over the reception area, either looking for help or hoping no one was eavesdropping. "I am not on trial, missy," she spluttered. "I told the police everything. If you can't get that through your thick skull, that's too bad." She rolled her shoulders and then tossed her hair over them. "You have to leave. I'm working."

"Are you having an affair with my father?"

CHAPTER 37

Reeling my words back in wasn't an option.

Regina's reaction: Priceless. Her slathered mauve lips formed a perfect O.

"How dare you." From shocked to irate, she tore off her glasses, flinging them over the desk. Her eyeballs sliced side to side, still making sure people weren't listening. "You have plenty of nerve. Get out," her silent snarl was for my ears alone.

Hands secured my shoulders, moving me from my unyielding posture. I clawed my taloned fingers onto the desk, holding on. "You're lying." I leaned at a ninety-degree angle into her face. Then, not caring if the entire building heard me, I yelled, "Tell me the truth!"

"I'm calling security to kick your ass out of here."

"Leo, chill. Come on." Becket wrenched my talons from the desk and stepped in front of me, blocking my sight. Hugging me to his chest, he didn't allow me an inch of space until we exited the glass doors and were on the congested sidewalk.

I didn't cry because my tear ducts were drier than the Sahara Desert. Becket guided me against the cool frontage of the building. "Not what I anticipated," he said. "What's going on?" Becket bracketed his arms on either side of my head, and his shoulders stooped so he could peer into my face. So near, the rim of his cap shadowed our faces, darkening his periwinkle eyes. "Did you get what you were looking for?"

"I think so. But that wasn't what I was going to say. Those words…" I shook my mixed-up head. "I don't know why I acted like that. It's like Mom…" His eyes narrowed, and my thoughts coagulated on my tongue. "Never mind."

"If it's true, it doesn't help. It only breaks your heart." He separated his hand from the building and stroked the tips of his fingers on my cheek. "Are you alright to meet those guys at Sharf's, or should I get them and take you home?"

"I'm fine." He reached for my hand, tying our fingers together. Even though his hands were huge, it was a perfect fit. We walked across the street and into the diner. Reggie and Nona were nowhere in sight. The hostess led us to a table for four, and I tried not to think about Dad going postal when he came home from work.

Becket assisted me with my jacket, which was kind of awesome. He shoved off his leather jacket, arranging both on the ridge of his chair. Before taking a seat, he removed his baseball cap and roughed a hand into his lengthy hair, teasing it into placid beauty. He seemed oblivious to the admiring stares, even mine, as he cracked the menu. His long-sleeved, vermillion T-shirt cried at the seams as he bent his elbow and nicked a strand of hair from his eye.

"What are you having?" he inquired.

"I couldn't eat a thing. Just coffee." Recalling his comment about my hair being on fire, I hazarded onto a touchy subject. "Becket?" His gaze deviated from the menu to look at me. "My mother kept some of her student's journals over the years, and I'd been going through them, and guess what I found?"

If it were possible, his achingly attractive features heightened with an eyebrow hitch. "Mine. You found my journal. I remember when your mom asked if she could keep it at the end of the year. I was going to trash it, so I didn't care." The rim of his mouth curled. "How embarrassing. Did you read it?"

"Some." *Am I coming across like a stalker?*

"You should burn that sucker." He flicked the corner of the menu. "You felt it was necessary to confront your father's secretary today. You're going through those journals. You're up to something, aren't you?"

It needed to be said, and persevering, I asked, "Who is the mature woman with the moon-spun hair? My teacher in body and soul?"

A muddled groove lined his forehead. "Moon-spun hair? My teacher in body and—" He brightened in recognition and then pressed the heel of his palms to his brow. "Ughh. I feel like a moron. Jesus, you read that shit? It was about Joyce Winters. She was a senior at the time."

I had to prove Nona wrong and felt rather stupid. The nagging assumption that Becket and Mom engaged in an improper affair had been eating at me. "I'm looking for my mother's journal," I explained with an uneasy chuckle. "I thought it might have been packed away with all the others."

He peered from under a firm brow. "You're searching for answers to your mom's murder, aren't you?"

"Am I that transparent?"

"It adds up. After the recent murders of Dave and Skipper, and with the police hanging around again, and…" He paused, hanging on a thought. "Did you think that shitty poem was about your mother?"

227

I plinked my antsy fingers on the table. "Nona thought—oh, never mind."

"Great, Nona read my journal, too."

"Sorry."

"If you thought that poem was about your mother, then I know exactly what you and Nona were thinking." Becket's look of revulsion streamed over his face. "Am I one of your suspects?"

"No." I stifled a giggle. "Not anymore."

"Good thing I cleaned up my torrid reputation, or else you'd have me behind bars."

I lowered my head, letting my hair curtain my face, hiding my embarrassment. "I can't take much more, and... and the nightmares."

His large hand swept under my dangling hair and smoothed his palm over my neck like a cool compress. "I feel the need to defend myself and reassure you." His voice softened. "Your mom was a great teacher, and I liked her. But, we never, ever had any kind of thing. Got that?" He glared and I nodded. "Leo, I'll help you if I can."

Unrolling my shoulders, his hand slipped from my neck. "Like I tried explaining before, and I know this mirrors madness," I said, "I feel like my mom is reaching from the grave, needling me to find her killer."

"Tell me what I can do for you?"

Against my better judgment, I described my latest dream and the ominous Lucien attic. After my hectic babbling, we lingered in subdued quiet. Wordless, absorbed in our thoughts, I was positive Becket had labeled me as demented.

He crossed his arms on the table in front of him. "I can never seem to catch a break," he said, his hypnotizing eyes holding me prisoner. "Or find the right time, so I'm just going for it." His tone serious, I held my breath waiting for his criticism. "Will you go out with me after this damn dance?"

Gloomy clouds parted and the heavens rejoiced while my heart blossomed into sweet nectar.

Reggie and Nona fractured the blissful moment, barging boisterously to the table. Reggie's arms were loaded with designer bags, and was admonishing Nona. "I can't believe how much you can buy in a matter of minutes."

"I don't get into the city that often," Nona said, plunking boxes and bags on the floor. She winked at me. "I need to store up with these goodies while I'm here. I put a severe dent in my mom's credit card, though."

"She's going to wring your neck," I said, grinning.

"You got that right." They settled into chairs and Nona jiggled in place. "I have an excuse. I'm telling her I did some early Christmas shopping and gift her a sweater I bought."

"You're doomed, baby," Reggie said and covered her hand with his. "Your mama's going to have a freak attack."

She whisked her hand out from under his, looking bitter, then turned toward me. "Were you successful? Did you get done what needed to get done?"

"That sounds pretty ambiguous," Reggie remarked. For decoding purposes, his head swiveled to Becket.

I kept my thoughts to myself as Becket's lips tightened and he shook his head.

Less than an hour later, Becket was dropping Reggie and Nona at their prospective homes. Evening had invaded the avenues, and stars glittered in a velvety dome when he'd turned into my driveway. In an instant, I fastened onto the glow of the living room window and my stomach curdled. *Dad is home.* I shuddered to think of what lay ahead.

Becket cut the motor and said, "I'm coming in with you."

"What good would that do?"

"He might not explode with me there."

"Not a good night for introductions and you'd eventually have to leave. It'll only prolong his wrath." I perceived a slight movement of the curtains. Dad had peeked.

Becket's balled fingers thumped the steering wheel. "Have you given any thought to what I asked you before Reggie and Nona interrupted us?"

"Yes."

"You thought about it. And?"

"And. Yes."

He exhaled as if he'd been holding his breath. Before he had a chance to say anything, I opened and shut the car door and walked toward the house. I turned and saw him standing outside of the car, his arm shelving the driver's side door.

"Call if you need me." His voice came to me on a breeze.

The aroma of roasted chicken hung in the air as I glanced at the table settings. True to his word, Dad had prepared dinner. The Headline News infiltrated the house as I toed out of my sneakers. I padded to the bathroom and saw him in the living room, sitting in the recliner.

"Leo, it's time to eat."

It was rare that we ate together at the kitchen table. Though, for some reason, Dad had laid out a spread of mashed potatoes, peas, and sliced chicken with buttery hard rolls. He was all fake smiles, which had me on edge, and I waited for the dam to break.

"This looks great."

"I can't take the credit. The grocery store had it ready for me. Warming it up is the easy part."

I devoured the tasty meal, though the pit of my stomach turned to rot when Dad severed the congenial silence by saying, "I heard you came downtown today."

In mid-swallow, I choked on a pea. He wasn't asking a question, just stating a fact. Clearing my throat, I thought about lying, but deigned there'd be little purpose. Regina had squealed.

"Was it to your advantage?" His eyes sealed onto my face as he lifted the paper napkin to his mouth, blotting his lips.

"I don't know what you want me to say," I said, wondering about his ulterior motives. Dad had a brilliant mind. He'd climbed the ranks of Mortimer, Gimley, and Ross as a top-notch investment securities officer. He was a good-looking man, physically fit. In the past year, grooves had begun creasing his eyes and mouth, aging under pressure.

"Of course, you figured I'd hear of the altercation?" His fork speared a pea. "And you haven't engineered a levelheaded excuse?"

"I...I needed to hear for myself." I set my fork on the plate, the food now tasteless.

"So what have you deduced?" Pushing his plate aside, he replaced the area with his elbows and his chin poised on his hands. "Tell me."

My vertebrae wedged into the chair, striving for distance from his acute glare. "Dad, I don't want to do this."

"Really? You've been poking your nose into my business, stirring the kettle. It's obvious you want to hear the sordid details that should've been buried with your mother."

"Mom knew?"

CHAPTER 38

"Our marriage was a sham." Rising from the table, he released a gust of air. "We tried working it out. But…" He bit his knuckle as if he didn't trust himself to say more.

He was stewing and I monitored his expression. "Is that why she wanted to move to California with Grandpa?"

"You put your mother on a pedestal. She's no saint."

"I never said she was a saint." I rubbed my hand on my chest, quelling my racing heart. "What does any of this have to do with her murder? That's what I want to know. Who killed Mom! Who killed her?"

His palms flattened on the surface of the table. "Do you think I'm capable—that I killed Lily?"

"No—I don't know." My heart bashed against my ribcage, breaking it apart. "That's the problem; I don't know." I recoiled to some extent when he circled his arms around me, pressing me into him.

"Why dredge it up? She's gone and nothing can bring her back. I love you. I don't want you to get hurt."

Too late. I've been hurting for a year.

Soon, and on a radical journey to la-la-land, Dad was dispensing a third jigger of bourbon, and I sought refuge in my bedroom. Scrolling through my cell, I'd missed four calls from Henry. He didn't leave a voicemail or a text, which indicated what he had to say was for ears alone. I keyed in his number, and when he picked up, I inquired, "Did you talk to Detective Dyl?"

"Before I answer that question," he volleyed, "I'd like to know where you've been all afternoon? I thought you'd be waiting to hear from me."

"I went for something to eat with Nona." Not a fib. "And muted my cell." I wasn't ready to unload the aspect of Dad's affair and that Becket drove us into the city. He'd find out soon enough.

"Why would you mute your cell?"

My brain dulled and I couldn't think fast enough. "You know how Nona gets. She hates when a call interrupts her." My reason seemed adequate and he didn't delved further. "Now, can you tell me if you talked to the detective?"

"Yes, he wasn't surprised. I think he believed you all along. Now I wish I'd never said anything."

"Thanks for backing me up. But what makes you think he believed me? All the proof was missing. It made me look loco."

"Just a hunch." He made a slurpy noise. "And the way he was looking at me. Like I was a lying bag of scum."

"We did lie."

"I'm coming over. Open your window," he ordered.

"No, you better not. My dad is splurging on Jack Daniels. If he catches you, I don't know what he'll do."

"Then you come out."

I looked at the time. "It's after nine."

"So?" His tongue clucked. "You turn into a pumpkin at midnight or something?"

"I need to hit the books. I promised my father I'd show a marked improvement this quarter."

"Please," he pleaded, "just for an hour."

Why not? The house was smothering me. "Alright, an hour. We'll meet in front of your house."

I changed into my thick cable-knit sweater and threw on my jacket. Before abandoning my bedroom, I called Nona like I'd promised to tell her what happened downtown. She hemmed into the receiver and then killed my eardrum when I told her Becket asked me out.

"I told you. He's not interested in Marcy," she said, all cheery. "We can double date. Won't that be fun?"

"You're getting ahead of yourself."

"No, hun. I'm thinking positive. You've got to get that negativity bug out of that skull of yours."

"I'm trying. We'll talk later." I left out the part of meeting Henry. She'd have a cow and I wasn't in the mood.

I tiptoed through the hallway and into the kitchen. Dad was snoring on the couch, a sure symptom of over-imbibing and conked for the night. Exiting by the side door, I went along the sidewalk to Henry's.

A flame ignited in his car, depicting him behind the wheel. I swung open the door and climbed in. The tip of the rolled joint sizzled red as he inhaled, then he handed it off to me.

"Your parents can see us from here." I examined the draped windows.

"Who the eff cares?" He poked the joint at me. "Here, take it."

"What's wrong?" My finger and thumb pinched the joint as the car sped from the curb, squealing the tires.

"My parents, 'nough said."

"I have one of those too." I inhaled liberally. "Where we going?"

"Anywhere." He reached for the smoldering joint. "Let's take a ride through the Hallow, see what's happening."

"We're too late for the last show at Regal Theater. If you have the munchies, we could stop at Earl's for a doughnut."

"Yeah, they have those cider doughnuts at this time of year, don't they?" He gutted the joint in the ashtray and extracted a second one.

"Don't light that for my sake." I buttoned my jacket. "I have to study when I get home. Besides, Earl's is right around the corner if you want to stop." Exercising the joint like a baton, he twirled it in the air. "This baby will help you concentrate. I get uptight before a test, and after a few tokes, my body and mind relax."

"You smoke in school?"

"Doesn't everybody?"

"I doubt it."

"I'll save it for later." He sported a lopsided grin and tucked it into his pocket.

My cell booped with a text. I retrieved a message from Nona saying not to forget my uniform for the rival game at Kensington tomorrow night. She'd borrow her mom's car for the day and would be picking me up for school. "I won't need a ride to school in the morning. Nona's picking me up," I said to Henry.

"Where's the boyfriend?"

"I don't know." I brushed the side of my finger across my upper lip, pondering that question.

Henry had parked the car, and we walked past the picture window of Earl's. Henry's feet braked, and he discreetly announced, "Kane and Marcy are here."

Surveying the eatery, I couldn't miss his glimmering golden hair caused by the fluorescent lights. His spine curved, leaning on the table. Marcy's eyes were glued to his face and her mouth was working nonstop. I performed a hasty spin.

"Where are you going?" Henry said.

"Not in there."

"Why, 'cause you're jealous of Marcy?"

"I'm not hungry." It had been a harrowing day. The solitary spark of goodness was when Becket asked to go out with me. For some reason, I'd taken it for granted that Marcy had coaxed him into taking her to the dance. Now I wasn't so sure.

"Since you mentioned cider doughnuts, I won't be able to sleep unless I eat one. I'm going in."

A bell tinkled as Henry opened the glass door to Earl's, and my effort to shrink behind him didn't work. Greetings hailed from a few kids as we shuffled in line to the counter. He ordered two doughnuts and two cups of hot cider and then turned to check out the seating arrangements. *Oh cripes, he plans on staying.* Even amid the appetizing bouquet of fresh-brewed coffee, a hint of Becket's yummy aftershave sailed under my nose. I hadn't seen him move but felt his presence behind me.

"Would you and Henry like to sit with us?" The strong tone of his voice was unmistakable. "There's room at our table."

I glimpsed up at Becket, who was peering at Henry.

"Sure, man," Henry said.

We'd taken our seats when Mrs. Torkelson arrived with our hot mugs of apple cider and doughnuts. "I'm telling everyone," she said. "Earl and I are closing early tonight." She skimmed her palms down her checkerboard apron. "As soon as you kids are done, skedaddle so we can lock up for the night." Then threading among the tables, she preceded to repeat her message while shelving dirty plates and mugs into her overflowing arms.

"Leo, are you cheering in the game tomorrow night?" Marcy asked.

"I plan on it. What makes you think I won't be there?"

Becket reclined into his chair and folded his arms. His long legs spread under the table, nudging my feet. My gaze quickened to meet his as a smug smile trickled into his face. Our exchange did not go unnoticed.

"You've missed so many practices." Her snide attitude was conspicuous. "Rumor has it, Mrs. Sweeny is kicking you off the squad."

As if I cared. "Was there practice today?"

"Nona missed it too. But, as the team captain, I could persuade Sweeny to change her mind," she said, a snooty crimp to her lips. "If you still want to be part of the team."

"How 'bout I show up tomorrow and if she kicks me off, well then—I'm off." Her nose scrunched, offended by my apathetic retort.

Becket spoke up, "There's only a couple games left."

Blowing over his mug of cider, Henry entered the exchange, "Star Hallow is tied for first place, right?"

"Kensington's tough." Becket pulled on his fingers, one after the other, calculating. "I'd be surprised if we came away with a win."

Marcy took the opportunity to caress Becket's forearm and squeezed. "Oh, you'll win, honey. No doubt." Becket awarded her one of his beaming smiles. Her term of endearment triggered a vein of jealousy to needle through me.

"We're going to have a good time Saturday night." Henry flipped the conversation. "I heard the school doled out money for a decent DJ."

"Do you have plans after the dance?" Marcy looked from me to Henry. "Becket and I are driving into the city and staying the night at the Hyatt Regency."

Becket shot forward on his chair. "Marcy, I already said no to that."

"The plans are made. We can't back out now."

"Why not?"

"Because everyone's supposed to chip in for the rooms. You don't want to screw them, do you? They'll be pissed."

Becket's composure slipped, wiping a hand over and under his jaw.

"Leo and I are staying the night at the Lucien place," Henry staggeringly said.

CHAPTER 39

Becket clutched the edge of the table while I sputtered, "W-When did you plan on telling me?"

"Cool idea, huh?" His head joggled, lifting his brow above the rims of his glasses.

"That is an awesome idea!" Marcy added to my shock. "Why didn't we think of that!" Her hand sought Becket's, now clenching the table, knuckles whitening. "See, Becket, I told you that Henry and Leo were hooking up."

"No, we're not," I blurted. "Henry and I are friends."

Her catty eyes spoke volumes, determined to break Becket and me apart, no matter the consequences. "The two of you hang twenty-four seven. Everybody assumes you're together. So perfect for each other." Marcy threw Becket a clever, lipless grin, her proof I was lying.

"Henry, I hope you're done with that doughnut because I'm going home." The shoddy day was getting shoddier, and the legs of my chair screeched on the tile as I stood. Marcy's comment had gifted Henry a jolly expression, which bugged the crap out of me. He issued Becket an, I-told-you-so leer, and I restrained myself from slapping that leer off his face.

Walking in my wake, Henry opened the car door. Sniggering jangled his throat. "I said that to yank Marcy and Becket's chain."

"I'd never spend a night with you and certainly not in that haunted house." I fumed.

"Thanks for sticking a knife through my heart." His snickering died on his tongue. "I think Marcy's right. We are perfect for each other."

"Not in this lifetime." I'd struck a nerve, activating a ruthless downturned mouth, and his squinty eyes cut into me. He drilled the car in gear, tires smoking on the stony lot, hurtling pebbles, bouncing off Earl's brick wall, and rebounding onto the car like the ting of bullets riddling metal.

Henry zoomed around Terrace Circle. The car tilted on its axis. I thought for sure we were going to crash into the village gazebo. My fingers dug into the vinyl seat, a measure of pure survival.

"Slow down," I yelped.

The car whizzed past Westgate Boulevard, and I wondered where he was going. "Take me home, Henry."

He averted his gaze from the road to me, eyes fierce, hard as quartz. "I didn't think you were a gullible girl. But you're just like all the rest of them."

"Henry James, what are you talking about? And slow down before you get a speeding ticket." The car slowed and I breathed easier.

"You're a sucker for Kane's looks. But, he's a player."

"A player?"

"He's one of those guys that likes to have more than one girl at a time. I see how much you idolize him."

"I don't idolize, Becket." I pulled up the collar of my jacket to hug my chilled neck. "I don't know him that well."

"I'm not obtuse." He surfed the palm of his hand along the steering wheel. "I've learned enough about this stinking village in three months than you'll ever know. Leo, you're a dope. Kane's humping Marcy and has you waiting in the wings." He hesitated, throwing me a repugnant glance. "Unless you've already—you and Kane?"

"Henry, you are so sick. Even if I were, I wouldn't tell you." I didn't appreciate his smack talk. "Just take me home."

"I want to check something out at the mansion."

"Henry, it's late. You promised I'd only be gone for an hour and it's past that now."

"Appease me...please." He prevailed, plotting a course onto Lucien Court. "It'll only take a minute."

Feeling like a kidnap victim, I wanted to jump from the moving car. Then he stupefied me by saying, "Your mom's picture is back."

Parking, he leapt out.

Hooked like a floundering trout, I trotted after him. The place was much easier to get in since the police eliminated the bolted chain. Henry removed a flashlight from somewhere as if he'd charted this little investigation from the moment he called.

"Why didn't you bring me here right away if you'd known about her picture reappearing. Why take the long route to Earl's?"

"Before I called, I was driving around and saw Kane and Marcy. I wanted you to see them together, with your own eyes."

Was I supposed to be grateful?

We climbed the all-too-familiar staircase, and it groaned beneath our footsteps, rejecting our presence. My body jolted with the ring of my cell. I fished in my pocket and read the name. Henry saw his name, wrinkling his nose. I muted Becket's call.

Hearing a wail, I froze.

"It's the wind," he whispered and linked his arm through mine.

A dark shadow snared my eye. "That's not the wind." Henry shone the light into the elongated hallway. Running footsteps and a reverberating thud banged against the wall.

My voice quavered. "Let's get out of here. The ghosts are restless."

"Not until you see this." He persisted and manipulated an anchoring hold on my arm, redirecting us into the shadows.

"Aren't we going to the attic?"

"No, it's not there."

The flashlight scarcely made an impression into the windowless hallway. Exerting it like a machete, he chopped through pesky cobwebs and halted by a six-paneled doorframe. "I could've sworn I blocked this door open with a pillow before I left," he whispered, more to himself than to me. "It's in here." The door squeaked as he flashed the light into the room.

A gargantuan canopied bed commandeered the bedroom, flaunting inlaid carvings on the four pillars, headboard, and matching armoire on the far wall. Henry pulled me farther into the room and centered the light on Mom's picture.

There it is—relocated.

"Since we're here, we can make use of the bed."

I hadn't digested his objective until his arms strapped my waist, scrabbling backward to the canopied bed. When his grip slackened, I thrust him off. "I'm going to punch the living daylights out of you."

Henry laughed and loped like a gazelle onto the bed. He hammered his fist on the mattress, inviting me to join him. "Spring loaded for lots of pounding. Let's try it out."

"Like that is ever going to happen?" I berated insultingly. "Did you hang the picture in here?"

"No, I didn't. But you can coax it out of me."

"You dung heap. It's been you all along, hasn't it?"

"I said no. C'mere, and I'll tell you what I know."

"Go eff yourself." I booted the bedframe with my sneaker.

"That hurt." He frowned. "I knew it had to be here somewhere."

Skeptical, I analyzed his face for the lie. "Why didn't Dyl tear this place apart?"

"How do we know he didn't?" he said, cradling his head in his hands. "Maybe this is a trap to cull out the murderer?"

I unbuttoned my jacket. "Do you think so?"

"It wouldn't prove who killed your mom." He looked content on the bed. "An admirer could've put it here, someone like Kane."

"What makes you say that?"

"You'd be surprised what I dug up on him." He snicker-snorted.

"Put it to rest. Becket and my mother—No way." I neared Mom's picture, staring at her. "But, you might be on the right track. Why would the killer memorialize her like this?"

"A real sicko, that's who."

"Detective Dyl thinks her killer is connected to Dave and Skip."

He moved to the edge of the mattress. "He told you that?"

"He said it was confidential. I wasn't supposed to say anything."

"I'm like your best friend. Best friends kind of confide in one another," he said, testy. "I bet you told Nona."

I didn't want to argue. "Let's get out of here. Something's not kosher. I'm going to call the detective and tell him what we found."

"He might think we planted it here."

"Oh, I never thought of that."

The hefty, six-paneled door suddenly slammed shut.

CHAPTER 40

"Who's out there?" Henry bounced off the bed and shined the flashlight on the door. Neither one of us moved as the heebie-jeebies trounced over me. "Probably a draft," he said, voice hushed.

"That would be some draft to heave that door," I said in a subdued whisper and thought of hiding underneath the bed. "I think someone's in here. Those were real footsteps we heard earlier."

"Whoever—doesn't want to hurt us." Henry's hand was shaking because the beam of light juddered on the door.

"What makes you say that?" My timbre wavered. "I feel pretty vulnerable right now, like a sitting dead duck."

"He shut us in to make a getaway."

"If you're right," I said, sounding inconclusive, "we wait here."

Resembling immobile statues, the only parts of my body that moved were my eyes, sluing from Henry to the doorknob. In all the horror movies, it was the turning of the knob that would spark my pulse to rise because it meant something horrifying was going to happen.

I jolted at the sound of Henry's voice. "He has to be gone."

"What makes you so sure?"

"The guy would have to be a bumbling cripple not to be gone by now. Let's go."

I wasn't as confident as him. "He could be hiding in any one of the dozen rooms."

"If he's hiding, then he's not after us. We'll run. Don't stop."

"Don't worry," I said, "even if Lucien and Monique get in my face, I'm breezing right through them."

Slinking like conjoined Siamese twins, Henry broke the seal of the door. Together, we peeked around the frame, and he targeted the light along the pitch-dark passage.

Manipulating his arm similar to a crowbar, he applied leverage to dislocate my clinging body, shoving me into the hall.

"Run," he prompted quietly.

I gaped at him, feeling like the sacrificial lamb. "Are you shitting me?"

"You go first and I'll follow." He shined the light in my face, exposing me to whoever was lurking in the mansion.

"Why should I go first?"

"I have your back."

"Fine." My hand darted, robbing him of the flashlight. "I'll take this." I took off like my life depended on the sixty-second dash. If Star Hallow's track and field coach could see me running down the stairs, they'd be begging me to join their team. I didn't slow until I was outdoors and skidding to the car.

A chuckle split my mouth as Henry executed a windmill finish, his arms oscillating. He plowed into the hood of the car, his arms catching him from face-planting.

"Hilarious," he said breathily. "Get in."

The interior of my house was dark when I walked in. Dad wasn't on the couch. His bedroom door was shut, meaning he was sleeping, and he undoubtedly checked my room beforehand and discovered I wasn't home. Getting ready for bed, I dialed Nona's number three times, and three times I didn't press send. I'd wait to speak to her in person.

There were moments when I hated exhuming memories. Whenever I'd closed my eyes, it was the bad ones that seeped from the impenetrable cage where I'd secured them. Tonight, I stared at the ceiling, reflecting. There had been someone in the mansion tonight. Mom's killer. I was sure of it.

Wired and bewildered, I sprang up. I'd been trying to quit my addiction; although I knew I wouldn't sleep a wink if I didn't take my prescribed sleeping pill. Waiting for it to kick in, I delved through my closet for a dress to wear for the dance. I came across the dress I'd worn for Becket on our first coffee date. I ripped it from the hanger, dropped it on the floor, and gave it a good kick.

My eyelids grew heavy, and with thoughts of Becket's jeweled eyes and his sweeter-than-honey kisses, I ditched the dress notion and crawled into bed, sinking into a timeless abyss…

I passed a warren of rooms until a faint shine bled beneath a six-panel door. On its own accord, it parted to reveal a canopy bed, hosting two canoodling bodies, lustfully sniggering. Pale golden locks branched over his muscled back, and rumpled sheets sheathed Becket's hips. Marcy's raven hair spread across a white pillowcase. I gasped and Becket turned toward me. A beguiling smirk sharpened his face as he extended his arm.

In my dreamscape, I had a sinking feeling that dredged over my ribs.

My eyes snapped opened and kneaded the intolerable ache happening in my chest. Henry's words returned to haunt me. "He's a player."

CHAPTER 41

I didn't get out of bed until Dad's departure. He left a squiggly note on the table. It read: *Made an appointment with Dr. Mathias. With the anniversary coming up, it's necessary. You're not handling it well, kid.*

Miffed, I tore the paper into strips.

Finishing my last bite of peanut-butter toast, a text jingled on my cell. Nona was in the driveway. Flying out the door and into the car, I said, "How did you luck out with your mom's car today?"

Nona was readjusting the driver's seat. "I asked nicely and—" She held up a piece of paper. "A note from Mom to mollify Sweeny or piss her off."

"Awwesome." We fist-pumped. "Now we won't have to suffer with Marcy and Blair in the school van."

"You got that right."

October mornings were dark as night, which took effort rallying for a sunny mindset. Then I saw a streetlight showering Henry's SUV parked at the curb. It unleashed the previous night's escapades in the mansion and my dreams. I grit my teeth, girding those flashes of recall because it was too early to sink into the deep.

Forging ahead, I said, "Would it be alright if Grace came with us?" Nona checked the rear-view mirror and switched lanes to turn toward the high school. "She's had it with our not-so-charming captain. We'll all be happy to see them graduate."

"Definitely, and, of course, Grace can come." Nona grinned.

"Mom left me with a full tank of gas. I promised to fill it up, though."

"Umm…you didn't show her your purchases, did you?"

"Are you kidding? She'd kill me." In Nona fashion, she changed the subject. "I'm looking forward to getting spruced up for the dance. What are you wearing?"

"I scrounged through my closet last night and got depressed. I'm not that thrilled. Actually, I wish I wasn't going."

"I don't blame you. You never should have told Henry you'd go with him. You'd be excited if it was Becket."

I mulled over her remark and then said, "Are you sure Becket isn't involved with Marcy?"

"Not by what Reggie tells me." Her head shot in my direction, brow askew. "I think he'd know. Don't you?"

Unconvinced after that disgusting dream, my mouth scrunched. "Remember when you said Becket was one of those love 'em and leave 'em type of guys?"

"You're hedging at something," she said. "Out with it. What's tumbling in that head of yours?"

"Do you think I'm next on his list of conquests after he's done playing with Marcy?" I would've preferred a rapid response, but she hesitated. "You do—don't you?"

She squirmed. "If I didn't have Reggie, I'd shove you so fast you'd hit pavement, and I'd grab onto Becket for all it's worth."

"For all it's worth?" My fingers danced unevenly on the seat. "Like a one-nighter?"

"No, that's not what I meant." She found a space to park in the school lot, which was filling with cars. "He's dated mostly older girls that graduated and moved onto college."

My fingers stilled. "Yeah, more experienced girls."

"There were a few scandalous rumors." She tittered, her eyes shining. "Do you remember?"

"Like getting drunk and waking up naked with Joyce Winters on the football field," I said, remembering. "Or when Becket climbed to the top of the rollercoaster in the middle of the night to prove he wasn't scared of heights, and then—"

"Okay, okay, that was years ago," Nona held her hand up and stopped my long-winded montage of his antics. "Becket's not an angel. But, Reggie says he's a good guy and I believe him."

"So you asked Reggie for Becket's credentials?"

"Yes, for my best friend." She looked earnest. "Leo, I basically did."

Throughout my day, I roamed from class to class, always on the lookout for that tall body with sleek hair. I hadn't come in contact with Becket; however, the obnoxious Marcy strutted into view.

"Hey, Leo. I put a good word in for you. Mrs. Sweeny said you can participate in the pep rally today, and we're riding together in the school's van to Kensington."

As if I care. "Thanks. But I'm hitching a ride with Nona."

"Mrs. Sweeny won't allow that," said a caustic Marcy. "We're supposed to go in the van. School rules."

"Nona will clear it with Sweeny, I'm sure."

"Is it true?" she gushed, clamping her book and folders to her chest. "Are you and Henry staying at the mansion tomorrow night? I've only been in there once and it freaked me out."

Whether it was pure envy or downright stubbornness, I said, "Marcy, no matter what I say, you'll twist my words to suit your goals."

"You're a meany today." She flicked the corner of a purple folder. "It really is a good idea. All those bedrooms." A faraway look came over her as she murmured, "We could each have our own room for the night."

I ruined her reverie. "I thought you were staying at the Hyatt Regency?"

She blinked and refocused on me. "That's the plan. But we could only afford two rooms, and there's like ten of us going. We have to double up on the beds." Piety wasn't her forte. "A little uncomfortable, if you know what I mean."

A trilling bell signaled the end of the school day. "Saved by the bell," I said. "We'd better get ready for the rally."

Concluding an entertaining kickass rally, our relief was infectious as the squad headed for the school van while Grace, Nona, and I pranced to the car. What took us by surprise was a beefy, squat man decked in a tweed sports coat waddling from out of nowhere.

"Are you Leocadia Nelson?"

I kept walking and asked, "Who wants to know?"

"I'm Carm Castellano. A reporter for the Gazette." He unbridled his reporter's badge in my face like an FBI agent. "I have some questions for you."

Startled and reminiscent from a year ago, I queried, "Like what?"

His breathing accelerated, striving to keep up with me. "Detective Mark Dyl is concentrating on the David Galbraith and Skipper Townsend murder case. Does it upset you that your own mother's murder case has yet to be solved?"

Coming to an abrupt halt, I stared at the man with a bad comb-over. "That's a no-brainer, Mister." I watched Nona and Grace getting into the car without me.

"Are you aware there is a connection to your mother's murder and these two?" Beady eyes stared from his plump, perspiring face.

"How do you know that?" Detective Dyl had been adamant not to tell a soul; although I'd snitched to one person.

"So you are aware?" He was jotting words in a spiral notepad. "Have you heard there is a possibility of two accomplices in both crimes? It's been leaked to the press that two incongruent prints had been discovered at the scenes."

CHAPTER 42

"Why are you here, Mister?" My oversensitive blood pressure skyrocketed. "There is nothing I can tell you about either case. Leave me alone." I managed a couple of strides on rickety legs.

He rushed in front of me, blocking my path.

"Leocadia, how have you been coping now that the anniversary of your mother's murder is next week and there are no suspects?" he said like a sharp-shooter. "In retrospect, in your opinion, do you think Detective Dyl should be pulled from the case? What will you do if the murderer isn't apprehended? It came to our attention the police recently questioned you. Are you a suspect in these investigations?"

"It's none of your damn business," I said disdainfully. "We're done."

"One last thing. May I take your picture for the Gazette?" Using his phone, he clicked several shots before I plastered my hands over my face.

"Get the fuck out of here, buddy." Nona's cantankerous reproach moved the air. "Leave my friend alone." Her arm rounded my back and pulled me away, saving me from the reporter. "I should've come sooner. You don't have to talk to those jerks."

I glanced over my shoulder. He was stooped over his notebook writing. "Let's get out of here."

Once in the car, Nona rummaged in her duffle bag, producing a pack of cigarettes. "Here, I think you need this."

I was thinking of something stronger, but a smoke would have to do. "Is this the same pack from a week ago?" I knocked out a cigarette.

"I'm trying to quit. Reggie doesn't smoke. He said he hates kissing an ashtray."

I proffered the pack to Grace in the back seat. "You want one?"

"I don't smoke, but thanks."

"Good, girl. Don't start," Nona said. "Causes lung cancer."

"Thanks for the tidbit as I light up." Striking the match, I lit the smoke and blew out the match head with a gray stream. "That's why weed should be legalized and it will be; mark my words."

"I doubt that's a solution," Grace rebutted. "You're still inhaling smoke, and it'll cause cancer, too."

"Alright, enough. You convinced me." I closed my eyes, drawing deep on the cigarette as if it were a high. Tipping my head back, a smokey cloud slithered from my mouth. "My last drag." I rolled down the window and flicked the cigarette into the street. "Nona, if you're quitting, then so am I."

Nona's head bobbed and upped the volume to the radio. Straying from our assigned route for unhealthy fast food, we sang tunelessly along with our favorite songs, then onto Kensington High School for the big game.

I felt like an interloper on the opposing team's sidelines. The bleachers were jam-packed and the mob riotous. Kensington's marching band orchestrated a stimulating performance while the cheerleaders practiced on the sidelines. The weather held at a brisk forty-five degrees with no rain in sight. For the most part, I stayed clear of Marcy and Blair; although I was the recipient of several noxious glances.

Nona had also intercepted the girl's spiteful eyes. She said to me, "Let's have fun." Then insisted I ignore them.

Except for the officious reporter putting a bitter taste in my mouth, I was revved and my routines were right-on. Executing a proficient round-off and backflip, Mrs. Sweeny gave me a thumbs up and a smug grin.

After halftime, Star Hallow got their act together, tying the game. Nona saddled next to me on the bench for a brief interval. "Did you tell anyone about Becket asking you out?" she asked, tone discreet.

"No, no one, why?"

"Becket might've said something to Marcy. She's spitting bullets."

Nona's statement lifted my spirits somewhat. Marcy tilted forward on the bench and her olive complexion had morphed to scarlet red. Totally pissed and talking, or more like glowering at Blair.

"I see that teeny-weeny smile," Nona teased. "Shout it out. Becket's hot for you, girl. Your dreams are coming true." Excited, she squeezed and wiggled my arm.

"I certainly hope not." I had a flash of my funky dream. Nona's eyebrows knitted in confusion, and I clarified, "I had a doozy of a dream before I woke up this morning. I caught Becket in bed with Marcy."

"That's not the dream I'm talking about, hun."

"I know. But now you understand why I'm so messed up?"

"You got to cleanse those thingamajigs from your brain."

"Did I tell you Dad's making me see Dr. Mathias? She'll put me back on meds."

"It's your body, Leo." She advised. "Nobody can make you take them. We can't go through that again."

"Hey, we're supposed to be having fun." I hadn't meant to bum out the evening. Hopping from the bench and cuffing my pom-poms in the air, I cheered, "Let's get our heads in the game."

With sixty seconds left, we were losing by four points. It was Kensington's ball and it looked hopeless. However, their offense coughed up the ball, and Star Hallow's Rob Janko intercepted before being tackled. Our offense took the field and initiated one running play. Becket threw a completion to Reggie for the touchdown.

Nona and I tackled each other, hugging and screaming, jumping up and down. It was Marcy that caught my eye, galloping onto the field and throwing herself into Becket's arms. She ripped off his helmet and fervently kissed him.

What magnified my dismay was that he was a passionate recipient.

CHAPTER 43

"Take me home, Nona, please."

"But we're going out to celebrate. This is our night; Star Hallow is on top. We haven't beaten Kensington since we were in eighth grade."

"It's not my night." I was glad Grace had decided to return to school with the other cheerleaders in the van. She wouldn't have to witness my theatrical demise. "I'd be a dud anyway."

"I have to pick Reggie up at the school."

"No, I'm not going." I clawed fingernails over my arms. "Drop me at home, and then go back for him. With all the hype and publicity, they'll be late coming back from Kensington."

Disgruntled, she agreed to my demands.

My house was completely black when Nona turned into the drive. *Dad isn't home.* "I'm glad we won," I said, a bleaker than bleak grin crept across my face. "It was a good game."

"It was," Nona said, knowing it was best to let me be. "Call me. I'm here for you. I'll see you at the dance tomorrow night, right?"

"Yep, I'll be there with Henry."

After unbolting the door, I called to make sure no one was home. "Dad, are you here?" I turned on the kitchen lights. The house phone was blinking with a message.

"Leo, I'm going out after work. I'll be late."

Gnashing my teeth, I wondered if he were with Regina or if he found a new lady friend. I was sinking lower by the minute. I went into my bedroom, turning on lights as I went. A triangular edge of a composition notebook was sticking out from beneath my bed. Getting to my hands and knees, I looked at the disorganized piles.

"Mom, what should I do with these?"

Scritch...scritch. Focusing on my ears, I listened for the noise to repeat. My footfalls deadened on the shabby carpet as I retraced my steps to the living room.

Scritch...scritch. I pivoted toward Dad's bedroom. He had always kept the door shut. I'd never set foot in his room since moving to Westgate.

There was the noise again coming from inside. Cracking the door, it was pure blackness. I swept fingers on the side wall and clicked on the center-dome light. Breathing in stagnant air, I ran a hand across my nose.

Dad's bed was a bundle of disheveled blankets and sheets. Shoes, ties, and clothes littered the room as if we'd recently moved in, and he'd thrown his belongings wherever. Making a passage through his garbage, I headed to the chest of drawers that at one time had been Mom's.

Drawer upon drawer, I opened to find it overflowing with Dad's junk. I'd been desperate to seek a piece of her, a cherished remembrance. Browsing the room, there wasn't even a photograph of her or them together.

Scritch...scritch. I glimpsed the baseboard where a composition notebook was tenting the furnace duct. With the weather turning frosty, Dad had switched on the furnace to warm the house, and air sailing through the ducts rustled the pages.

I knew what it was—Mom's journal. It had been in here the whole time. I gaped at the notebook as spider legs scuttled across the nape of my neck. I presumed it was replete with undiagnosed clues. Squatting, I promptly hugged it to my chest. When I rose, I spied corrugated boxes situated on the upper ledge in his closet. If he'd been hiding her journal, what else had he kept secret? As if I were in possession of an ancient artifact, I placed Mom's journal on the dresser and headed for the boxes.

The first box resisted my attempts to heave it from its perch by catching on a nail or something. Mustering strength, I managed to hoist up the box. Its contents were chock full of memories. Mom was the picture taker, the movie mongrel, the scrapbooker. In complete disarray were framed family photographs of happier times, DVDs, and a treasure trove of her favorite books and more personal journals.

I savored the notion of unearthing every single item with loving care. But now was not the time because Dad would have a hissy fit if he knew I had infringed on his privacy. There was a second box on the ledge. In red magic marker, I recognized Mom's artistry. A skull and crossbones.

The box wasn't heavy. Setting it atop the first, I flipped it open. Dad's army uniform. I removed the uniform and stared at a worn pair of black combat boots and a knife.

CHAPTER 44

The incriminating knife and boots appeared undisturbed. My hands shook as I replaced the uniform over them and returned the box onto the shelf.

Revisiting the contents of Mom's boxed memories, I regrettably returned it to the ledge, too. I claimed Mom's journal and wondered if Dad would notice it was missing? Hardly, considering his wasted nights. I intended on leafing through it and then put it back where I found it.

By reshuffling his junk into its messy state, I disguised my break-in. *First things first, don't become a wackadoodle; keep it together.* I scoured my desk for the detective's business card. "Where did I put it?" I found it tucked under my desk lamp. My body was one nerve bundle as I keyed in his number.

"Leo, what's wrong?" His voice came through loud and clear.

"I found something."

"Where are you?"

"At home."

"Where's your father?"

"He's out."

"What's going on?"

"I found a pair of boots and…and a knife in his bedroom." My voice pitched an octave as I paced back and forth.

"We know your father was in the military."

"Did you check his stuff?" I exhaled deeply. "Like for prints or whatever you do?"

"Yes."

"He…he was there," I said, fraying by the minute. "I know he's lying."

"It was normal to find prints of you, your mom, and your father in the house. I'm coming over. We'll discuss this."

"He might be home soon. He'll know I called you."

"I'm in my car. I'll be there in a few minutes."

The line went dead and I regretted calling him. *What am I doing? I'm stirring the kettle into a bubbling brew; that's what!* Dad would never…would he? Waiting for the detective, I fingered the pages in Mom's journal and went into the lighted kitchen.

October first. No one loves the man whom he fears. (Aristotle)

Mom crossed out he and added she. The very next passage was dated October fifth:

What tangled webs we weave. (Sir Walter Scott)

On October sixth, she concluded the popular quote:

When we practice to deceive. (Sir Walter Scott)

Her journal was a litany of literary quotes and one-liners. I jerked when the doorbell chimed knowing it was the detective.

"I gather your father's not home?"

"Not yet." He trailed me into the kitchen.

"You look frazzled. Are you alright?"

"Not really," I said, weepiness coating my words, "I can't believe I'm having doubts about my father. He'd never, ever slaughter her in their bed."

"Sit." He indicated a chair at the table. "I wanted to tell you this in person instead of over the phone." He didn't say anything; instead he tarried, slowly unbuttoning his trench coat before taking a seat. "Forensics went over the house with a fine-tooth comb. Your father's military uniform and accruements were discovered and tested. The items were returned to him shortly thereafter."

My body withered in my chair, feeling like a phobic child.

He went on, tempering my panic. "There's no proof that your father was at the house on the day of her murder. As you know, he supplied us with an airtight alibi, and the other person involved has authenticated his whereabouts."

"It was his secretary, Regina, right?" His eyebrows heightened. "I know he was having a thing with her."

"That's why I came over. I didn't want to drop the bomb over the phone. Detective Dyl inquired, "When did you find out?"

"Recently." I didn't elaborate.

"Has your father given you any reason to doubt his alibi?"

I shook my head, saddened. "I am so...so miserable. Like we weren't living in the same house. How could I be so blind to what was happening around me?" Detective Dyl smiled, and he didn't look nearly as hardnosed; in fact, he was a good-looking man.

"Leo, you're a teenager. Teenagers tend to thrive in their own world."

"I'd hardly say I'm thriving."

He pointed to the composition notebook under my arm. "What's that?"

"My homework journal." There was no way I was handing it over, not yet. I slid the book onto my lap, away from him.

"You're going to the Homecoming dance with Henry James tomorrow?"

Now it was my turn to look baffled. "How did you know?"

"It's my job to know." He massaged his eyes, brow, and forehead, in an uncharacteristic indicator of dismay, and then moved his hand over the crown of his head. A slash of sorrow crossed his face. It happened so fast I might have imagined it. "You should stay away from the boy. He's got problems." He rose from the chair and turned to leave.

"Wait!" I barked and he stalled in his tracks. "Henry and I went back into the mansion. Mom's picture is still there. It's now in one of the third-floor bedrooms. I checked it out this morning."

His fingers crunched the lapels of his coat.

I wanted confirmation and asked, "Henry told you about everything he saw in the attic, didn't he?"

"Yes, and for the record, I believed your story from the beginning."

"He thought you did." I blustered out a breath. "Do you have any clues or suspicions?"

Again, he raked fingers on the side of his head over his temple. "We believe your mom's murder wasn't premeditated." His lips flattened against his teeth, assessing what he was going to say next. "Perhaps, a lover's dispute that got deadly."

The pit of my stomach turned to rot. "No. Not true… I can't—"

"Leo, you're old enough to face facts. You must've known they were having marital problems."

"They fought a lot." I didn't want to believe him. "But…I never would've thought…Mom."

Detective Dyl stepped behind my chair and placed his hands on my shoulders. "Buck up, kid. You'll get through

263

this." He applied kind pressure. "Stay out of the Baskerville place. It's not safe."

"Henry wants to spend the night there after the dance." Why did I vomit that?

"Really?" He released my shoulders. "My professional recommendation is to stay as far from that place as possible. Why would you take chances like that when you know somebody's skulking around in there? Leave the investigation to me."

His retort drew my ire. "Find my mother's killer and I'll stop! And what about Dave and Skipper? Someone said there might be two accomplices. Is that true?"

His eyes sparked, narrowing. "Who the hell told you that?"

"A reporter practically tackled me at school today. His name is Carm Castellano."

He crammed his hands into his pockets. "Is that the guy from the Gazette, that rinky-dink paper?"

"That's what he said."

"He's stirring up trouble. If he comes around again, kick him in the nuts for me."

I smirked.

"I wish you'd taken my advice and not hooked up with Henry. But go to your dance. Have fun. Forget about murder for one night." Buttoning his coat while walking toward the door, he said, "And don't go to the mansion. Just in case, a squad car will be patrolling Lucien Court."

I lay in bed feeling lousy. The detective had sliced a scar into my heart, unseating Mom from her chaste throne. The buzz of incoming texts vibrated on the nightstand. I rolled over the mattress and snatched my cell.

Nona wrote: *Call me.*

Don't Forget to Breathe

There was also a message from Becket: *We need to talk.*

And a text from Henry: *I guarantee a good time at the dance.* Whatever that meant.

Dad hustled into the house at two-twenty. The mourning phase was over. It didn't take long for him to convert into a whoremonger, or was he always like this?

CHAPTER 45

Since it was Saturday and considering his late night, Dad would sleep till noon. Cozy in my sweats, I sat in bed riveted to Mom's journal. While I read about the months prior to her death, her emotions came through on each turned page.

Mom jotted cryptic messages through quotes and essays, most likely assuming Dad would conspire to read her journals. I diligently went through the first few entries:

It was not into my ear you whispered, but into my heart. It was not my lips you kissed, but my soul. (Judy Garland)

Then I found an entry about me and many more:

Each time I look into my daughter's eyes, I see unconditional love. Leo is my greatest gift to the world. My heart and soul lie alone with my daughter.

She was livid or irritated by the hard slant and indentations in the paper:

Beware of the copper-headed snake. It slithers and tempts you into submission until its fangs sink deep into your throat, ejecting venomous seduction. It twists and turns, strangles, and suffocates—Here, she left off leaving half of the page blank. There was another entry on the next page days later, indicated by the date. I wondered if she'd meant to return to the previous entry to finish what she'd started?

The journal had page after page of internal strife. In her beautiful, cursive handwriting I read:

My love lies—bleeding (Thomas Campbell)

On October twenty-fourth, the day before she was murdered, she'd boldly printed:

Part of loving you is learning to let go.

Her very last entry was dated October, twenty-fifth. I would never know the time it had been written:

The copper-headed snake threatens to strike. I'm terrified.

"Mom, you led me into Dad's room. I thought it was to find the boots and knife, but the clue must be here. I'm missing something in your journal," I mumbled into the pages. "What am I looking for?" Wet droplets splashed the ledger paper, smearing ink. My long sleeve soaked up the wetness before my tears caused unreadable damage. I reclined against my headboard and closed my eyes.

Since October twenty-fifth, and to my detriment, I'd periodically recreated the murder. To be in her shoes. To experience her terror. I'd reenacted the scene, like a horror movie where you watch between your fingers, only this time it was the real deal. Over and over, replaying it in my head. No wonder I needed drugs to forget.

My ribcage ached, choking down bile. I had to stop. The psychiatrist had said it wasn't healthy. *Hah—really?* I pressed the thermal blanket to my face conquering the urge to bawl.

A bad juju day was unfolding.

Drained and feeling like an invalid, I poured out of bed and groaned. Tonight is Homecoming. After I read Henry's last text, it seemed like he had things organized. My first Homecoming Dance with a boy, and it was going to be a real bummer. Foraging into my closet, I unhooked an olive-green dress. *It will do.*

Fully alert, I needed to get out of the house. Dad didn't have work, which meant the car was available. Snotty snores reverberated from his room, making life easier; there'd be no begging. Emptying corn flakes into a bowl and adding milk, I leaned against the kitchen sink. *Keep a clear head.* I concentrated on the crunchy flakes and cold milk.

The day was cold and frosty as I drove along Westgate, passing Henry's place, which appeared quiet. When my cell rang, I figured it was Nona because I'd been ignoring her calls. She'd be ticked-off. I swiped my cell, lacking to check the screen, and said, "Hey, what's up?"

"What's up with you?"

Positively not Nona. "Becket?"

"I'm coming to your house," he stated point-blank. "Just thought I'd warn you, in case you're still in your pj's."

A smile pulled on the edges of my mouth. "I'm not home."

"Where are you?"

"Cruising."

"Can you be more specific?"

"I don't have a destination in mind. I'm just riding around."

He hemmed into his cell. "Meet me at Earl's."

"I'm sick of Earl's."

"Where then? Pick a place."

I loved the inflection of his voice, rich and velvety, making me all gooey inside. Then the image of Marcy swapping spit with him stiffened the goo. "We really don't have anything to talk about."

"Are you afraid of me?"

"Why would I be afraid of you?"

"Afraid of my persuasive personality, that is."

I thought of his flashing eyes, blue like a new spring day in May. "Your head couldn't get any bigger. It won't fit into your football helmet." A faint snicker generated a superb tingle in my ear.

"Leo, I'm parked in front of your house and Henry's perched on his car looking shifty-eyed. I'm not leaving. You have to come home sooner or later."

"Are you really at my house?"

"Come home and find out."

I bargained with him and said, "Meet me at Earl's."

I was seated and drinking a cup of coffee when Becket sauntered into Earl's. As I eyed the succulent piece of boy candy, my heart fluttered.

He shrugged off his jacket and straddled the chair next to me. The tips of his hair were damp and he smelled terrific like an ocean breeze. I was kind of grungy with my unmanageable hair, and I didn't recall putting a brush to the mess. I fingered my strands, sedating their disobedience.

"You look great, Red," he said.

In his astral eyes, I could see my gaze staring back at me. "Liar."

"I never lie." A roguish grin slipped onto his face. "Your boyfriend followed me."

"Henry?" I scanned Earl's. "He's not here."

"He will be. Give him a minute to stew. So you admit Henry's your boyfriend?"

"Those words came out of your mouth, not mine." I outlined the rim of my mug, thinking how Henry called Becket my boyfriend and vice versa. "And I could say the same to you—about Marcy."

"I planned on asking you to the dance, and then Henry—"

I raised my hand, cutting him off. "My tongue wasn't lashing Henry's tonsils last night."

He snorted. "I would've tongued the coach. We weren't picked to beat Kensington. I was psyched."

Clutching the mug with both hands, I hummed a sour, wordless retort and then said, "She latched onto you like a damn bloodsucker." He slanted over the table, eyes twinkling. "What?"

"So, you do like me—a little?"

I brought the mug to my mouth, and my smile betrayed me. I gazed at Becket over the rim and sparks ignited.

CHAPTER 46

"What's going on?"

Henry's voice pulled me from Becket's eyes. "Hi, Henry, want a cup of coffee or cider?"

"Why are you here with Kane?" His eyes thinned, and he rooted his hands into his jean pockets, shoulders hunched.

"Having a cup of coffee with a friend."

"I warned you about him," Henry said, grinding his teeth.

From his relaxed body, Becket aligned his back, straightening. "Henry, you have a problem with me?" he said, a satirical sharpness to his voice.

Henry's cheeks turned chili-pepper red, body rigid. I recognized his tantrum-like scowl, his temper was at a critical phase.

I scuffed the chair back with my legs. "I'm leaving." I drew his rage from Becket, and Henry turned to me.

Becket also stood, towering over both of us. "Well then." He sounded defeated and arranged his jacket over his shoulder. "We'll see each other tonight, at the dance."

Henry threw him a contemptible glower. "Not if I can help it."

I pirouetted in place and marched from Earl's with hound-dog Henry at my ankles. Striding past the eatery's picture window, I captured Becket's blazing eyes.

"Are you mad at me?" Henry asked.

I cringed hearing his whiny voice. A confrontation on the sidewalk in front of Earl's, in clear view of meandering villagers, wasn't appropriate. I wanted to end it now, but he'd blame Becket. Tomorrow, after the dance, I would break ties with Henry. Attempting a casual tone, I said, "What time should I be at your house tonight?"

"Don't you want me to pick you up?"

I thought of Dad's comments about staying clear of Henry. "I'd rather just walk to your house. The dance starts at seven, so I'll come by at six-thirty. Is that alright with you?"

"Sure, fine," he said, dispirited. "I better tip you off. My Dad's...different."

"What do you mean by different?"

"I never wanted to dump my problems on you." He stubbed the toe of his sneakers into the pebbly stones. "My Dad...he's...well...kinda—"

"You don't have to explain." I already despised his father for hitting him and who knew what else. "I'll see you later."

My blood pressure was at a subtle simmer when I turned onto Westgate and spotted Detective Dyl's sedan parked in front of my house. *Oh, no.* What else could possibly go wrong today?

I rushed into the side door and sensed the strain. Dad and the detective were standing by the table. "What's going on?"

"Leo, this is your fault," Dad thundered. "Why can't you let it go? It's over. You can't bring her back."

A splash of anguish twinged the detective's eyes. It had been a year without any leads, and Detective Dyl was feeling the burden of Mom's unsolved murder and now dealing with two more. The media had been callously reporting the police department's ineptitudes.

Interrupting Dad's outburst, Detective Dyl said, "I went to the Baskerville place this morning and found Lily's picture just like you said. I've been informing your father that everything you'd experienced in the attic was evidently true. I also found a burr hole in the attic where the picture once hung, and there was evidence of something like the legs of a bed scuffing the wooden floor. Someone was in a hurry to clean it out."

"So I'm not delusional," I said, vindicated. Dad's previous hotheaded, flushed complexion turned pasty as he sank to the chair.

"I was driving by and thought you might want to know." The detective swerved to leave and added, "Leo, have a good time at the dance and stay clear of the Baskerville place, understand?"

CHAPTER 47

I shimmied into the form-fitting, olive-green dress and slipped my feet into my black heels, then a last-minute touch up in the mirror. For once my hair didn't retaliate; razored layers were flawlessly tousled. For the occasion, I chose my knee-length raincoat and went into the living room to say goodbye to Dad.

He was high on a bender, weary-eyed and stinking of booze. I kissed him on the cheek. "Are you coming home tonight?" he inquired, tongue thick.

"I don't know what the post plans are, so don't wait up for me."

His body wobbled, attempting to sit. "You look stunning. Just like Lily." Water welled in his eyes and he outspread his arms.

I moved into his embrace. "Thanks, Dad."

"That kid bothers me. Be careful." His slurred warning.

"It's just a dance." Hedging from his arms, I said, "Make sure you eat something." I believed we'd switched roles, me mothering my father. It was a little after six, too early to knock on Henry's door. Yet, the dance couldn't pass fast enough as far as I was concerned.

A crescent moon hung in the darkening sky, a perfect Halloween night. My heels *click-clacked* to the end of the driveway, where a gust nearly knocked me off my feet. I cinched my winging coat, leaned into the wind, and managed to make it to Henry's in one piece; albeit, my flawless hair was toast.

"Come in, come in," Ethan James said, opening the door as if he'd been waiting for me. "I saw you crossing the street." I stepped into the four-by-four foot foyer. Mr. James boarded his body to my back, and I instantly felt icky. "Go on in, Leo."

His hand smoothed the back of my coat, ushering me into the kitchen. With twanging thoughts of those hands beating Henry, I shivered.

"Keep going, into the living room."

I faltered at the border of a plush beige carpet. "I should take off my shoes."

"Oh, no, dear, come on in," a docile voice heralded from the living room.

Mr. James moved around me and, intoning eloquence, said, "Look who we get to meet again, Lily's daughter."

"Come closer, dear," a female voice said. "Let me see you."

Mr. James urged me into the living room. A skeletal woman seated in a wheelchair had a grin plastered on her face.

"Hello, Leo." She held aloft a welcoming hand.

"Nice to meet you, Mrs. James." I took hold of her cold hand, her fingers were stiff and unresponsive.

"Call me Martha and this is Ethan," she greeted, then dropped my hand. "Lily was instrumental in acquiring a position for my Ethan at Star Hallow Elementary. Did she tell you?"

"You met my mother?"

"On one occasion." Her chin tipped, lowering her gaze. "Ethan talks about Lily quite a bit."

"Lily never mentioned me?" Ethan said, incredulous and intrusive.

"No, I'm sorry. Not that I remember." The resemblance between father and son was uncanny. Ethan removed his glasses and blotted his eyes with his fingers.

"The administration at my school laid off dozens of teachers. My position was tenuous. Lily implored me to pull up stakes and come to Star Hallow. It was the summer before..." His voice turned hoarse, pausing. "Lily emailed me concerning a teacher retiring at the elementary school, said the position had yet to be filled." He rearranged his glasses over his ears. "So dreadful...so dreadful. Poor Lily."

His account didn't make sense. "Mr. James, I mean Ethan." He recovered from his emotional condition. "My mother's been deceased... It'll be a year in a few days."

"It was like yesterday." Water winked from his eyes. "You and I talked at the funeral. Don't you remember?"

"I...I wasn't in the best frame of mind."

"Perfectly understandable," Martha accentuated with little compassion. She twined her fingers onto her lap. "Ethan, let it rest. You're upsetting the poor thing."

I wasn't upset. Though, I wondered why Henry hadn't provided all the specifics.

"Would you like a beverage?" Ethan asked.

"No, thank you."

"You are lovely, like Lily." Ethan's grin cocked to the side of his mouth, inspecting me from my hair to my heels. I was on display and uncomfortable. "Isn't she, Martha?"

A passing smile honed Martha's angular cheekbones. She parroted, "Yes. Lovely." When her smile shrunk, she was a skeleton with flaccid skin. "You are just like your mother, dear." A ghost of a shadow fled through her eyes.

I didn't like how she said that as if accusing me of something.

"May I take your coat?" Ethan offered, and I felt the warmth of his hands on the collar of my raincoat.

"I'm still cold. I think I'll leave it on."

Rather than disengaging his hands, Ethan palmed the nape of my neck. His touch warranted a ping of caution.

"Your skin is cold."

My voice had a meek tremor to it when I said, "Is Henry ready?"

"He's a dilly-dallier," Martha said. "Go up to his room." When I turned to look at the staircase leading to the second story, Ethan detached his fingers.

"I'll show you the way."

"Ethan," Martha said in a spanking pitch. "I think the young lady is capable of handling the stairs on her own."

"It's my pleasure. Come, Leo, this way." Again, he secured his hand to my lower back as if I might tumble. Ethan had no choice but to remove his hand as I hastened up the stairs.

"Henry," Ethan called. "I have a pretty surprise for you."

There was an explicit clank of a lock, and then Henry stepped into the hallway. Lacking his hipster glasses, he looked rather cute. Coppery hair feathered pleasingly over his ears and in a white, button-down shirt overlaid with a V-neck, burgundy sweater. "You're early."

"I know, sorry."

He twitched his head, and I took that as an invitation. As elegant as possible in heels, I entered his room. Prior to crossing the threshold, I intercepted a look of repulsion on Henry's face, directed at his father. He then worked on relocking the door, not one but three locks.

"Wow." He finished dead bolting the door. "Are those really necessary in your own home?"

"They are if you live here."

"Is something wrong?" I wondered if the locks were to keep his dad at bay or for another reason.

"No," he remarked. "What makes you think something's wrong?"

"I dunno." My eyes coasted over his room. If I didn't count Jimmy Gautier when I was in kindergarten, this was my first time in a boy's bedroom and ten times worse than mine ever was. Henry was in the process of booting clothes, creating a channel for me to walk.

"Sorry 'bout the mess. I didn't expect you'd be coming up here."

"No problem." He persevered in lobbing clothes into his closet. "Stop that, Henry, it's okay."

He swiveled and said, "Isn't my dad a tool?"

I didn't disagree, merely shrugged, glancing around. There was a computer and a pile of papers that laid disorganized on a desk, a decent-sized television and an attached game system, and even a compact fridge sitting kitty-corner. "You have a refrigerator in your bedroom?"

"Doesn't everybody?" he said sarcastically. "Want a soda?"

"Sure, what do you have?"

"Coke."

I redistributed a pile of books from his bed to the desk and stared at the morose posters on the wall. "Did you paint these?"

"Years ago." He handed me a paper cup with fizzing soda. "Cool, huh?"

"Bloody and kind of sinister."

I drank the bubbling soda, tickling my nose. Henry's gaze was fixated on me. I speculated whether he was still fuming over Becket and me at Earl's this morning.

Nevertheless, I didn't want to mention Becket's name. "Are you sure nothing is wrong?"

"My parents are getting on my nerves."

Phew, at least he's not angry because of Becket. "Are they fighting?" I realized too late that it was none of my business.

"Have been for years, but that's not it." He paced to his dresser and retrieved his glasses.

"You never told me that your mom was in a wheelchair."

"She's a frigging hypochondriac. She was fine until three months ago, having luncheons with her hoity-toity friends in the city. I think it's a play to rein Dad in. Besides, she's not my mom."

"She's not?"

"I don't remember my real mother. My father married Martha when I was six. She's a rich bitch. My father married her for her money. She's an antique."

"She seemed...okay." Although, the sound of her voice when she said, *You are just like your mother, dear*, was peculiar.

"An act. My dad is more of a scumbag than she is, though." Using the hem of his V-neck sweater, he obsessively cleaned the lenses of his glasses. "If I had some cash, I'd take you to the city."

Amid a nervous chuckle, I said, "You're going to break those glasses if you keep rubbing so hard."

His fingers ceased and his eyes clicked to my face. "Since you're early, let's have a pregame warm-up." He had the joint in his lips before I had a chance to protest.

"Your parents can probably smell that."

"I couldn't care less." He offered me the joint. "I do what I want."

"I don't want to smoke anything tonight."

"Why not?" He looked stricken. "I plan on getting wasted and having a riot."

"Then maybe I should drive if you're getting wasted." I balanced the paper cup in my right hand and swirled what remained of the soda. "I'll go home and get my father's car."

"No, don't do that. I'll be good," he gasped, holding in a lungful of smoke. Exhaling, he said, "Hey, drink up. We have to leave."

Tipping the cup to my mouth, I downed the last of the soda and licked my lips. It tasted good, quenching my tongue. For the second time, he was watching me with interest. "Okay," I said, finally figuring it out, "what did you put in it?"

"I guaranteed you a good time, didn't I?"

"You drugged me?" I squashed the cup in my hand. "You're unbelievable."

"Chill, Leo, it's a mild ride. Just enough ecstasy to make you giddy." He balanced what remained of the joint into an ashtray. "You've been so uptight, thinking of your Mom chaperoning the dance last year and all."

"I told you that?"

He wavered with a sheepish tick to his lips. "Yes, don't you remember? That night in the cemetery, you were crying on my shoulder. That's when I made up my mind to take you to the dance. I understand what's eating your brain and I want to help." I didn't recollect the circumstances, but in his defense, this was his weird style of helping me.

Throwing the cup into an overflowing wastebasket, I said, "We should call this dance thing off."

"I paid for the tickets. We'll leave when you say the word." Conflict swelled over his face as he tugged on his sweater.

I felt wretched. Henry was legit messed up, like me, and I was a huge sap. "Then let's go before I get too loopy."

"Wait here." He hastily unbolted the locks. "I'll be right back." He clunked the door closed behind him.

Infuriated by the setback, I'd been coping without indulging in drugs, even during my recurring dreams. I'd handled more than a little ecstasy over the year. *I can do this.* Maybe he was right. A bit of a pick-me-up might be the ticket to get me through the dance. I had incessantly been reminiscing about last year's Homecoming. To my utter dismay, Mom had volunteered as a teacher chaperone. Poor Nona, having to tolerate my ragging because I'd assumed we wouldn't have any fun with Mom standing guard. It was just the opposite. We had a great time.

I moseyed to a shelving unit to check out Henry's books, DVDs, and CDs. The heel of my shoe struck a hard object. I crouched into a pile of crud and grasped the tongue of a black boot.

CHAPTER 48

"You—you were wearing these—that night—in the graveyard?" I said when Henry walked in. I held onto the boot like it were a lethal weapon.

"What the fuck, Leo. Every guy in school has a pair of those." He knocked the boot from my hand. "You're losing it. Do you think I gutted Dave and Skipper? Don't forget I didn't live here when your mom bit the bullet."

My tongue clicked free. "Your father did." His brow pulled, shaking his head. "How come you didn't tell me your dad knew my mom?"

"Because." He folded his arms, caving in on himself. "My Dad knows lots of women."

Henry turned from me. He was battling demons, too. His shoulders de-tensed and he swung an indifferent hand as if nothing mattered. Then, tucking his shirttail into the waistband of his trousers, he said, "Martha and I liked the city. She had her acquaintances and I had freedom. Dad made me move here after…" He paused while opening his closet to hunt for something.

I finished his statement. "After you got into trouble?"

"I suck at this. This soul-healing junk." He plundered through a tier of hangers.

"Tell me. I'd like to know."

"No—you don't." He withdrew a jacket and put it on. "Let's go."

When we bid Henry's parents goodbye, Martha didn't appear as frail as I'd originally thought. In fact, she'd transferred from the wheelchair to the couch.

"Son," Ethan said, "can we speak in private?"

Henry expressed sheer hatred, though relented and followed his father. Vicious undertones drifted into the living room and I shifted from foot to foot.

"Henry causes my Ethan such misery." Martha's voice unraveled like a thinning thread. "Always a problem child. We'd hoped Star Hallow would calm him."

I turned to the emaciated woman.

"Henry is temperamental," she said. "A bane to my existence." She gained strength with each word. "Prone to violent episodes." Then, as if playing a major Hollywood role, she clutched her chest and wheezed.

"Do you need help?"

Grasping her chest, squeezing her eyelids, she then reopened them. "I'm fine, dear." It sounded rehearsed. "I paid your mom a visit once. Did she ever tell you about that?"

Talk about a punch below the belt. "No."

"It was—unpleasant and undignified. I wouldn't want you to get the wrong impression of me." She dabbed at the corner of her eyes. "Don't tell Henry I've been spilling secrets. I'd hate for him to lose his temper."

She attempted a smile and I averted my gaze from her trampled face. *How do I appraise Martha James, and why the hell does it matter what impression I have of her?*

Henry charged out from wherever they'd been arguing and grabbed my hand. "Ready?" He towed me like I were deadweight.

As we passed the hallway, Ethan was leaning on the wall, his body that of a broken man; his glasses dangled from his fingertips. At least that was what it looked like until his eyes flickered to meet mine. Dark and pernicious.

Once in the car, Henry completely transformed and was almost buoyant. He amped up the radio and sung, "Let's get this party started."

We zoomed along Westgate as if the previous minutes never existed. His buoyancy filled me from the inside out. Knotted muscles and coiled nerves loosened, and I knew why. Whatever he'd slipped into my soda had taken effect. I reveled in the sensation. Weeks of shitass anxiety eclipsed behind a masquerade of euphoria.

"Have any more weed?" I asked on a whim.

He manufactured a cockeyed grin. "It's about frickin' time." He retrieved a joint from his pocket, offering it to me. "Light up."

"Just what the doctor ordered." The chill of the car evaporated and I unbuttoned my raincoat. I'd decided to go with the flow instead of against the current. "I'm feeling much better."

"I've driven around the school three times; we're late," Henry said, sooner than I'd anticipated.

"So what?" I laid my head on the seat and rubbed my eyes, forgetting about my mascara. "Let's not go."

"We're going in," he said with determination.

"Why is this stupid dance so important to you?"

He'd parked and swerved his shoulders to peer at me. "For once, the hottest girl in school will be in my arms and I want everyone to see it."

I broke down into a giggling fit. "You're joking, right?"

"Leo, you underestimate yourself." Staggering from the car, the heel of my shoe punctured a pothole. Before hitting the asphalt, Henry nailed me to his side. "Hey, straighten up or the teachers will be suspicious."

"I'm fine." I gobbled the nighttime air like a famished kitten, defragging my brain.

Perceiving Mr. Slepe guarding the doors of the gymnasium, I gave an inaudible growl.

"Henry, I'm going to the restroom. I'll meet you back here in a minute." Grateful for the vacant room, I browsed my complexion in the mirror and groaned: smudged mascara and tragic hair. After a retouch, I spied my phone and made a snap decision.

I'd added him to my contacts and pressed his name. It rang three times before he answered. "Leo, what's wrong?"

"Why do you always think something's wrong?"

"It's the only time you call."

I breathed in and said, "Henry has a pair of black boots in his bedroom."

"I can't get a search warrant for every house in the village," Detective Dyl uttered into the phone.

"You should check them out. His father knew my mother. Did you know that?"

There was only silence.

I thought I lost the signal and asked, "Are you there?"

"Are you at the dance with Henry?" His voice came through with a strange steely edge.

"Yes, we just got here."

"Be careful. I'll see what I can do." Devoid of paraphrasing, he hung up. I walked out of the restroom and collided with Henry.

"Let me hang up your coat," he suggested. Coat racks had been placed in the school's hallway, and he located a free hangar and mashed our coats into the disorder. We went up to Mr. Slepe and Henry handed him the tickets.

"You kids are over a half-hour late." Mr. Slepe stared into my eyes and then Henry's. "Have you been drinking?"

"Of course not, Mr. Slepe," I said, more astute than I felt. "Do you remember when my mom was chaperoning last year? It was the last time I saw her laughing and dancing before…" I sniffed and wiped a finger under my nose.

A strip of pink saturated his cheeks. "Go on in, Leo."

We penetrated a throng of bedlam. Music pumped into the gym, overriding the bellowing laughter and noisy jabbering. Rectangular tables and metal chairs lined the outskirts of the shellacked flooring, clearing the center for dancing. Students demonstrating their moves clogged the area.

A range of seconds passed before I found Becket dancing with Marcy. He was infallibly groomed and a total dreamboat, in a baby-blue sweater adorning his broad shoulders, which complemented the color of his eyes.

Henry linked his arm through mine, conducting me frontward. Circuiting chairs and tables like a pair of clinging snakes, I chucked my purse onto the nearest surface.

"You're taller than me in those high-heels," he said and wrapped his arms around me.

Finding his statement hilarious, I snickered and voiced like a vamp, "The better to see you with, my dear."

"You look great, by the way." He brushed the tip of his nose to mine.

During the song's final stanza, a familiar voice said, "Leo, where have you been? I've been calling and calling. Are you ignoring me?"

I turned to face an irate Nona and a jaunty Reggie.

"We can talk later," I said and fashioned a rueful grin. "Hey, Reggie, how's it going? Nona is swanky tonight, isn't she?"

His gaze was for Nona alone. "That's my babe. One swanky lady." He pressed her tighter to his side. "I'll be right back, babe." He pecked a kiss on Nona's cheek and, in a friendly gesture, he tweaked my nose and snubbed Henry altogether.

By the tart glare on Henry, he wasn't fond of Reggie either.

"I saved two chairs." Nona gestured for us to follow.

"Leo, I'm going to get us something to eat." Henry's thumb glided over my knuckles. "I have the munchies."

"Me too, bring something back."

Henry veered toward the refreshment table and I registered Nona's analytic gaze.

"You using again? See, that boy is not good for you."

"No grief, Nona. I'm trying hard to get through this night. Let it go for now." She puffed air from her nose and led me through a hive of tables. "We're nowhere near Marcy and Becket, are we?"

"Girl, do you think I can keep those boys apart?" Aggravated, she shook her head. "You're forgetting, this is my first dance with Reggie and I want it to be special. Reggie nixed the table by the dance floor to sit way-the-heck back here with Becket and Marcy. Do you think that makes me happy?"

I felt like such a creep, always thinking of myself. "I don't know what Henry will say when he sees Becket."

"Henry has to deal with it," she said, exasperated. "Grace came without a date. Maybe there's some way we can hook them up."

"That'd be nice. But Henry's not that bad. He's looking better and better every day; don't you think?"

"What the hell! You're high, so don't be giving me that bullshit."

"I am feeling really, really good right now. Let's dance." I clasped her wrists and hauled her into the mix, putting an end to her squawking. The impelling tempo sent us in motion, and my inhibitions dispelled like a feather on a contented breeze. My body kept the beat; however, Nona was the dancer. I mimicked her gyrating torso and, giggling, we competed with each other. The intoxicating drug had stayed the course, distorting my vision. The world revolved upside down and right-side up. Happy again. No thoughts, just the rhythm, music, and laughter.

Five songs later, Nona breathed weightily, "Let's sit."

"No. Not yet." Swaying with the song in my head, I grasped her arm. "Stay with me."

"It's a slow song, anyway. I'm going to get Reggie."

"I thought I'd never get the chance to hold you." The words sailed sweetly by my ears. Strong arms swallowed me and I curled into Becket's chest.

Unlike Henry, I had to tilt my head to gaze into his perfect face, and his irresistible smile had my heart performing somersaults. "Hi, Becket. You're looking good. How's Marcy?"

"Let's not go there." He fingered a loose strand of hair that had fallen over my eye, moving it to the side of my forehead. His fingertips continued to glide across my collarbone and over the sensitive skin beneath my hair, hooking onto the nape of my neck. He leaned and his hair tickled my cheek. "You are incredibly beautiful."

I melted like butter over fire as his hands molded me into him. It took a moment for his words to register, and I said, "I bet you say that to yall the goils."

"Are you alright?" He pulled back and examined my eyes.

"Don't I look alright? You just said I was 'credible booiful."

"You're slurring and your eyes. Are you high?"

"Becket. I'm...I'm...messed..." My ankle twisted, and I would've fallen, but he held on to me.

He slowed our lazy sidestepping. "I'm taking you home."

"No, you can't do that." My arms circled his neck like a life preserver, and I stared at his tormenting lips. "I came with Hen-nery. He'll take me home when I'm good and ready."

"Is he alright to drive?"

My gaze traveled from his mouth to his impeccable eyes, but they merged into an eye of a Cyclops. "You have one big eyeball." I snorted through my nose, then making him envious, I said, "I don't think we're going home."

"What do you mean you're not going home?"

The floor tilted. "Are we dancing?"

"Leo, answer me," he said, voice unyielding. "What do you mean you're not going home?"

I tried focusing on his big eye. "'Member, Lucien's place..."

Someone charged into Becket and I stumbled to my knees. Two bodies plunged to the floor. Everyone scattered. Girls screeched and I sloppily got my feet under me. Henry was all over Becket like tarpaper. Becket recovered from the blindsided tackle, reeling in Henry's flailing fists with one hand. Then after Becket caged his other arm around Henry's waist, they staggered to their feet. Kids were fencing them in.

"I don't want to fight you." Becket liberated Henry with a jerking thrust.

"She's mine, Kane. Leo's with me." Glasses uneven on his nose, rage warped Henry's face. "You have no right to touch her." In a linebacker move, he rammed into Becket with his shoulder. Henry was neither equivalent in height nor strength, so Becket had rooted his feet to the ground, taking the full brunt of his weight.

Becket then propelled Henry to the floor.

Henry gasped, the wind knocked out of him. Behind his lenses, his eyelashes fluttered. I started for him, but Becket blocked my path.

"You have to stop." I placed my hand on Becket's chest, holding him off. "You're hurting him."

"I didn't start this." He sheltered an arm over my shoulder. "He's in no condition to take you home. Let's go before the teachers nab us."

A shout emitted, "Blow me, Kane!" From the edge of my vision, Henry had gotten to his feet. It happened fast, yet, in slow motion. Henry lurched, walloping Becket in the upper shoulder. Red liquid drenched the threads of Becket's sweater, and pain slashed across his face. I caught a wink of a silver jackknife in Henry's hand before he hid it in his pants pocket.

"Becket," his name passed breathily from my lips, "Becket." He'd clasped a hand to the spreading flood, and his hand came away coated in blood.

CHAPTER 49

In my nightmarish haze, I hadn't a choice but to comply as Henry nabbed my arm, jogging us from the gym. *Where are the chaperones? What is happening to Becket?* The car door cracked open and Henry flung me onto the seat, then raced behind the wheel.

Coatless and in semi-shock, iciness bled into my skin. The car smoked from the parking lot and I finally looked at him. In the quiet dimness, he concentrated on the road ahead. He was adrift in his own mind of discord.

"Henry." My teeth chattered. "Wha...what did you do?" Foremost in my thoughts was the image of Becket and the blood. "You stabbed him. You stabbed Becket."

The airy hum of the heaters filled the interior, though, not squelching the ice encasing my bones. He avoided Terrace Circle, detouring through the outskirts of Star Hallow.

"Henry, we have to go back," I ordered. "Where are you going?"

When he eventually sought my eyes, a cavalcade of emotions flashed over him. "I...I'm screwed." That was when we heard the drone of sirens.

"You have to take me home." I recognized the back route and knew where he was heading. "Henry, you can't hide there." He crossed over the middle of the intersection and made a right. There was a screeching of metal on metal and sparks exploded underneath the car's chassis. My body joggled as the wheels trundled over the railroad ties.

On the eastern side of the tracks was the preliminary section to Hallow Saint's Cemetery. He traversed further ahead, then yanked the wheel to the left. The car nosedived over the ground into a field of brambles, trees, and shrubbery.

"Watch out for the tree." I pointed. "You're not going to make it through this."

Henry began skidding out of control, and the tires became entrenched in mangled brushwood, strangling the axel. Henry cranked the gear into park and shut off the engine.

"Get out!" he barked.

The gravity of our plight sent my worthless functioning body into overdrive, and I pushed on the door. It budged an inch as twigs clawed the metal frame. "I can't get out."

"Come over to my side."

I climbed over the center console into the driver's seat. He held out his hand and took me into his arms. I wrestled from his binding grip. "Let me go."

"This way." He rotated, paying little heed to my distress and yanked my arm. With each woeful step, my heels burrowed holes into the ground, making my trek hazardous and dawdling. Undergrowth grazed my legs as Henry's fingers dug into my forearm. We made it to the gazebo, and my heels clunked on the wood as he continued lugging me forward. I gathered a hefty breath of air in hope of cleansing my drug-altered brain.

Henry's cell rang. He slowed to trawl into his pants pocket. I peeked at the bright screen. His father. He muted the call. In less than a minute, his cell buzzed again, and this time the screen said Dyl.

"Everyone's looking for us," I said and thought of my only form of communication. My phone was in my purse still on the table at school.

By the light of the moon, we managed to tread upon the ornamental slate pathway that encompassed the mansion. The grounds were overrun with nettling greenery, and my heel snagged a vine, sending me to my knees. A stinging pain lanced into my thighs as Henry wrenched me up and off the path toward the house. We huddled together and watched a spotlight scouring the ground and then it disappeared.

"What the fuck?" Henry cussed.

"Detective Dyl told me to stay away from the mansion. Police are patrolling the Court."

Putting his arm around my shoulders, we inched far enough to perceive the rear headlights vanishing around the corner.

"They're gone," he whispered.

We scampered to the front of the mansion and halted. Someone had reattached a new, shiny, metal chain to the doors.

"Think we can get in through the back?" he asked.

"Not a chance." I twisted from his hold, but he held firm. "That's been boarded and bolted for as long as I can remember." Henry had muted his cell, but his pocket vibrated unceasingly. "It would be better if we—"

"Stop talking." He elbowed me to move to the porch. "Walk over to our hole."

"They boarded that up too."

He ushered me around the far corner of the mansion. "Stand back." Using the heel of his shoe, he thwacked the planks. When they didn't break, he booted it again and again. The weatherized planks surrounding the newly applied panel splintered.

"You first," he commanded.

"Henry, please." With his fingers manacling my wrist, his other hand cupped the top of my head, and he pushed me down. I didn't have a choice except to funnel myself through the broken gap. My thigh-high dress hampered my worming skills, and slivers of wood tore the material. I plummeted onto the floor like a beached whale.

"Why are we here?" It was dark, and I couldn't see a thing.

Henry was right behind me and then went to the couch and slid his hand underneath the shawled covering. He extracted a heavy-duty flashlight and dispersed the blackness. "I bought this a week ago and left it here just in case." The lenses of his glasses veiled his eyes. "It's important that I explain."

"Explain?"

"Follow me." He signaled with the light. "The cops might come back."

"Where are we going? You can't hide here forever."

He shored up my left elbow, and I believed for my stiletto's sake, he proceeded at a measured pace up the stairs. "This wasn't supposed to happen," he said, shining the flashlight on the steps. "I went berserk when I saw you in Kane's arms."

Wary of setting him off like a stick of dynamite, I remained silent.

"My father says I was born with this wrath inside of me. He blames my druggie mother. He said I inherited her psychosis. Even when I was an infant, he said my tantrums were off the wall. When I was five, my father said she committed suicide." When we made it to the third-story landing, he flipped the light to his face, looking ghoulish. "I never believed she committed suicide."

"Why don't you believe him?" Clarifying his neurosis, did Henry think I'd feel empathy after he stabbed Becket? "Because—he killed my mother."

CHAPTER 50

"What makes you think your father killed your mother?" After a pregnant pause and still bearing my elbow, he walked with purpose. We ventured to the room where we'd last seen Mom's picture.

"I know."

"You said she died when you were only five." My toes were beginning to cramp in my shoes. "Kind of young to suspect your father of murder."

Skin stretched like parchment over his angular cheekbones, and shadows invaded the contours of his face. His chest rose up and down, breathing deep. "He never stops—never, all these years. Physically punishing me because of her." Behind his lenses, his eyes were black sockets. "And it's him. It's all him."

Henry's fingers clamped tighter on my arm, suspecting I'd run away. We turned into the bedroom. A beam of light sluiced over the fourposter bed, landing on Mom's picture. On the chest of drawers was a vase with multicolored lilies.

"He's been here," he uttered.

My eyes rebounded from the lilies to Henry. "What'd you say?" His face developed into a fusion of alarm and abhorrence. Lacking a forewarning, he forced me onto the bed.

"You haven't figured it out yet?" He set the flashlight on the bedframe and tore off his glasses. Glossy eyes blinked. "My father—my father." His arms lashed out, pointing to the flowers and Mom's picture. "He hung that here. He puts flowers on her grave. Now, do you understand?" His features grew into muddling strife.

"Are you trying to tell me that—your father...he... killed..." My thoughts died in my throat.

Henry reached into his pocket and answered his vibrating cell. I listened to the one-sided conversation.

"I have to tell her. No, I don't care what you say. It doesn't matter anymore—Go to fucking hell!" He threw the phone and retrieved the jackknife still stained in Becket's blood. *Is he going to stab me too?*

He placed it onto the bedframe next to his glasses and the flashlight. His mouth pressed into an obstinate line. "Did you know my dad and your mom hooked up years ago?"

"I...I don't believe you." Blood stormed through my arteries, and I couldn't think straight.

"Your mom was a piece of work, a real shit starter." He licked his lips. "My father told me he'd groveled at her feet like an effing weakling. She liked to humiliate him. A typical tramp like all the rest of them."

"My mom wasn't like that. You're lying."

"We used to watch. From the attic." His fingers clipped my chin. "All women are flirtatious skanks."

"We?"

"I liked to surprise my father with a visit. I followed him one day. Their favorite spot was the Lucien attic." His thumb skimmed my cheekbone. "Then I started watching you. I thought you'd be different. But you played me, just like all the other sluts."

Henry spread my knees and wedged himself between them, only to thrust me backward onto the mattress. Then I took the full weight of his body as he fell on top of me.

"Henry! What are you doing?"

"Do you know the real reason I moved here?" He mouthed less than an inch from my nose. "I can't believe Dyl didn't tell you."

"Get off; you're scaring me."

"My pregnant girlfriend was murdered." He brushed his cheek against mine to speak into my ear. "They wanted to blame me because my DNA and another dudes was inside her. We were screwing around before she left." His arm slithered underneath my back, tacking me to his chest. "They found her in the trash, where she belonged."

He trapped my right arm behind me and affixed my left arm to my chest, between us.

"She was a sadistic bitch, teasing me like her personal patsy." Warm breath circulated around my ear. "But, I had an alibi."

I shuddered, revolted.

"Get off!" I writhed, trying to break his grip. His mouth covered mine in a ruthless attempt to quash my cries. I felt a hand on my thigh, roughly tearing my dress up and over my hips.

"Give it to me, Leo. Just like you give it up for that jockhead," he snapped. "I want to do you before..."

"You're crazy." Screaming wouldn't help since only ghosts lived here. With the right side of my body pinned to the mattress, I tried shoving him off. I never thought of Henry as strong until now.

"Dyl couldn't save your mother." He continued talking like he needed to solve the mystery for me. "He tried to warn her. But, like the arrogant whore that she was, she didn't listen, and then, it was too late. He made me watch."

"Who made you watch?" Each word was a cleaver to my heart. "Who made you do it—Dyl?"

He pinched my inner thigh and his knees moved my legs farther apart. I jerked my hips, thwarting his exploration, but it made him travel faster and harder.

A loud splintering crash terminated his fumbling fingers. His body shifted upright, lessening his weight, and my opportunity to bolt. I made it to the boundary of the mattress when his arms shackled me. The vase of flowers had shattered on the floor. Long, flowerless stems littered the area, and the petals inexplicably scattered a trail to the bed.

Henry's gaze skittered around the room, looking for someone.

Just the distraction I needed. My intention was not to goad him, though, to entice him. "Henry, let's go to the attic."

"The attic?" he said, eyes neutral.

"That's where it all began, right? We'll make plans—for...for the Halloween party." He wasn't taking the bait, instead, adding further pressure he shoved me back onto the mattress.

Astoundingly an incandescent glow struck his face. "Hold still, Henry James. Don't make a move."

Huffing sighs of relief, I then bit down on my bottom lip to stop it from quivering.

"Leo, are you alright?" Detective Dyl asked.

"Yes," I squeaked.

"Henry, slowly, very slowly—get off the bed."

The enormity of Henry's embrace increased, his body inflexible. Placing his palm on my forehead, he pressed my head onto his shoulder. Into my ear, he said, "Leo, don't let him take me. Don't."

"Henry," Dyl said. "Let her go."

I squinted into the detective's light, not able to tell if he were pointing a gun at us.

"Leo, you have to believe me," Henry's voice clutched in his throat. "I had to—"

"Son?" A familiar voice swelled the nightmare.

"Dad? Get the fuck away from me," Henry sobbed. "Why are you here?"

The light was blinding, and I couldn't see Ethan in the hallway next to the detective.

"Now, Henry, release her," Detective Dyl instructed, "or you'll leave me no option but to take extreme measures."

"Please, son, listen to the detective."

"But he...he made me." Henry was openly crying.

I didn't know what he was stuttering about, but his arms mechanically snapped off me as if somebody pressed the magic button.

"Leo, walk toward me," the detective said.

I slid from the bed, righting my bedraggled dress and realized I was barefoot. During my struggle, my heels had fallen off. I glimpsed around and decided to leave them.

"Stop!" Detective Dyl shouted. "Henry, stop whatever it is that you're doing."

"I'm just getting my glasses." I turned and watched him fingering his glasses.

"May I put them on?" He held them aloft.

"Leo, walk towards me," the detective said, his tone cautious.

Henry was suddenly mauling me from behind as the sharp tip of his jackknife pierced my neck.

"I didn't want this to happen," Henry's voice was laden in controversy. "Back away, Dyl."

CHAPTER 51

"I got you this time, boy." Malice emanated from the detective. "Playtime is over."

"Try me, pig. I'll cut her jugular. She'll be dead in minutes." The prick of the blade punctured my skin, and blood dribbled along my throat.

Henry crooned in my ear. "I'm not going to kill you. Not yet." He said the exact words from a year ago. Stars ruptured my brain. Light-headed, my vision blurred.

The beam faded as Detective Dyl shied away.

"Further, Dyl, go back further." Henry felt like a brick wall, holding onto me. "You too, Dad. Back up, or I'll slice her throat in half."

His arms bound my body, the knife biting into my neck. We edged past the door lintels. There was a tick and everything went black as Dyl switched off his flashlight, blinding us. Henry's garroting hold slackened, and felt his hand on my back. He launched me in the direction of his father and the detective.

"Henry!" Ethan yelled.

I reflexively splayed my arms and, as my kneecaps struck the floor, a pair of hands softened my fall. Dyl hauled me upright as Henry absconded into the hallway. The detective's flashlight clicked on. "Stay here."

A beam of light knocked up and down as he took off after Ethan and Henry.

"No way." I dashed into the bedroom and snatched Henry's heavy-duty flashlight.

In bare feet, I hurried toward the staircase. Shrill bickering echoed from the upper level. I scuffed the pads of my feet on the stairs to the attic. The door was slightly ajar and murky light streaked the stairwell.

Don't breathe, don't breathe, don't make a sound. I wondered if they could hear my clanging heart ripping out of my chest.

"I had to do it." Henry's sobering cry trickled from the attic. "I had too. He made me."

"Henry," Ethan's voice. "Think about what you're saying. We talked about this."

"Let the boy speak." Detective Dyl sounded fierce. "When Lily came to me for a restraining order for Henry, it was the best and the worst day of my life. But you already know that. Don't you, Ethan?"

Ethan James said, "Just slit my throat and be done with it."

Did I hear *Lily*? He said Lily. *Mom*.

"Leo, I know you're standing there." I breathed in and held it. "Come in," Detective Dyl ordered.

Frozen with fear, I couldn't move. There were footsteps, and then the door to the attic opened wide. An inky figure framed the doorway. "Get in here where I can keep an eye on you."

I stepped on the creaky floorboards. Henry's heavy-duty flashlight slipped from my fingers. It clunked to the wood and united with an eerie glow. Elongated shadows banded the walls. Henry had his father in a headlock. He was wielding a curved, unique dagger, and beads of blood necklaced Ethan's throat. Detective Dyl had his flashlight pointed toward them and in his other hand his Glock.

My gaze coasted over Ethan's face, gnarled in fury, with his arms tensing by his sides.

"Leo, over there." Detective Dyl tipped his head, not taking his eyes off his prey. "Toward the window."

Inept and frightened, I routed to the circular stained-glass window.

"Now what?" Henry's voice scraped from the bottom of his diaphragm. "If you don't kill him, I will."

Instead of answering, Detective Dyl repositioned himself around the room. His body was blocking the doorway. "Leo, I cautioned you to stay away from Henry James." he said. "You kept snooping, asking questions, wanting answers."

"This is all your fault," Henry cried. His hand trembled, shearing Ethan's throat.

"Henry. Son. I love you. Don't do anything rash," Ethan said, begging for his life. "I've always helped you. Didn't I?"

"You never loved me like a son. You used me like an incestuous prick." Henry was disintegrating. "You abusive sonofabitch!"

I affixed my arms on my chest and muffled my whimpering with my hands. Why did I feel a tinge of regret for him?

"Not true, Henry." His son's accusations reddened Ethan's injured expression. He talked through the side of his mouth. "You're blaming the wrong man. It's Dyl that's messing with your head. He's the man who will take away our freedom. You can still have Leo, son."

Henry's insufferable gaze darted to me. "I'm not your son. You used me. You used me like...like—"

"Calm down, Henry. I was biding my time," Detective Dyl placated. "Waiting for you to make the right decision. Give yourself up without any more bloodshed. Give me Ethan James, your abusive father."

"Don't listen to him, son." Ethan stood like a stone effigy. "I got you cleared from being prosecuted for that girl's murder, remember? I can take care of this too. Just let me go."

"Like you took care of your skank." Henry's eyes were wild, peering over his father's shoulder. "And the drug dealers."

"Thank you, Henry." Hatred resounded from Detective Dyl. "Not precisely accurate. I doubt Ethan could've run that fast to catch up to David Galbraith on Tarpon. Your hand is all over that one."

"I had to. He would have gutted me if I didn't do it."

Detective Mark Dyl's bottom lip stiffened. "With a dagger to his throat, I think your father is ready to confess. Aren't you, Ethan?"

"Lily was screwing you behind my back." Ethan's body sucked in on itself. "Lily and I used to make love. Right there." His eyes indicated the attic bedroom. "How does that make you feel, Dyl?"

I looked away from the squeamish Ethan to Detective Dyl. "What's going on? I...I don't understand," I asked, finding my tongue.

"I advised Lily to leave for a while." Dyl was talking to Ethan. "She was panicking about everything." His face sagged into a canopy of grief. "I should've protected her better." As if he were being emotionally crushed, his entire body quaked. "I thought she was talking about Henry, but it was you, Ethan. She called you a slimy copper-headed snake."

The detective veered his eyes to me and said, "Ethan murdered your mother."

Beware of the copper-headed snake. It threatens to strike. The magnitude of his statement felled my legs. Mom was warning me in her journal.

"He made me," Henry cried. "He made me watch."

Ethan sniveled, "She was leaving me. I—"

"I knew Henry was bat-shit crazy," Detective Dyl severed Ethan's words. "But you, Ethan, you are the inherent seed. Like father, like son. For the past year, you've been expecting me to take Henry in."

"If I'm a psycho," Henry yelled, "it's because of him." He tightened his grip on Ethan's throat, and the dagger cut a yawning gap, blood gushed.

"I'm done playing pat-a-cake," Detective Dyl expressed defiantly. "Henry, either slit your father's throat and save the taxpayers a ton of money on a trial, or drop the dagger and come with me."

"Henry." Ethan inched his hand up to grasp Henry's wrist. "Don't listen to him. He'll shoot you dead especially after I tell him how Lily begged. She wanted me, not you Dyl—Me. She groaned in ecstasy until I stabbed her in the heart."

"Shut up!" The detective heaved a groaning shout.

"Why? You're going to kill me anyway," Ethan said. "See, Henry. See how he's shaking."

"I'm warning you, Ethan." Dyl pressed the Glocks trigger.

In a swift fluent feat, Ethan clasped Henry's wrist and yanked the dagger from his son's fingers. With dire accuracy, he flung the knife at the detective.

A gunshot boomed, along with my spine-chilling scream, the bullet shearing Ethan's arm. But shockingly, the dagger had buried deep into Detective Dyl's stomach. His flashlight rolled to the floor as his hand clutched the blade's hilt. The Glock teetered on his fingertips, struggling to remain conscious.

Ethan barreled into the detective, stealing the piece. "Who's in control now, Dyl?" An expression of contaminated greed swelled his mouth.

Detective Dyl dropped to his knees, and seeking me with his excruciating eyes, he gasped. "Run."

Ethan kicked the detective to the floor and blood creeped from beneath his body. I swallowed a gut-wrenching scream as my fingers groped the wall for support, endeavoring to stand.

"Where do you think you're going, my dear?" Ethan's eyelids reduced to mere slits.

"She's mine." Henry rushed toward me.

Ethan whirled, pointing the gun at his son. "Henry, Henry." Ethan backpedaled to keep both of us in his sight. "I wish this could end differently. Your savage temper not only killed Lillian Nelson, those drug dealers, the good detective here, and now Leo."

"You're setting me up?" Henry sucked his teeth. "I'll tell them everything. You're going down with me."

"Sorry, Henry, I can't keep saving you. I'll put on a good show. Devastated as I tell the police how mentally volatile you've been. Martha will back me up. They'll read about your past in the police reports. Oh, thanks for this." He wiped blood from his neck where he'd cut him. "It validates my testimony. My son tried to kill me."

Henry's eyes were threatening as he stepped toward his father. "Go to hell."

"No doubt. But you first son." With rapid precision, Ethan plowed the gun beneath Henry's jawline and pulled the trigger.

Henry's face exploded.

CHAPTER 52

"I'm sorry, Leo." Ethan revolved toward me. "I have to make this quick. Over the years, forensics has upped its game. It's vital to substantiate your time of death within the hour." He then retracted a few steps.

"You killed your son!" Hysteria had set in. "You're a deranged murderer!"

"He was a burdensome piece of shit. His pregnant girlfriend thought she could bled me dry, then threatened to tell the cops that Henry had raped her. I had to get rid of that whore because he didn't have the balls to do it. The police blamed Henry, but he was acquitted due to insufficient evidence." Ethan said. "I loved Lily. She was everything. I begged like a damn buffoon for her to love me and she had the gall to laugh." Sweat glistened on his face. "She knew too much. My past...How dare she... How dare she!" He was focusing on me and waving the gun. "Now, stand up."

"No."

He pitched forward. Fingers knotting into my hair, pulling me to my feet. "You shouldn't have poked your nose into my business. This isn't going to end well for you." He twisted the roots of my hair, making me sob in pain. "You're going to fly out that window behind you. Understand?"

In wide-eyed terror, I searched the darkened crevices for an escape.

"I know what you're thinking and it's not going to happen." The shaft of the gun dented my neck. Recoiling, I waited for the bullet to shred my insides. We shifted away from the circular stained glass, and using his elbow as a battering ram; he shattered the smaller window.

"I won't go down without a fight." I sounded braver than I felt and kicked my leg, catching him in the shin.

The vile man pressed my forehead into his fire-breathing mug, and spittle flew from his mouth. "You want to do this the hard way?"

He whacked me in the face with the butt of the gun. Starbursts ignited and then darkened my vision. *Don't pass out! I'll be done for.* Fraught with fear, shards of glass cut into my fingers as I held onto the window frame.

"Henry's known in the precinct for his fiery temper." Glass crinkled underfoot as he shoved me. "Everyone will believe he went berserk, punching you in the face and throwing you out the window." His mouth twisted in satisfaction. "I won't be needing your cooperation after all."

The sound of sprinting footfalls startled Ethan. In the course of turning, a flying object hit him. I caught a hint of a pale head of hair. The boards shook as they crashed to the floor. The attic's atmosphere intensified with grunting and groaning, bodies tussling for power. I shrieked, hearing gunfire. Becket's body jolted, but he continued to wrestle for the handgun. My sight was lured to the window by a conflagration of police cars.

With his slight advantage, Becket's expression became pinched while trying to restrain Ethan. Thick brushstrokes of blood painted the floorboards. He was surviving on pure adrenaline. Ethan pistol-cuffed Becket in the jaw, spooling him sideways. It provided Ethan the ability to wobble upward and targeted Becket with the Glock.

Provoked into action, I hurdled onto Ethan's back, lassoing my arms around his neck, foiling his aim. The gun misfired, affording Becket ample time to recover. He implemented an uppercut to Ethan's unprotected jaw. The deed caused both of us to reel backward and the gun flipped from Ethan's fingers.

My backside crashed into the magnificent window, smashing panes of colorful glass. I fell, bashing into the sturdy casement and into the midst of showering glass. Becket managed to circle my waist, hurtling me from harm's way. I lay sprawled in a disgusting pool of Henry and Detective Dyl's blood, initiating my gag reflex. Regrettably, this distraction caught Becket unaware as Ethan struck again.

In a battle of fists, their muscles convulsed as Becket and Ethan scuffled over glass shavings. Their entangled bodies came dangerously close to the window. As if reading my mind, Ethan unshackled his arms from Becket and pushed him over the casement.

"Becket, watch out!" I screamed.

He dipped backward, teetering on the ledge.

Ethan instigated one last deadly strike. He pounced just as Becket regained his equilibrium. Becket swerved sideways and Ethan tripped, falling over the sill. Becket plunged after him, binding his wrist.

Ethan dangled in the air with Becket as his lifeline. "You can't save me. Nobody can save me," Ethan said.

"Hold. On." Becket's jaw clenched as blinding agony etched across his face. "Give me your other hand."

"Let me fall. I'd rather die here than in prison."

Spotlights were showering us from below when I leaned over the broken ledge, stretching my arms to help.

"Leo, get out of here," Becket forced a plea.

I stepped back and heard a devastating crack. Gazing upward, an immense hunk of the stained-glass waved in the breeze. "The glass is falling!" Encaging my arms around Becket's waist, I tugged with every ounce of contained energy.

"Nooo," he wailed.

Together, as one, we lurched backward. A sheet of glass detached from its moorings, slicing the air like a guillotine and crystal particles shattered around us.

As if someone had cut the strings on the marionette, Becket slumped to the floor, a bloody angel.

"Becket." I fell to my knees, leaning over him. His eyes were closed. I stripped a skein of hair that cloaked his face, gleaming in sweat. "Becket, please don't be dead, please—"

"I'm not dead. I hurt like a mother." He extracted a wheeze and then his eyelids flickered open.

"How...?"

"You told me. Henry was...bringing you here," he said, breathless. "Sorry, it took me so long, but—"

Placing my fingertips to his mouth, I said, "Shush, stop talking, save your strength. The police are here."

The attic was teeming with pounding boots; the cavalry had arrived.

⁂

My bedroom was drenched in light when I woke to find Nona dozing on the chair. I whispered to rouse her, "Hey."

Her eyelashes fanned open. "Hey, Leo." Sluggish and groggy, she staggered next to me on the bed. "Your dad said you didn't get home until the wee hours of the morning. I wanted to wake you up because this is all freaking me out. I have so many questions." She took a breath. "Your poor face is all black and blue."

I propped my elbows on the mattress and chased sleep from my eyes, only to feel the sting of my cheekbone where Ethan had hit me. "Yes, lots of questions. But the people who knew all the answers died last night." I fell into Nona's arms.

Being my tenderhearted comforter, she drew me to her chest, supporting me.

"I heard Becket's in the hospital," she said. Her head moved side to side, tsking. "After Hen...Henry stabbed Becket, he refused anyone's help. Then airhead Marcy was screaming and crying as if she were the one bleeding." Nona tried to diminish the fiasco by circling her hands to her throat, imitating a chokehold. "The teachers were out of their minds. Then Becket took off like a bat out of hell. He wouldn't even let Reggie come with him."

"We went to see him at the hospital before coming home," I said. Remembering the sight, it triggered a burn behind my eyes. "He fought with Mr. James for the gun. The doctor said he was lucky, the bullet just grazed his ribs. He lost a lot of blood and then... Detective Dyl... Henry."

Nona hugged me tighter and I bawled like a baby.

After she left, and like a girl on fire, I hunted for my embroidered box. Lifting the lid, I stared at the array of drugs, tempted to forget the past. I fingered the tiny packet Henry had given me less than a month ago. My discipline had been tested. Tentatively, I went to the bathroom and dumped the contents into the toilet bowl and flushed.

I followed up at police headquarters and realized then that the chair I was instructed to sit in had a permanent indentation of my butt. "I told you everything last night." I was in a hurry to get to the hospital to visit Becket. I didn't want to be put on the rack again. "I don't know what more you want from me."

"Sorry, Leo." Officer Simmons peered at me with lamenting, spider-veined eyes. She shuffled paperwork. "We're putting together the pieces. Detective Dyl is...was... one of our finest. I was able to speak with him before he died." Clearly distraught, she wiped down her face. "He explained in detail. No need to rehash the scene at the mansion."

My memories had lived in a polluted smog of imprisonment for a year. After Mom's murder, I had disliked Detective Mark Dyl and thought him incompetent. He'd suspected Henry from the beginning; however, he was confident of an even more deviant accomplice. Ethan might have gotten away with murder if Dyl jumped the gun and detained Henry. If Henry implicated his father, Ethan could've easily brought up his psychiatric evaluations, and being a suspect in an unsolved murder of a young girl, it could have proved him legally insane.

Officer Simmons nudged me back to the present, speaking into a microphone. "Detective Mark Dyl stated, Ethan James and his accomplice Henry James confessed to murdering Lillian Nelson on October twenty-fifth, 2013. On October fourth, 2014, Ethan James, and Henry James murdered Skipper Townsend and David Galbraith. For the record, do you corroborate with Detective Mark Dyl's statement?"

"Yes," I said, too soft as she recorded my deposition.

"Leocadia, you have to speak up." The officer pushed the mic closer to me. "We have reason to believe that there is another accomplice or person involved."

"I...I thought Henry..." Why did I feel as if I were on trial?

"Leo, this is not meant to upset you, but I'd like you to listen to the 911 call you placed to the police on October twenty-fifth of last year." Her observant eyes watched me. "It was after you discovered your mother. Can you do this for me?"

My face went numb, nodding.

She pressed a button and a female's voice came through the speakers. "Help! Somebody killed my mom! I'm at 3 Lucien Court!"

"Leocadia, did you make that call?"

"I don't remember." My restless fingernails grated over the metal table. "I passed out after…"

"Leo, this isn't your voice."

"What?"

"Voice analysis proves it to be someone else entirely. Possibly a woman's tone trying to sound girlish."

"How come it took a year to figure that out?"

"A year ago, when you suffered from retrograde amnesia, we accepted the fact it was your voice. I've been studying the case files and decided to test my theory." Officer Simmons tucked her lips into her mouth for a second. "Dyl was thorough but admitted he didn't make a voice analysis." Assembling the paperwork, she shut the manila folder.

"I think we're through here, for now."

"Is Mom's murder investigation finally closed?"

"We found the boots in Henry's bedroom and the dagger which incriminates them to the murders." Officer Simmons ended her supposition, expressing a firmly lined mouth.

"So, what are you trying to tell me?"

"I'm not ready to close the case."

I wanted it to be over.

CHAPTER 53

A week later, a convalescing Becket and I shared a roast beef sandwich and chips at Earl's. I smiled into his intense blue eyes.

"You're looking better today," I said.

"I thought I looked good yesterday." His gaze was mirthful. "Is that your classic eye roll?"

"Get used to it, bud." I pulverized a chip with my teeth. "You'll be seeing a lot of it."

"I'll drive you to the game tonight if that's alright."

"I thought the doctors said you shouldn't be driving with the meds?"

"Screw the doctors, I'm fine. It's bad enough I can't finish out the season."

"The doctors won't let you play?"

"I'm done for the season; go figure." He took a bite of his sandwich and, with a mouthful, said, "There are only two games left anyway."

"That's good. The weather's going downhill. It's been freezing lately." He tossed the last chip into his mouth. "Ready to go?"

"Yep." Since Becket arrived home from the hospital, we'd been spending time together—as friends. I'd talked endlessly with Nona over his change of attitude, and her advice was to give him time to heal. After lunch, I chauffeured him to Hallow Saint's Cemetery. I unloaded the pot of hardy mums I'd purchased, and we wandered over the dewy lawn.

"Come here; I want you to see this cool statue." I directed him to the Saint Michael statue with his sword piercing the air.

"Kind of looks like me, don't you think?" he jested.

"Exactly like you." His eyes darkened, looking down at me. His hand came up and tenderly held my chin between his thumb and forefinger. Becket drew near. Our lips bonded, a timeless kiss of perfection setting my heart on fire. I fell into his kiss and my toes curled.

"I've been wanting to do that all week," he whispered.

"And I've been waiting all week." With accuracy, he hungrily recaptured my mouth. The potted mum acted as a barrier, yet I gravitated my right arm beneath his leather jacket, gliding up his back. This time, I pulled away. "Mom's waiting."

"Oh—right," he said, breathing shallow.

We passed a row of headstones, then I halted and knelt, fixing the pot underneath her carved name. "Hi, Mom. I want you to meet Becket." He stood above, and then squatted beside me, grimacing. He liked to pretend he was fine, but he wasn't fooling me. It would take time to heal his aching wounds.

"Leocadia," he said after a meditative calm. "She wants you to be happy." He then smoothed a hand under my hair and kissed my cooled cheek.

On Sunday afternoon, Dad's fist banged the kitchen table, rife with animosity. "What the hell is wrong with our judicial system? This is over. This is over! They found Lily's killer. Why did they haul me in asking the same damn questions over and over?" He rose, capsizing the chair. "You're in the middle of this?"

"I didn't make that call." I illuminated again.

"Well, it wasn't me." He turned with fire flaring in his eyes. "It was probably Henry disguising his voice. That's what I told them." He pointed a finger in my face. "I ordered you not to hang around with that flaky kid. I ordered you!"

"Dad, stop it." If he wanted to play the harassment game, I was done walking on eggshells around him. Fueling courage, I aimed for maturity. "Admit it. Just admit it."

His fiery expression extinguished.

"Dad, please. Then it's over." I remained seated, afraid my legs wouldn't support me. "I've remembered for a while now. You were there. I don't know why you were there—at that time of day, especially with Regina."

I guessed about the woman, and his splotchy complexion gave me my answer. "Unless...unless you knew Mom was in trouble." Internally I prayed, *No, it's not true—prove me wrong.*

Eliciting a twinge of grief and grasping for absolution, his body deflated and crumpled in on himself.

"It was horrible—gruesome—my God," he yowled in a desolate whimper. "There was nothing I could do. Your mother was dead. I couldn't handle it. I just want this all to go away."

I wasn't through interrogating. "Why didn't you tell the police you were there?"

"I...I didn't have time to think. I was scared. I was being audited at work for financial discrepancies...and...and they'd have me pegged as her killer because of...of..." Riddled with guilt, his eyes pleaded for sympathy, which wasn't forthcoming. "You saw how they treated me...afterward."

"Because you were screwing your business partners? And your secretary. You left me to lay there, alone?" I pulled in a jagged breath. "For a whole year, you knew."

"That's unfair." Two handedly, he grasped his head. "Lily hooked up with that demented neighbor. It was her fault. I never suspected Dyl. I swore to you she was no saint, remember?"

My stiff fingers keyed in Officer Simmons' phone number.

EPILOGUE

Somehow Dad had finagled it. He had been granted immunity. As a result, he would not be prosecuted for withholding evidence and systematically was exonerated by a voice-mail message he'd saved on his cell:

"*Paul, when Leo gets home from school, we're leaving for California. It's been over between us for a while. I'll retain a lawyer to discuss custody. I can't stay in the Hallow another day. I should have explained sooner. I'm worried and...scared.*" She had paused, breathing raspy. "*I thought I could handle it. There is someone... He's—*" Then there was a clanging doorbell and hammering and Mom's frightened whisper, "*Oh God, he's here.*" The message ended, and no one ever recovered Mom's phone.

Dad, completely shaken, couldn't drive; hence Regina drove him home. They found me passed out in the hallway and Regina phoned 911 from my cell. He hadn't provided the evidence when the police were grilling him. He thought it might incriminate him as a partner in crime due to his work discrepancies. He fled the murder scene, traumatized, dazed, and scared shitless.

It had been Ethan who had tackled me in the attic that day when I unexpectedly showed up. The day I'd found

Mom, it had been Henry who said, "I'm not going to kill you. Not yet." The feel of his clammy hands covering my mouth and the marijuana odor had been prevalent then and the day Detective Dyl died.

If the vase hadn't broken in the Lucien mansion, deterring Henry, it made me ill to think what would have happened. I believed Mom had a hand in that. She'd been with me the whole time and knew I'd be the next victim. She saved me and helped to uncover her killers.

It was over. Case closed.

People are flawed—big time. I learned it the hard way, a lesson that sliced a cavernous scar into my heart. A scar that swells and blisters on occasion.

In Dad's defense, I'd been a prime witness to his self-punishment. He loved me. Would I ever forgive him for remaining mum, for leaving me alone, for being a coward? It had been complex to shorten Mom's saintly pedestal. My love for her would be everlasting.

The brisk autumn afternoon and Losson Park were aglow with a vestige of colorful leaves. We'd gathered for the traditional Turkey Bowl, a tag football game. My first year competing and I was hyped, much more improved than cheering on the sidelines. Participating in the game, I set my sights for my boyfriend.

"C'mon, Becket." Reggie acted as a defensive linebacker. "Throw the ball. I don't give a rat's ass if you're hurting, bro. My teammate will take it easy on you when she comes in for the sack. Won't you, Leo?" He rascally winked.

"Sure, I will, Reg."

Becket shouted to his teammate, "Nona, go long." The petite spitfire sprinted downfield to our makeshift goal, cans of soda lining the zone.

Reggie was in hot pursuit and I made a beeline for Becket. He lobbed the ball and crouched low, taking the full impact of my body into his arms. We tumbled and rolled onto pliable grass, laughing.

Crutched on his elbows, Becket gazed into my face, eyes vibrant and alive. He delicately plucked a piece of hair from my lips and whispered, "Leocadia, I'll always love you."

I smiled and shivered in anticipation, and to seal his promise, he kissed me.

ABOUT THE AUTHOR

Cathrina Constantine lives in West Seneca, a suburb of Buffalo, New York, with her husband, five grown children, and 8 grand-babies. She loves the four seasons, though, fall, with all its glorious colors and fragrances, is her favorite time of year. The winters are long and bitterly cold, but it's during those snowy months when her writing flourishes like the snowflakes.

Cathrina is an award-winning, bestselling author. Don't Forget to Breathe received Reader's Favorite International Book Award, Literary Classics Gold Award, Literary Classics Seal of Approval, New Apple Medalist Award, and TopShelf 1st place winner for YA/Mystery. Tallas received the Literary Classics Seal of Approval, and Literary Classics Silver Award. Her books have also been awarded Readers Favorite five star reviews. Her writing veers toward young adult stories that definitely appeals to adults. From fantasy, dystopian, contemporary, mystery, paranormal, and ghost stories, she is fond of all genres, and can't pick a preference to read or to write.

You can find Cathrina here:

www.facebook.com/wickedly333
cathrinaconstantine.blogspot.com

www.ingramcontent.com/pod-product-compliance
Lightning Source LLC
LaVergne TN
LVHW042252070526
838201LV00106B/302/J